# The Mystery of "The Yellow Room"

# The Mystery of "The Yellow Room"

Gaston Leroux

MINT EDITIONS

*The Mystery of "The Yellow Room"* was first published in 1907.

This edition published by Mint Editions 2021.

ISBN 9781513282930 | E-ISBN 9781513287959

Published by Mint Editions®

 **MINT EDITIONS**

minteditionbooks.com

Publishing Director: Jennifer Newens
Design & Production: Rachel Lopez Metzger
Project Manager: Micaela Clark
Typesetting: Westchester Publishing Services

# Contents

# I

## In Which We Begin Not to Understand

It is not without a certain emotion that I begin to recount here the extraordinary adventures of Joseph Rouletabille. Down to the present time he had so firmly opposed my doing it that I had come to despair of ever publishing the most curious of police stories of the past fifteen years. I had even imagined that the public would never know the whole truth of the prodigious case known as that of the "Yellow Room", out of which grew so many mysterious, cruel, and sensational dramas, with which my friend was so closely mixed up, if, propos of a recent nomination of the illustrious Stangerson to the grade of grandcross of the Legion of Honour, an evening journal—in an article, miserable for its ignorance, or audacious for its perfidy—had not resuscitated a terrible adventure of which Joseph Rouletabille had told me he wished to be for ever forgotten.

The "Yellow Room"! Who now remembers this affair which caused so much ink to flow fifteen years ago? Events are so quickly forgotten in Paris. Has not the very name of the Nayves trial and the tragic history of the death of little Menaldo passed out of mind? And yet the public attention was so deeply interested in the details of the trial that the occurrence of a ministerial crisis was completely unnoticed at the time. Now the "Yellow Room" trial, which, preceded that of the Nayves by some years, made far more noise. The entire world hung for months over this obscure problem—the most obscure, it seems to me, that has ever challenged the perspicacity of our police or taxed the conscience of our judges. The solution of the problem baffled everybody who tried to find it. It was like a dramatic rebus with which old Europe and new America alike became fascinated. That is, in truth—I am permitted to say, because there cannot be any author's vanity in all this, since I do nothing more than transcribe facts on which an exceptional documentation enables me to throw a new light—that is because, in truth, I do not know that, in the domain of reality or imagination, one can discover or recall to mind anything comparable, in its mystery, with the natural mystery of the "Yellow Room".

That which nobody could find out, Joseph Rouletabille, aged eighteen, then a reporter engaged on a leading journal, succeeded in discovering. But when, at the Assize Court, he brought in the key to the whole case, he did not tell the whole truth. He only allowed so much of it to appear as sufficed to ensure the acquittal of an innocent man. The reasons which he had for his reticence no longer exist. Better still, the time has come for my friend to speak out fully. You are going to know all; and, without further preamble, I am going to place before your eyes the problem of the "Yellow Room" as it was placed before the eyes of the entire world on the day following the enactment of the drama at the Chateau du Glandier.

On the 25th of October, 1892, the following note appeared in the latest edition of the "Temps":

"A frightful crime has been committed at the Glandier, on the border of the forest of Sainte-Genevieve, above Epinay-sur-Orge, at the house of Professor Stangerson. On that night, while the master was working in his laboratory, an attempt was made to assassinate Mademoiselle Stangerson, who was sleeping in a chamber adjoining this laboratory. The doctors do not answer for the life of Mdlle. Stangerson."

The impression made on Paris by this news may be easily imagined. Already, at that time, the learned world was deeply interested in the labours of Professor Stangerson and his daughter. These labours—the first that were attempted in radiography—served to open the way for Monsieur and Madame Curie to the discovery of radium. It was expected the Professor would shortly read to the Academy of Sciences a sensational paper on his new theory,—the Dissociation of Matter,—a theory destined to overthrow from its base the whole of official science, which based itself on the principle of the Conservation of Energy. On the following day, the newspapers were full of the tragedy. The "Matin," among others, published the following article, entitled: "A Supernatural Crime":

"These are the only details," wrote the anonymous writer in the "Matin"—"we have been able to obtain concerning the crime of the Chateau du Glandier. The state of despair in which Professor Stangerson is plunged, and the impossibility of getting any information from the lips of the victim, have rendered our investigations and those of justice so difficult that, at present, we cannot form the least idea of what has passed in the 'Yellow Room' in which Mdlle. Stangerson, in her night-dress, was found lying on the floor in the agonies of death. We have, at least, been able to interview Daddy Jacques—as he is called in the country—a old servant in the Stangerson family. Daddy Jacques entered the 'Yellow Room' at the same time as the Professor. This chamber adjoins the laboratory. Laboratory and 'Yellow Room' are in a pavilion at the end of the park, about three hundred metres (a thousand feet) from the chateau.

"'It was half-past twelve at night,' this honest old man told us, 'and I was in the laboratory, where Monsieur Stangerson was still working, when the thing happened. I had been cleaning and putting instruments in order all the evening and was waiting for Monsieur Stangerson to go to bed. Mademoiselle Stangerson had worked with her father up to midnight; when the twelve strokes of midnight had sounded by the cuckoo-clock in the laboratory, she rose, kissed Monsieur Stangerson and bade him good-night. To me she said "bon soir, Daddy Jacques" as she passed into the "Yellow Room". We heard her lock the door and shoot the bolt, so that I could not help laughing, and said to Monsieur: "There's Mademoiselle double-locking herself in,—she must be afraid of the 'Bete du bon Dieu!'" Monsieur did not even hear me, he was so deeply absorbed in what he was doing. Just then we heard the distant miawing of a cat. "Is that going to keep us awake all night?" I said to myself, for I must tell you, Monsieur, that, to the end of October, I live in an attic of the pavilion over the "Yellow Room", so that Mademoiselle should not be left alone through the night in the lonely park. It was the fancy of Mademoiselle to spend the fine weather in the pavilion; no doubt, she found it more cheerful than the chateau and, for the four years it had been built, she had never failed to take up her lodging there in the spring. With the return of winter, Mademoiselle returns to the chateau, for there is no fireplace in the "Yellow Room".

"'We were staying in the pavilion, then—Monsieur Stangerson and me. We made no noise. He was seated at his desk. As for me, I was sitting on a chair, having finished my work and, looking at him, I said to myself: "What a man!—what intelligence!—what knowledge!" I attach importance to the fact that we made no noise; for, because of that, the assassin certainly thought that we had left the place. And, suddenly, while the cuckoo was sounding the half after midnight, a desperate clamour broke out in the "Yellow Room". It was the voice of Mademoiselle, crying "Murder!—murder!—help!" Immediately afterwards revolver shots rang out and there was a great noise of tables and furniture being thrown to the ground, as if in the course of a struggle, and again the voice of Mademoiselle calling, "Murder!—help!—Papa!—Papa!—"

"'You may be sure that we quickly sprang up and that Monsieur Stangerson and I threw ourselves upon the door. But alas! it was locked, fast locked, on the inside, by the care of Mademoiselle, as I have told you, with key and bolt. We tried to force it open, but it remained firm. Monsieur Stangerson was like a madman, and truly, it was enough to make him one, for we heard Mademoiselle still calling "Help!—help!" Monsieur Stangerson showered terrible blows on the door, and wept with rage and sobbed with despair and helplessness.

"'It was then that I had an inspiration. "The assassin must have entered by the window!" I cried;—"I will go to the window!" and I rushed from the pavilion and ran like one out of his mind.

"'The inspiration was that the window of the "Yellow Room" looks out in such a way that the park wall, which abuts on the pavilion, prevented my at once reaching the window. To get up to it one has first to go out of the park. I ran towards the gate and, on my way, met Bernier and his wife, the gate-keepers, who had been attracted by the pistol reports and by our cries. In a few words I told them what had happened, and directed the concierge to join Monsieur Stangerson with all speed, while his wife came with me to open the park gate. Five minutes later she and I were before the window of the "Yellow Room".

"'The moon was shining brightly and I saw clearly that no one had touched the window. Not only were the bars that protect it intact, but the blinds inside of them were drawn, as I had myself drawn them early in the evening, as I did every day, though Mademoiselle, knowing that I was tired from the heavy work I had been doing, had begged me not to trouble myself, but leave her to do it; and they were just as I had left them, fastened with an iron catch on the inside. The assassin, therefore, could not have passed either in or out that way; but neither could I get in.

"'It was unfortunate,—enough to turn one's brain! The door of the room locked on the inside and the blinds on the only window also fastened on the inside; and Mademoiselle still calling for help!—No! she had ceased to call. She was dead, perhaps. But I still heard her father, in the pavilion, trying to break down the door.

"'With the concierge I hurried back to the pavilion. The door, in spite of the furious attempts of Monsieur Stangerson and Bernier to burst it open, was still holding firm; but at length, it gave way before our united efforts,—and then what a sight met our eyes! I should tell you that, behind us, the concierge held the laboratory lamp—a powerful lamp, that lit the whole chamber.

"'I must also tell you, monsieur, that the "Yellow Room" is a very small room. Mademoiselle had furnished it with a fairly large iron bedstead, a small table, a night-commode; a dressing-table, and two chairs. By the light of the big lamp we saw all at a glance. Mademoiselle, in her night-dress, was lying on the floor in the midst of the greatest disorder. Tables and chairs had been overthrown, showing that there had been a violent struggle. Mademoiselle had certainly been dragged from her bed. She was covered with blood and had terrible marks of finger-nails on her throat,—the flesh of her neck having been almost torn by the nails. From a wound on the right temple a stream of blood had run down and made a little pool on the floor. When Monsieur Stangerson saw his daughter in that state, he threw himself on his knees beside her, uttering a cry of despair. He ascertained that she still breathed. As to us, we searched for the wretch who had tried to kill our mistress, and I swear to you, monsieur, that, if we had found him, it would have gone hard with him!

"'But how to explain that he was not there, that he had already escaped? It passes all imagination!—Nobody under the bed, nobody behind the furniture!—All that we discovered were traces, blood-stained marks of a man's large hand on the walls and on the door, a big handkerchief red with blood, without any initials, an old cap, and many fresh footmarks of a man on the floor,—footmarks of a man with large feet whose boot-soles had left a sort of sooty impression. How had this man got away? How had he vanished? Don't forget, monsieur, that there is no chimney in the "Yellow Room". He could not have escaped by the door, which is narrow, and on the threshold of which the concierge stood with the lamp, while her husband and I searched for him in every corner of the little room, where it is impossible for anyone to hide himself. The door, which had been forced open against the wall, could not conceal anything behind it, as we assured ourselves. By the window, still in every way secured, no flight had been possible. What then?—I began to believe in the Devil.

"'But we discovered my revolver on the floor!—Yes, my revolver! Oh! that brought me back to the reality! The Devil would not have needed to steal my revolver to kill Mademoiselle. The man who had been there had first gone up to my attic and taken my revolver from the drawer where I kept it. We then ascertained, by counting the cartridges, that the assassin had fired two shots. Ah! it was fortunate for me that Monsieur Stangerson was in the laboratory when the affair took place and had seen with his own eyes that I was there with him; for otherwise, with this business of my revolver, I don't know where we should have been,—I should now be under lock and bar. Justice wants no more to send a man to the scaffold!'"

The editor of the "Matin" added to this interview the following lines:

"We have, without interrupting him, allowed Daddy Jacques to recount to us roughly all he knows about the crime of the 'Yellow Room'. We have reproduced it in his own words, only sparing the reader the continual lamentations with which he garnished his narrative. It is quite understood, Daddy Jacques, quite understood, that you are very fond of your masters; and you want them to know it, and never cease repeating it—especially since the discovery of your revolver. It is your right, and we see no harm in it. We should have liked to put some further questions to Daddy Jacques—Jacques—Louis Moustier—but the inquiry of the examining magistrate, which is being carried on at the chateau, makes it impossible for us to gain admission at the Glandier; and, as to the oak wood, it is guarded by a wide circle of policemen, who are jealously watching all traces that can lead to the pavilion, and that may perhaps lead to the discovery of the assassin. 'We have also wished to question the concierges, but they are invisible. Finally, we have waited in a roadside inn, not far from the gate of the chateau, for the departure of Monsieur de Marquet, the magistrate of Corbeil. At half-past five we saw him and his clerk and, before he was able to enter his carriage, had an opportunity to ask him the following question:

"'Can you, Monsieur de Marquet, give us any information as to this affair, without inconvenience to the course of your inquiry?'

"'It is impossible for us to do it,' replied Monsieur de Marquet. 'I can only say that it is the strangest affair I have ever known. The more we think we know something, the further we are from knowing anything!'

"We asked Monsieur de Marquet to be good enough to explain his last words; and this is what he said,—the importance of which no one will fail to recognise:

"'If nothing is added to the material facts so far established, I fear that the mystery which surrounds the abominable crime of which Mademoiselle Stangerson has been the victim will never be brought to light; but it is to be hoped, for the sake of our human reason, that the examination of the walls, and of the ceiling of the "Yellow Room"—an examination which I shall tomorrow intrust to the builder who constructed the pavilion four years ago—will afford us the proof that may not discourage us. For the problem is this: we know by what way the assassin gained admission,—he entered by the door and hid himself under the bed, awaiting Mademoiselle Stangerson. But how did he leave? How did he escape? If no trap, no secret door, no hiding place, no opening of any sort is found; if the examination of the walls— even to the demolition of the pavilion—does not reveal any passage practicable—not only for a human being, but for any being whatsoever— if the ceiling shows no crack, if the floor hides no underground passage, one must really believe in the Devil, as Daddy Jacques says!'"

And the anonymous writer in the "Matin" added in this article— which I have selected as the most interesting of all those that were published on the subject of this affair—that the examining magistrate appeared to place a peculiar significance to the last sentence: "One must really believe in the Devil, as Jacques says."

The article concluded with these lines: "We wanted to know what Daddy Jacques meant by the cry of the Bete Du Bon Dieu." The landlord of the Donjon Inn explained to us that it is the particularly sinister cry which is uttered sometimes at night by the cat of an old woman,—Mother Angenoux, as she is called in the country. Mother Angenoux is a sort of saint, who lives in a hut in the heart of the forest, not far from the grotto of Sainte-Genevieve.

"The 'Yellow Room', the Bete Du Bon Dieu, Mother Angenoux, the Devil, Sainte-Genevieve, Daddy Jacques,—here is a well entangled crime which the stroke of a pickaxe in the wall may disentangle for us tomorrow. Let us at least hope that, for the sake of our human reason, as the examining magistrate says. Meanwhile, it is expected that Mademoiselle Stangerson—who has not ceased to be delirious and only pronounces one word distinctly, 'Murderer! Murderer!'—will not live through the night."

In conclusion, and at a late hour, the same journal announced that the Chief of the Surete had telegraphed to the famous detective, Frederic Larsan, who had been sent to London for an affair of stolen securities, to return immediately to Paris.

# II

## In Which Joseph Rouletabille Appears for the First Time

I remember as well as if it had occurred yesterday, the entry of young Rouletabille into my bedroom that morning. It was about eight o'clock and I was still in bed reading the article in the "Matin" relative to the Glandier crime.

But, before going further, it is time that I present my friend to the reader.

I first knew Joseph Rouletabille when he was a young reporter. At that time I was a beginner at the Bar and often met him in the corridors of examining magistrates, when I had gone to get a "permit to communicate" for the prison of Mazas, or for Saint-Lazare. He had, as they say, "a good nut." He seemed to have taken his head—round as a bullet—out of a box of marbles, and it is from that, I think, that his comrades of the press—all determined billiard-players—had given him that nickname, which was to stick to him and be made illustrious by him. He was always as red as a tomato, now gay as a lark, now grave as a judge. How, while still so young—he was only sixteen and a half years old when I saw him for the first time—had he already won his way on the press? That was what everybody who came into contact with him might have asked, if they had not known his history. At the time of the affair of the woman cut in pieces in the Rue Oberskampf—another forgotten story—he had taken to one of the editors of the "Epoque,"—a paper then rivalling the "Matin" for information,—the left foot, which was missing from the basket in which the gruesome remains were discovered. For this left foot the police had been vainly searching for a week, and young Rouletabille had found it in a drain where nobody had thought of looking for it. To do that he had dressed himself as an extra sewer-man, one of a number engaged by the administration of the city of Paris, owing to an overflow of the Seine.

When the editor-in-chief was in possession of the precious foot and informed as to the train of intelligent deductions the boy had been led to make, he was divided between the admiration he felt for such detective cunning in a brain of a lad of sixteen years, and delight at being able to exhibit, in the "morgue window" of his paper, the left foot of the Rue Oberskampf.

"This foot," he cried, "will make a great headline."

Then, when he had confided the gruesome packet to the medical lawyer attached to the journal, he asked the lad, who was shortly to become famous as Rouletabille, what he would expect to earn as a general reporter on the "Epoque"?

"Two hundred francs a month," the youngster replied modestly, hardly able to breathe from surprise at the proposal.

"You shall have two hundred and fifty," said the editor-in-chief; "only you must tell everybody that you have been engaged on the paper for a month. Let it be quite understood that it was not you but the 'Epoque' that discovered the left foot of the Rue Oberskampf. Here, my young friend, the man is nothing, the paper everything."

Having said this, he begged the new reporter to retire, but before the youth had reached the door he called him back to ask his name. The other replied:

"Joseph Josephine."

"That's not a name," said the editor-in-chief, "but since you will not be required to sign what you write it is of no consequence."

The boy-faced reporter speedily made himself many friends, for he was serviceable and gifted with a good humour that enchanted the most severe-tempered and disarmed the most zealous of his companions. At the Bar cafe, where the reporters assembled before going to any of the courts, or to the Prefecture, in search of their news of crime, he began to win a reputation as an unraveller of intricate and obscure affairs which found its way to the office of the Chief of the Surete. When a case was worth the trouble and Rouletabille—he had already been given his nickname—had been started on the scent by his editor-in-chief, he often got the better of the most famous detective.

It was at the Bar cafe that I became intimately acquainted with him. Criminal lawyers and journalists are not enemies, the former need advertisement, the latter information. We chatted together, and I soon warmed towards him. His intelligence was so keen, and so original!—and he had a quality of thought such as I have never found in any other person.

Some time after this I was put in charge of the law news of the "Cri du Boulevard." My entry into journalism could not but strengthen the ties which united me to Rouletabille. After a while, my new friend being allowed to carry out an idea of a judicial correspondence column, which he was allowed to sign "Business," in the "Epoque," I was often able to furnish him with the legal information of which he stood in need.

Nearly two years passed in this way, and the better I knew him, the more I learned to love him; for, in spite of his careless extravagance, I had discovered in him what was, considering his age, an extraordinary seriousness of mind. Accustomed as I was to seeing him gay and, indeed, often too gay, I would many times find him plunged in the deepest melancholy. I tried then to question him as to the cause of this change of humour, but each time he laughed and made me no answer. One day, having questioned him about his parents, of whom he never spoke, he left me, pretending not to have heard what I said.

While things were in this state between us, the famous case of the "Yellow Room" took place. It was this case which was to rank him as the leading newspaper reporter, and to obtain for him the reputation of being the greatest detective in the world. It should not surprise us to find in the one man the perfection of two such lines of activity if we remember that the daily press was already beginning to transform itself and to become what it is today—the gazette of crime.

Morose-minded people may complain of this; for myself I regard it a matter for congratulation. We can never have too many arms, public or private, against the criminal. To this some people may answer that, by continually publishing the details of crimes, the press ends by encouraging their commission. But then, with some people we can never do right. Rouletabille, as I have said, entered my room that morning of the 26th of October, 1892. He was looking redder than usual, and his eyes were bulging out of his head, as the phrase is, and altogether he appeared to be in a state of extreme excitement. He waved the "Matin" with a trembling hand, and cried:

"Well, my dear Sainclair,—have you read it?"

"The Glandier crime?"

"Yes; The 'Yellow Room'!—What do you think of it?"

"I think that it must have been the Devil or the Bete du Bon Dieu that committed the crime."

"Be serious!"

"Well, I don't much believe in murderers* who make their escape through walls of solid brick. I think Daddy Jacques did wrong to leave behind him the weapon with which the crime was committed and, as he occupied the attic immediately above Mademoiselle Stangerson's

---

* Although the original English translation often uses the words "murder" and "murderer," the reader may substitute "attack" and "attacker" since no murder is actually committed.

room, the builder's job ordered by the examining magistrate will give us the key of the enigma and it will not be long before we learn by what natural trap, or by what secret door, the old fellow was able to slip in and out, and return immediately to the laboratory to Monsieur Stangerson, without his absence being noticed. That, of course, is only an hypothesis."

Rouletabille sat down in an armchair, lit his pipe, which he was never without, smoked for a few minutes in silence—no doubt to calm the excitement which, visibly, dominated him—and then replied:

"Young man," he said, in a tone the sad irony of which I will not attempt to render, "young man, you are a lawyer and I doubt not your ability to save the guilty from conviction; but if you were a magistrate on the bench, how easy it would be for you to condemn innocent persons!—You are really gifted, young man!"

He continued to smoke energetically, and then went on:

"No trap will be found, and the mystery of the 'Yellow Room' will become more and more mysterious. That's why it interests me. The examining magistrate is right; nothing stranger than this crime has ever been known."

"Have you any idea of the way by which the murderer escaped?" I asked.

"None," replied Rouletabille—"none, for the present. But I have an idea as to the revolver; the murderer did not use it."

"Good Heavens! By whom, then, was it used?"

"Why—by Mademoiselle Stangerson."

"I don't understand,—or rather, I have never understood," I said.

Rouletabille shrugged his shoulders.

"Is there nothing in this article in the 'Matin' by which you were particularly struck?"

"Nothing,—I have found the whole of the story it tells equally strange."

"Well, but—the locked door—with the key on the inside?"

"That's the only perfectly natural thing in the whole article."

"Really!—And the bolt?"

"The bolt?"

"Yes, the bolt—also inside the room—a still further protection against entry? Mademoiselle Stangerson took quite extraordinary precautions! It is clear to me that she feared someone. That was why she took such precautions—even Daddy Jacques's revolver—without telling him of it. No doubt she didn't wish to alarm anybody, and least of all, her father. What she dreaded took place, and she defended herself. There was a struggle, and she used the revolver skilfully enough to wound the assassin in the hand—which explains the impression on the wall and on the door of the large, blood-stained hand of the man who was searching for a means of exit from the chamber. But she didn't fire soon enough to avoid the terrible blow on the right temple."

"Then the wound on the temple was not done with the revolver?"

"The paper doesn't say it was, and I don't think it was; because logically it appears to me that the revolver was used by Mademoiselle Stangerson against the assassin. Now, what weapon did the murderer use? The blow on the temple seems to show that the murderer wished to stun Mademoiselle Stangerson,—after he had unsuccessfully tried to strangle her. He must have known that the attic was inhabited by Daddy Jacques, and that was one of the reasons, I think, why he must have used a quiet weapon,—a life-preserver, or a hammer."

"All that doesn't explain how the murderer got out of the 'Yellow Room'," I observed.

"Evidently," replied Rouletabille, rising, "and that is what has to be explained. I am going to the Chateau du Glandier, and have come to see whether you will go with me."

"I?—"

"Yes, my boy. I want you. The 'Epoque' has definitely entrusted this case to me, and I must clear it up as quickly as possible."

"But in what way can I be of any use to you?"

"Monsieur Robert Darzac is at the Chateau du Glandier."

"That's true. His despair must be boundless."

"I must have a talk with him."

Rouletabille said it in a tone that surprised me.

"Is it because—you think there is something to be got out of him?" I asked.

"Yes."

That was all he would say. He retired to my sitting-room, begging me to dress quickly.

I knew Monsieur Robert Darzac from having been of great service to him in a civil action, while I was acting as secretary to Maitre Barbet Delatour. Monsieur Robert Darzac, who was at that time about forty years of age, was a professor of physics at the Sorbonne. He was intimately acquainted with the Stangersons, and, after an assiduous seven years' courtship of the daughter, had been on the point of marrying her. In spite of the fact that she has become, as the phrase goes, "a person of a certain age," she was still remarkably good-looking. While I was dressing I called out to Rouletabille, who was impatiently moving about my sitting-room:

"Have you any idea as to the murderer's station in life?"

"Yes," he replied; "I think if he isn't a man in society, he is, at least, a man belonging to the upper class. But that, again, is only an impression."

"What has led you to form it?"

"Well,—the greasy cap, the common handkerchief, and the marks of the rough boots on the floor," he replied.

"I understand," I said; "murderers don't leave traces behind them which tell the truth."

"We shall make something out of you yet, my dear Sainclair," concluded Rouletabille.

# III

## "A Man Has Passed Like a Shadow Through the Blinds"

Half an hour later Rouletabille and I were on the platform of the Orleans station, awaiting the departure of the train which was to take us to Epinay-sur-Orge.

On the platform we found Monsieur de Marquet and his Registrar, who represented the Judicial Court of Corbeil. Monsieur Marquet had spent the night in Paris, attending the final rehearsal, at the Scala, of a little play of which he was the unknown author, signing himself simply "Castigat Ridendo."

Monsieur de Marquet was beginning to be a "noble old gentleman." Generally he was extremely polite and full of gay humour, and in all his life had had but one passion,—that of dramatic art. Throughout his magisterial career he was interested solely in cases capable of furnishing him with something in the nature of a drama. Though he might very well have aspired to the highest judicial positions, he had never really worked for anything but to win a success at the romantic Porte-Saint-Martin, or at the sombre Odeon.

Because of the mystery which shrouded it, the case of the "Yellow Room" was certain to fascinate so theatrical a mind. It interested him enormously, and he threw himself into it, less as a magistrate eager to know the truth, than as an amateur of dramatic embroglios, tending wholly to mystery and intrigue, who dreads nothing so much as the explanatory final act.

So that, at the moment of meeting him, I heard Monsieur de Marquet say to the Registrar with a sigh:

"I hope, my dear Monsieur Maleine, this builder with his pickaxe will not destroy so fine a mystery."

"Have no fear," replied Monsieur Maleine, "his pickaxe may demolish the pavilion, perhaps, but it will leave our case intact. I have sounded the walls and examined the ceiling and floor and I know all about it. I am not to be deceived."

Having thus reassured his chief, Monsieur Maleine, with a discreet movement of the head, drew Monsieur de Marquet's attention to us. The face of that gentleman clouded, and, as he saw Rouletabille approaching, hat in hand, he sprang into one of the empty carriages saying, half aloud to his Registrar, as he did so, "Above all, no journalists!"

Monsieur Maleine replied in the same tone, "I understand!" and then tried to prevent Rouletabille from entering the same compartment with the examining magistrate.

"Excuse me, gentlemen,—this compartment is reserved."

"I am a journalist, Monsieur, engaged on the 'Epoque,'" said my young friend with a great show of gesture and politeness, "and I have a word or two to say to Monsieur de Marquet."

"Monsieur is very much engaged with the inquiry he has in hand."

"Ah! his inquiry, pray believe me, is absolutely a matter of indifference to me. I am no scavenger of odds and ends," he went on, with infinite contempt in his lower lip, "I am a theatrical reporter; and this evening I shall have to give a little account of the play at the Scala."

"Get in, sir, please," said the Registrar.

Rouletabille was already in the compartment. I went in after him and seated myself by his side. The Registrar followed and closed the carriage door.

Monsieur de Marquet looked at him.

"Ah, sir," Rouletabille began, "You must not be angry with Monsieur de Maleine. It is not with Monsieur de Marquet that I desire to have the honour of speaking, but with Monsieur 'Castigat Ridendo.' Permit me to congratulate you—personally, as well as the writer for the 'Epoque.'" And Rouletabille, having first introduced me, introduced himself.

Monsieur de Marquet, with a nervous gesture, caressed his beard into a point, and explained to Rouletabille, in a few words, that he was too modest an author to desire that the veil of his pseudonym should be publicly raised, and that he hoped the enthusiasm of the journalist for the dramatist's work would not lead him to tell the public that Monsieur "Castigat Ridendo" and the examining magistrate of Corbeil were one and the same person.

"The work of the dramatic author may interfere," he said, after a slight hesitation, "with that of the magistrate, especially in a province where one's labours are little more than routine."

"Oh, you may rely on my discretion!" cried Rouletabille.

The train was in motion.

"We have started!" said the examining magistrate, surprised at seeing us still in the carriage.

"Yes, Monsieur,—truth has started," said Rouletabille, smiling amiably,—"on its way to the Chateau du Glandier. A fine case, Monsieur de Marquet,—a fine case!"

"An obscure—incredible, unfathomable, inexplicable affair—and there is only one thing I fear, Monsieur Rouletabille,—that the journalists will be trying to explain it."

My friend felt this a rap on his knuckles.

"Yes," he said simply, "that is to be feared. They meddle in everything. As for my interest, monsieur, I only referred to it by mere chance,—the mere chance of finding myself in the same train with you, and in the same compartment of the same carriage."

"Where are you going, then?" asked Monsieur de Marquet.

"To the Chateau du Glandier," replied Rouletabille, without turning.

"You'll not get in, Monsieur Rouletabille!"

"Will you prevent me?" said my friend, already prepared to fight.

"Not I!—I like the press and journalists too well to be in any way disagreeable to them; but Monsieur Stangerson has given orders for his door to be closed against everybody, and it is well guarded. Not a journalist was able to pass through the gate of the Glandier yesterday."

Monsieur de Marquet compressed his lips and seemed ready to relapse into obstinate silence. He only relaxed a little when Rouletabille no longer left him in ignorance of the fact that we were going to the Glandier for the purpose of shaking hands with an "old and intimate friend," Monsieur Robert Darzac—a man whom Rouletabille had perhaps seen once in his life.

"Poor Robert!" continued the young reporter, "this dreadful affair may be his death,—he is so deeply in love with Mademoiselle Stangerson."

"His sufferings are truly painful to witness," escaped like a regret from the lips of Monsieur de Marquet.

"But it is to be hoped that Mademoiselle Stangerson's life will be saved."

"Let us hope so. Her father told me yesterday that, if she does not recover, it will not be long before he joins her in the grave. What an incalculable loss to science his death would be!"

"The wound on her temple is serious, is it not?"

"Evidently; but, by a wonderful chance, it has not proved mortal. The blow was given with great force."

"Then it was not with the revolver she was wounded," said Rouletabille, glancing at me in triumph.

Monsieur de Marquet appeared greatly embarrassed.

"I didn't say anything—I don't want to say anything—I will not say anything," he said. And he turned towards his Registrar as if he no longer knew us.

But Rouletabille was not to be so easily shaken off. He moved nearer to the examining magistrate and, drawing a copy of the "Matin" from his pocket, he showed it to him and said:

"There is one thing, Monsieur, which I may enquire of you without committing an indiscretion. You have, of course, seen the account given in the 'Matin'? It is absurd, is it not?"

"Not in the slightest, Monsieur."

"What! The 'Yellow Room' has but one barred window—the bars of which have not been moved—and only one door, which had to be broken open—and the assassin was not found!"

"That's so, monsieur,—that's so. That's how the matter stands."

Rouletabille said no more but plunged into thought. A quarter of an hour thus passed.

Coming back to himself again he said, addressing the magistrate:

"How did Mademoiselle Stangerson wear her hair on that evening?"

"I don't know," replied Monsieur de Marquet.

"That's a very important point," said Rouletabille. "Her hair was done up in bands, wasn't it? I feel sure that on that evening, the evening of the crime, she had her hair arranged in bands."

"Then you are mistaken, Monsieur Rouletabille," replied the magistrate; "Mademoiselle Stangerson that evening had her hair drawn up in a knot on the top of her head,—her usual way of arranging it—her forehead completely uncovered. I can assure you, for we have carefully examined the wound. There was no blood on the hair, and the arrangement of it has not been disturbed since the crime was committed."

"You are sure! You are sure that, on the night of the crime, she had not her hair in bands?"

"Quite sure," the magistrate continued, smiling, "because I remember the Doctor saying to me, while he was examining the wound, 'It is a great pity Mademoiselle Stangerson was in the habit of drawing her hair back from her forehead. If she had worn it in bands, the blow she received on the temple would have been weakened.' It seems strange to me that you should attach so much importance to this point."

"Oh! if she had not her hair in bands, I give it up," said Rouletabille, with a despairing gesture.

"And was the wound on her temple a bad one?" he asked presently.

"Terrible."

"With what weapon was it made?"

"That is a secret of the investigation."

"Have you found the weapon—whatever it was?"

The magistrate did not answer.

"And the wound in the throat?"

Here the examining magistrate readily confirmed the decision of the doctor that, if the murderer had pressed her throat a few seconds longer, Mademoiselle Stangerson would have died of strangulation.

"The affair as reported in the 'Matin,'" said Rouletabille eagerly, "seems to me more and more inexplicable. Can you tell me, Monsieur, how many openings there are in the pavilion? I mean doors and windows."

"There are five," replied Monsieur de Marquet, after having coughed once or twice, but no longer resisting the desire he felt to talk of the whole of the incredible mystery of the affair he was investigating. "There are five, of which the door of the vestibule is the only entrance to the pavilion,—a door always automatically closed, which cannot be opened, either from the outer or inside, except with the two special keys which are never out of the possession of either Daddy Jacques or Monsieur Stangerson. Mademoiselle Stangerson had no need for one, since Daddy Jacques lodged in the pavilion and because, during the daytime, she never left her father. When they, all four, rushed into the 'Yellow Room', after breaking open the door of the laboratory, the door in the vestibule remained closed as usual and, of the two keys for opening it, Daddy Jacques had one in his pocket, and Monsieur Stangerson the other. As to the windows of the pavilion, there are four; the one window of the 'Yellow Room' and those of the laboratory looking out on to the country; the window in the vestibule looking into the park."

"It is by that window that he escaped from the pavilion!" cried Rouletabille.

"How do you know that?" demanded Monsieur de Marquet, fixing a strange look on my young friend.

"We'll see later how he got away from the 'Yellow Room'," replied Rouletabille, "but he must have left the pavilion by the vestibule window."

"Once more,—how do you know that?"

"How? Oh, the thing is simple enough! As soon as he found he could not escape by the door of the pavilion his only way out was by the window in the vestibule, unless he could pass through a grated window. The window of the 'Yellow Room' is secured by iron bars, because it looks out upon the open country; the two windows of the laboratory have to be protected in like manner for the same reason. As the murderer got away, I conceive that he found a window that was not barred,—that of the vestibule, which opens on to the park,—that is to say, into the interior of the estate. There's not much magic in all that."

"Yes," said Monsieur de Marquet, "but what you have not guessed is that this single window in the vestibule, though it has no iron bars, has solid iron blinds. Now these iron blinds have remained fastened by their iron latch; and yet we have proof that the murderer made his escape from the pavilion by that window! Traces of blood on the inside wall and on the blinds as well as on the floor, and footmarks, of which I have taken the measurements, attest the fact that the murderer made his escape that way. But then, how did he do it, seeing that the blinds remained fastened on the inside? He passed through them like a shadow. But what is more bewildering than all is that it is impossible to form any idea as to how the murderer got out of the 'Yellow Room', or how he got across the laboratory to reach the vestibule! Ah, yes, Monsieur Rouletabille, it is altogether as you said, a fine case, the key to which will not be discovered for a long time, I hope."

"You hope, Monsieur?"

Monsieur de Marquet corrected himself.

"I do not hope so,—I think so."

"Could that window have been closed and refastened after the flight of the assassin?" asked Rouletabille.

"That is what occurred to me for a moment; but it would imply an accomplice or accomplices,—and I don't see—"

After a short silence he added:

"Ah—if Mademoiselle Stangerson were only well enough today to be questioned!"

Rouletabille following up his thought, asked:

"And the attic?—There must be some opening to that?"

"Yes; there is a window, or rather skylight, in it, which, as it looks out towards the country, Monsieur Stangerson has had barred, like the rest of the windows. These bars, as in the other windows, have remained intact, and the blinds, which naturally open inwards, have not been unfastened. For the rest, we have not discovered anything to lead us to suspect that the murderer had passed through the attic."

"It seems clear to you, then, Monsieur, that the murderer escaped—nobody knows how—by the window in the vestibule?"

"Everything goes to prove it."

"I think so, too," confessed Rouletabille gravely.

After a brief silence, he continued:

"If you have not found any traces of the murderer in the attic, such as the dirty footmarks similar to those on the floor of the 'Yellow Room', you must come to the conclusion that it was not he who stole Daddy Jacques's revolver."

"There are no footmarks in the attic other than those of Daddy Jacques himself," said the magistrate with a significant turn of his head. Then, after an apparent decision, he added: "Daddy Jacques was with Monsieur Stangerson in the laboratory—and it was lucky for him he was."

"Then what part did his revolver play in the tragedy?—It seems very clear that this weapon did less harm to Mademoiselle Stangerson than it did to the murderer."

The magistrate made no reply to this question, which doubtless embarrassed him. "Monsieur Stangerson," he said, "tells us that the two bullets have been found in the 'Yellow Room', one embedded in the wall stained with the impression of a red hand—a man's large hand—and the other in the ceiling."

"Oh! oh! in the ceiling!" muttered Rouletabille. "In the ceiling! That's very curious!—In the ceiling!"

He puffed awhile in silence at his pipe, enveloping himself in the smoke. When we reached Savigny-sur-Orge, I had to tap him on the shoulder to arouse him from his dream and come out on to the platform of the station.

There, the magistrate and his Registrar bowed to us, and by rapidly getting into a cab that was awaiting them, made us understand that they had seen enough of us.

"How long will it take to walk to the Chateau du Glandier?" Rouletabille asked one of the railway porters.

"An hour and a half or an hour and three quarters—easy walking," the man replied.

Rouletabille looked up at the sky and, no doubt, finding its appearance satisfactory, took my arm and said:

"Come on!—I need a walk."

"Are things getting less entangled?" I asked.

"Not a bit of it!" he said, "more entangled than ever! It's true, I have an idea—"

"What's that?" I asked.

"I can't tell you what it is just at present—it's an idea involving the life or death of two persons at least."

"Do you think there were accomplices?"

"I don't think it—"

We fell into silence. Presently he went on:

"It was a bit of luck, our falling in with that examining magistrate and his Registrar, eh? What did I tell you about that revolver?" His head was bent down, he had his hands in his pockets, and he was whistling. After a while I heard him murmur:

"Poor woman!"

"Is it Mademoiselle Stangerson you are pitying?"

"Yes; she's a noble woman and worthy of being pitied!—a woman of a great, a very great character—I imagine—I imagine."

"You know her then?"

"Not at all. I have never seen her."

"Why, then, do you say that she is a woman of great character?"

"Because she bravely faced the murderer; because she courageously defended herself—and, above all, because of the bullet in the ceiling."

I looked at Rouletabille and inwardly wondered whether he was not mocking me, or whether he had not suddenly gone out of his senses. But I saw that he had never been less inclined to laugh, and the brightness of his keenly intelligent eyes assured me that he retained all his reason. Then, too, I was used to his broken way of talking, which only left me puzzled as to his meaning, till, with a very few clear, rapidly uttered words, he would make the drift of his ideas clear to me, and I saw that what he had previously said, and which had appeared to me void of meaning, was so thoroughly logical that I could not understand how it was I had not understood him sooner.

# IV

## "In the Bosom of Wild Nature"

The Chateau du Glandier is one of the oldest chateaux in the Ile de France, where so many building remains of the feudal period are still standing. Built originally in the heart of the forest, in the reign of Philip le Bel, it now could be seen a few hundred yards from the road leading from the village of Sainte-Genevieve to Monthery. A mass of inharmonious structures, it is dominated by a donjon. When the visitor has mounted the crumbling steps of this ancient donjon, he reaches a little plateau where, in the seventeenth century, Georges Philibert de Sequigny, Lord of the Glandier, Maisons-Neuves and other places, built the existing town in an abominably rococo style of architecture.

It was in this place, seemingly belonging entirely to the past, that Professor Stangerson and his daughter installed themselves to lay the foundations for the science of the future. Its solitude, in the depths of woods, was what, more than all, had pleased them. They would have none to witness their labours and intrude on their hopes, but the aged stones and grand old oaks. The Glandier—ancient Glandierum—was so called from the quantity of glands (acorns) which, in all times, had been gathered in that neighbourhood. This land, of present mournful interest, had fallen back, owing to the negligence or abandonment of its owners, into the wild character of primitive nature. The buildings alone, which were hidden there, had preserved traces of their strange metamorphoses. Every age had left on them its imprint; a bit of architecture with which was bound up the remembrance of some terrible event, some bloody adventure. Such was the chateau in which science had taken refuge—a place seemingly designed to be the theatre of mysteries, terror, and death.

Having explained so far, I cannot refrain from making one further reflection. If I have lingered a little over this description of the Glandier, it is not because I have reached the right moment for creating the necessary atmosphere for the unfolding of the tragedy before the eyes of the reader. Indeed, in all this matter, my first care will be to be as simple as is possible. I have no ambition to be an author. An author is always something of a romancer, and God knows, the mystery of the "Yellow

Room" is quite full enough of real tragic horror to require no aid from literary effects. I am, and only desire to be, a faithful "reporter." My duty is to report the event; and I place the event in its frame—that is all. It is only natural that you should know where the things happened.

I return to Monsieur Stangerson. When he bought the estate, fifteen years before the tragedy with which we are engaged occurred, the Chateau du Glandier had for a long time been unoccupied. Another old chateau in the neighbourhood, built in the fourteenth century by Jean de Belmont, was also abandoned, so that that part of the country was very little inhabited. Some small houses on the side of the road leading to Corbeil, an inn, called the "Auberge du Donjon," which offered passing hospitality to waggoners; these were about all to represent civilisation in this out-of-the-way part of the country, but a few leagues from the capital.

But this deserted condition of the place had been the determining reason for the choice made by Monsieur Stangerson and his daughter. Monsieur Stangerson was already celebrated. He had returned from America, where his works had made a great stir. The book which he had published at Philadelphia, on the "Dissociation of Matter by Electric Action," had aroused opposition throughout the whole scientific world. Monsieur Stangerson was a Frenchman, but of American origin. Important matters relating to a legacy had kept him for several years in the United States, where he had continued the work begun by him in France, whither he had returned in possession of a large fortune. This fortune was a great boon to him; for, though he might have made millions of dollars by exploiting two or three of his chemical discoveries relative to new processes of dyeing, it was always repugnant to him to use for his own private gain the wonderful gift of invention he had received from nature. He considered he owed it to mankind, and all that his genius brought into the world went, by this philosophical view of his duty, into the public lap.

If he did not try to conceal his satisfaction at coming into possession of this fortune, which enabled him to give himself up to his passion for pure science, he had equally to rejoice, it seemed to him, for another cause. Mademoiselle Stangerson was, at the time when her father returned from America and bought the Glandier estate, twenty years of age. She was exceedingly pretty, having at once the Parisian grace of her mother, who had died in giving her birth, and all the splendour, all the riches of the young American blood of her parental grandfather, William Stangerson.

A citizen of Philadelphia, William Stangerson had been obliged to become naturalised in obedience to family exigencies at the time of his marriage with a French lady, she who was to be the mother of the illustrious Stangerson. In that way the professor's French nationality is accounted for.

Twenty years of age, a charming blonde, with blue eyes, milk-white complexion, and radiant with divine health, Mathilde Stangerson was one of the most beautiful marriageable girls in either the old or the new world. It was her father's duty, in spite of the inevitable pain which a separation from her would cause him, to think of her marriage; and he was fully prepared for it. Nevertheless, he buried himself and his child at the Glandier at the moment when his friends were expecting him to bring her out into society. Some of them expressed their astonishment, and to their questions he answered: "It is my daughter's wish. I can refuse her nothing. She has chosen the Glandier."

Interrogated in her turn, the young girl replied calmly: "Where could we work better than in this solitude?" For Mademoiselle Stangerson had already begun to collaborate with her father in his work. It could not at the time be imagined that her passion for science would lead her so far as to refuse all the suitors who presented themselves to her for over fifteen years. So secluded was the life led by the two, father and daughter, that they showed themselves only at a few official receptions and, at certain times in the year, in two or three friendly drawing-rooms, where the fame of the professor and the beauty of Mathilde made a sensation. The young girl's extreme reserve did not at first discourage suitors; but at the end of a few years, they tired of their quest.

One alone persisted with tender tenacity and deserved the name of "eternal fiance," a name he accepted with melancholy resignation; that was Monsieur Robert Darzac. Mademoiselle Stangerson was now no longer young, and it seemed that, having found no reason for marrying at five-and-thirty, she would never find one. But such an argument evidently found no acceptance with Monsieur Robert Darzac. He continued to pay his court—if the delicate and tender attention with which he ceaselessly surrounded this woman of five-and-thirty could be called courtship—in face of her declared intention never to marry.

Suddenly, some weeks before the events with which we are occupied, a report—to which nobody attached any importance, so incredible did it sound—was spread about Paris, that Mademoiselle Stangerson had at last consented to "crown" the inextinguishable flame of Monsieur Robert Darzac! It needed that Monsieur Robert

Darzac himself should not deny this matrimonial rumour to give it an appearance of truth, so unlikely did it seem to be well founded. One day, however, Monsieur Stangerson, as he was leaving the Academy of Science, announced that the marriage of his daughter and Monsieur Robert Darzac would be celebrated in the privacy of the Chateau du Glandier, as soon as he and his daughter had put the finishing touches to their report summing up their labours on the "Dissociation of Matter." The new household would install itself in the Glandier, and the son-in-law would lend his assistance in the work to which the father and daughter had dedicated their lives.

The scientific world had barely had time to recover from the effect of this news, when it learned of the attempted assassination of Mademoiselle under the extraordinary conditions which we have detailed and which our visit to the chateau was to enable us to ascertain with yet greater precision. I have not hesitated to furnish the reader with all these retrospective details, known to me through my business relations with Monsieur Robert Darzac. On crossing the threshold of the "Yellow Room" he was as well posted as I was.

# V

## In Which Joseph Rouletabille Makes a Remark to Monsieur Robert Darzac Which Produces Its Little Effect

Rouletabille and I had been walking for several minutes, by the side of a long wall bounding the vast property of Monsieur Stangerson and had already come within sight of the entrance gate, when our attention was drawn to an individual who, half bent to the ground, seemed to be so completely absorbed in what he was doing as not to have seen us coming towards him. At one time he stooped so low as almost to touch the ground; at another he drew himself up and attentively examined the wall; then he looked into the palm of one of his hands, and walked away with rapid strides. Finally he set off running, still looking into the palm of his hand. Rouletabille had brought me to a standstill by a gesture.

"Hush! Frederic Larsan is at work! Don't let us disturb him!"

Rouletabille had a great admiration for the celebrated detective. I had never before seen him, but I knew him well by reputation. At that time, before Rouletabille had given proof of his unique talent, Larsan was reputed as the most skilful unraveller of the most mysterious and complicated crimes. His reputation was world-wide, and the police of London, and even of America, often called him in to their aid when their own national inspectors and detectives found themselves at the end of their wits and resources.

No one was astonished, then, that the head of the Surete had, at the outset of the mystery of the "Yellow Room", telegraphed his precious subordinate to London, where he had been sent on a big case of stolen securities, to return with all haste. Frederic who, at the Surete, was called the "great Frederic," had made all speed, doubtless knowing by experience that, if he was interrupted in what he was doing, it was because his services were urgently needed in another direction; so, as Rouletabille said, he was that morning already "at work." We soon found out in what it consisted.

What he was continually looking at in the palm of his right hand was nothing but his watch, the minute hand of which he appeared to be noting intently. Then he turned back still running, stopping only when he reached the park gate, where he again consulted his watch and then put it away in his pocket, shrugging his shoulders with a gesture of discouragement. He pushed open the park gate, reclosed and locked it, raised his head and, through the bars, perceived us. Rouletabille rushed after him, and I followed. Frederic Larsan waited for us.

"Monsieur Fred," said Rouletabille, raising his hat and showing the profound respect, based on admiration, which the young reporter felt for the celebrated detective, "can you tell me whether Monsieur Robert Darzac is at the chateau at this moment? Here is one of his friends, of the Paris Bar, who desires to speak with him."

"I really don't know, Monsieur Rouletabille," replied Fred, shaking hands with my friend, whom he had several times met in the course of his difficult investigations. "I have not seen him."

"The concierges will be able to inform us no doubt?" said Rouletabille, pointing to the lodge the door and windows of which were close shut.

"The concierges will not be able to give you any information, Monsieur Rouletabille."

"Why not?"

"Because they were arrested half an hour ago."

"Arrested!" cried Rouletabille; "then they are the murderers!"

Frederic Larsan shrugged his shoulders.

"When you can't arrest the real murderer," he said with an air of supreme irony, "you can always indulge in the luxury of discovering accomplices."

"Did you have them arrested, Monsieur Fred?"

"Not I!—I haven't had them arrested. In the first place, I am pretty sure that they have not had anything to do with the affair, and then because—"

"Because of what?" asked Rouletabille eagerly.

"Because of nothing," said Larsan, shaking his head.

"Because there were no accomplices!" said Rouletabille.

"Aha!—you have an idea, then, about this matter?" said Larsan, looking at Rouletabille intently, "yet you have seen nothing, young man—you have not yet gained admission here!"

"I shall get admission."

"I doubt it. The orders are strict."

"I shall gain admission, if you let me see Monsieur Robert Darzac. Do that for me. You know we are old friends. I beg of you, Monsieur

Fred. Do you remember the article I wrote about you on the gold bar case?"

The face of Rouletabille at the moment was really funny to look at. It showed such an irresistible desire to cross the threshold beyond which some prodigious mystery had occurred; it appealed with so much eloquence, not only of the mouth and eyes, but with all its features, that I could not refrain from bursting into laughter. Frederic Larsan, no more than myself, could retain his gravity. Meanwhile, standing on the other side of the gate, he calmly put the key in his pocket. I closely scrutinised him.

He might be about fifty years of age. He had a fine head, his hair turning grey; a colourless complexion, and a firm profile. His forehead was prominent, his chin and cheeks clean shaven. His upper lip, without moustache, was finely chiselled. His eyes were rather small and round, with a look in them that was at once searching and disquieting. He was of middle height and well built, with a general bearing elegant and gentlemanly. There was nothing about him of the vulgar policeman. In his way, he was an artist, and one felt that he had a high opinion of himself. The sceptical tone of his conversation was that of a man who had been taught by experience. His strange profession had brought him into contact with so many crimes and villanies that it would have been remarkable if his nature had not been a little hardened.

Larsan turned his head at the sound of a vehicle which had come from the chateau and reached the gate behind him. We recognised the cab which had conveyed the examining magistrate and his Registrar from the station at Epinay.

"Ah!" said Frederic Larsan, "if you want to speak with Monsieur Robert Darzac, he is here."

The cab was already at the park gate and Robert Darzac was begging Frederic Larsan to open it for him, explaining that he was pressed for time to catch the next train leaving Epinay for Paris. Then he recognised me. While Larsan was unlocking the gate, Monsieur Darzac inquired what had brought me to the Glandier at such a tragic moment. I noticed that he was frightfully pale, and that his face was lined as if from the effects of some terrible suffering.

"Is Mademoiselle getting better?" I immediately asked.

"Yes," he said. "She will be saved perhaps. She must be saved!"

He did not add "or it will be my death"; but I felt that the phrase trembled on his pale lips.

Rouletabille intervened:

"You are in a hurry, Monsieur; but I must speak with you. I have something of the greatest importance to tell you."

Frederic Larsan interrupted:

"May I leave you?" he asked of Robert Darzac. "Have you a key, or do you wish me to give you this one."

"Thank you. I have a key and will lock the gate."

Larsan hurried off in the direction of the chateau, the imposing pile of which could be perceived a few hundred yards away.

Robert Darzac, with knit brow, was beginning to show impatience. I presented Rouletabille as a good friend of mine, but, as soon as he learnt that the young man was a journalist, he looked at me very reproachfully, excused himself, under the necessity of having to reach Epinay in twenty minutes, bowed, and whipped up his horse. But Rouletabille had seized the bridle and, to my utter astonishment, stopped the carriage with a vigorous hand. Then he gave utterance to a sentence which was utterly meaningless to me.

"The presbytery has lost nothing of its charm, nor the garden its brightness."

The words had no sooner left the lips of Rouletabille than I saw Robert Darzac quail. Pale as he was, he became paler. His eyes were fixed on the young man in terror, and he immediately descended from the vehicle in an inexpressible state of agitation.

"Come!—come in!" he stammered.

Then, suddenly, and with a sort of fury, he repeated:

"Let us go, monsieur."

He turned up by the road he had come from the chateau, Rouletabille still retaining his hold on the horse's bridle. I addressed a few words to Monsieur Darzac, but he made no answer. My looks questioned Rouletabille, but his gaze was elsewhere.

# VI

## In the Heart of the Oak Grove

W e reached the chateau, and, as we approached it, saw four gendarmes pacing in front of a little door in the ground floor of the donjon. We soon learned that in this ground floor, which had formerly served as a prison, Monsieur and Madame Bernier, the concierges, were confined. Monsieur Robert Darzac led us into the modern part of the chateau by a large door, protected by a projecting awning—a "marquise" as it is called. Rouletabille, who had resigned the horse and the cab to the care of a servant, never took his eyes off Monsieur Darzac. I followed his look and perceived that it was directed solely towards the gloved hands of the Sorbonne professor. When we were in a tiny sitting-room fitted with old furniture, Monsieur Darzac turned to Rouletabille and said sharply:

"What do you want?"

The reporter answered in an equally sharp tone:

"To shake you by the hand."

Darzac shrank back.

"What does that mean?"

Evidently he understood, what I also understood, that my friend suspected him of the abominable attempt on the life of Mademoiselle Stangerson. The impression of the blood-stained hand on the walls of the "Yellow Room" was in his mind. I looked at the man closely. His haughty face with its expression ordinarily so straightforward was at this moment strangely troubled. He held out his right hand and, referring to me, said:

"As you are a friend of Monsieur Sainclair who has rendered me invaluable services in a just cause, monsieur, I see no reason for refusing you my hand—"

Rouletabille did not take the extended hand. Lying with the utmost audacity, he said:

"Monsieur, I have lived several years in Russia, where I have acquired the habit of never taking any but an ungloved hand."

I thought that the Sorbonne professor would express his anger openly, but, on the contrary, by a visibly violent effort, he calmed himself, took off his gloves, and showed his hands; they were unmarked by any cicatrix.

"Are you satisfied?"

"No!" replied Rouletabille. "My dear friend," he said, turning to me, "I am obliged to ask you to leave us alone for a moment."

I bowed and retired; stupefied by what I had seen and heard. I could not understand why Monsieur Robert Darzac had not already shown the door to my impertinent, insulting, and stupid friend. I was angry myself with Rouletabille at that moment, for his suspicions, which had led to this scene of the gloves.

For some twenty minutes I walked about in front of the chateau, trying vainly to link together the different events of the day. What was in Rouletabille's mind? Was it possible that he thought Monsieur Robert Darzac to be the murderer? How could it be thought that this man, who was to have married Mademoiselle Stangerson in the course of a few days, had introduced himself into the "Yellow Room" to assassinate his fiancee? I could find no explanation as to how the murderer had been able to leave the "Yellow Room"; and so long as that mystery, which appeared to me so inexplicable, remained unexplained, I thought it was the duty of all of us to refrain from suspecting anybody. But, then, that seemingly senseless phrase—"The presbytery has lost nothing of its charm, nor the garden its brightness"—still rang in my ears. What did it mean? I was eager to rejoin Rouletabille and question him.

At that moment the young man came out of the chateau in the company of Monsieur Robert Darzac, and, extraordinary to relate, I saw, at a glance, that they were the best of friends. "We are going to the 'Yellow Room'. Come with us," Rouletabille said to me. "You know, my dear boy, I am going to keep you with me all day. We'll breakfast together somewhere about here—"

"You'll breakfast with me, here, gentlemen—"

"No, thanks," replied the young man. "We shall breakfast at the Donjon Inn."

"You'll fare very badly there; you'll not find anything—"

"Do you think so? Well, I hope to find something there," replied Rouletabille. "After breakfast, we'll set to work again. I'll write my article and if you'll be so good as to take it to the office for me—"

"Won't you come back with me to Paris?"

"No; I shall remain here."

I turned towards Rouletabille. He spoke quite seriously, and Monsieur Robert Darzac did not appear to be in the least degree surprised.

We were passing by the donjon and heard wailing voices. Rouletabille asked:

"Why have these people been arrested?"

"It is a little my fault," said Monsieur Darzac. "I happened to remark to the examining magistrate yesterday that it was inexplicable that the concierges had had time to hear the revolver shots, to dress themselves, and to cover so great a distance as that which lies between their lodge and the pavilion, in the space of two minutes; for not more than that interval of time had elapsed after the firing of the shots when they were met by Daddy Jacques."

"That was suspicious evidently," acquiesced Rouletabille. "And were they dressed?"

"That is what is so incredible—they were dressed—completely—not one part of their costume wanting. The woman wore sabots, but the man had on laced boots. Now they assert that they went to bed at half-past nine. On arriving this morning, the examining magistrate brought with him from Paris a revolver of the same calibre as that found in the room (for he couldn't use the one held for evidence), and made his Registrar fire two shots in the 'Yellow Room' while the doors and windows were closed. We were with him in the lodge of the concierges, and yet we heard nothing, not a sound. The concierges have lied, of that there can be no doubt. They must have been already waiting, not far from the pavilion, waiting for something! Certainly they are not to be accused of being the authors of the crime, but their complicity is not improbable. That was why Monsieur de Marquet had them arrested at once."

"If they had been accomplices," said Rouletabille, "they would not have been there at all. When people throw themselves into the arms of justice with the proofs of complicity on them, you can be sure they are not accomplices. I don't believe there are any accomplices in this affair."

"Then, why were they abroad at midnight? Why don't they say?"

"They have certainly some reason for their silence. What that reason is, has to be found out; for, even if they are not accomplices, it may be of importance. Everything that took place on such a night is important."

We had crossed an old bridge thrown over the Douve and were entering the part of the park called the Oak Grove, the oaks here were centuries old. Autumn had already shrivelled their tawny leaves, and their high branches, black and contorted, looked like horrid heads of hair, mingled with quaint reptiles such as the ancient sculptors have made on the head of Medusa. This place, which Mademoiselle found cheerful and in which she lived in the summer season, appeared to us as sad and funereal now. The soil was black and muddy from the recent rains and the rotting of the fallen leaves; the trunks of the trees were black and the sky above us was now, as if in mourning, charged with great, heavy clouds.

And it was in this sombre and desolate retreat that we saw the white walls of the pavilion as we approached. A queer-looking building without a window visible on the side by which we neared it. A little door alone marked the entrance to it. It might have passed for a tomb, a vast mausoleum in the midst of a thick forest. As we came nearer, we were able to make out its disposition. The building obtained all the light it needed from the south, that is to say, from the open country. The little door closed on the park. Monsieur and Mademoiselle Stangerson must have found it an ideal seclusion for their work and their dreams.

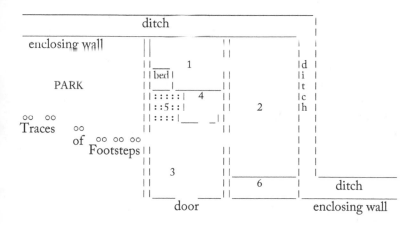

Here is the ground plan of the pavilion. It had a ground-floor which was reached by a few steps, and above it was an attic, with which we need not concern ourselves. The plan of the ground-floor only, sketched roughly, is what I here submit to the reader.

1. The "Yellow Room", with its one window and its one door opening into the laboratory.
2. Laboratory, with its two large, barred windows and its doors, one serving for the vestibule, the other for the "Yellow Room".

3. Vestibule, with its unbarred window and door opening into the park.
4. Lavatory.
5. Stairs leading to the attic.
6. Large and the only chimney in the pavilion, serving for the experiments of the laboratory.

The plan was drawn by Rouletabille, and I assured myself that there was not a line in it that was wanting to help to the solution of the problem then set before the police. With the lines of this plan and the description of its parts before them, my readers will know as much as Rouletabille knew when he entered the pavilion for the first time. With him they may now ask: How did the murderer escape from the "Yellow Room"? Before mounting the three steps leading up to the door of the pavilion, Rouletabille stopped and asked Monsieur Darzac point blank:

"What was the motive for the crime?"

"Speaking for myself, Monsieur, there can be no doubt on the matter," said Mademoiselle Stangerson's fiance, greatly distressed. "The nails of the fingers, the deep scratches on the chest and throat of Mademoiselle Stangerson show that the wretch who attacked her attempted to commit a frightful crime. The medical experts who examined these traces yesterday affirm that they were made by the same hand as that which left its red imprint on the wall; an enormous hand, Monsieur, much too large to go into my gloves," he added with an indefinable smile.

"Could not that blood-stained hand," I interrupted, "have been the hand of Mademoiselle Stangerson who, in the moment of falling, had pressed it against the wall, and, in slipping, enlarged the impression?"

"There was not a drop of blood on either of her hands when she was lifted up," replied Monsieur Darzac.

"We are now sure," said I, "that it was Mademoiselle Stangerson who was armed with Daddy Jacques's revolver, since she wounded the hand of the murderer. She was in fear, then, of somebody or something."

"Probably."

"Do you suspect anybody?"

"No," replied Monsieur Darzac, looking at Rouletabille. Rouletabille then said to me:

"You must know, my friend, that the inquiry is a little more advanced than Monsieur de Marquet has chosen to tell us. He not only knows that Mademoiselle Stangerson defended herself with the revolver, but he knows what the weapon was that was used to attack her. Monsieur Darzac tells me it was a mutton-bone. Why is Monsieur de Marquet surrounding this mutton-bone with so much mystery? No doubt for the purpose of facilitating the inquiries of the agents of the Sureté? He imagines, perhaps, that the owner of this instrument of crime, the most terrible invented, is going to be found amongst those who are well-known in the slums of Paris who use it. But who can ever say what passes through the brain of an examining magistrate?" Rouletabille added with contemptuous irony.

"Has a mutton-bone been found in the 'Yellow Room'?" I asked him.

"Yes, Monsieur," said Robert Darzac, "at the foot of the bed; but I beg of you not to say anything about it." (I made a gesture of assent.) "It was an enormous mutton-bone, the top of which, or rather the joint, was still red with the blood of the frightful wound. It was an old bone, which may, according to appearances, have served in other crimes. That's what Monsieur de Marquet thinks. He has had it sent to the municipal laboratory at Paris to be analysed. In fact, he thinks he has detected on it, not only the blood of the last victim, but other stains of dried blood, evidences of previous crimes."

"A mutton-bone in the hand of a skilled assassin is a frightful weapon," said Rouletabille, "a more certain weapon than a heavy hammer."

"The scoundrel has proved it to be so," said Monsieur Robert Darzac, sadly. "The joint of the bone found exactly fits the wound inflicted.

"My belief is that the wound would have been mortal, if the murderer's blow had not been arrested in the act by Mademoiselle Stangerson's revolver. Wounded in the hand, he dropped the mutton-bone and fled. Unfortunately, the blow had been already given, and Mademoiselle was stunned after having been nearly strangled. If she had succeeded in wounding the man with the first shot of the revolver, she would, doubtless, have escaped the blow with the bone. But she had certainly employeeed her revolver too late; the first shot deviated and lodged in the ceiling; it was the second only that took effect."

Having said this, Monsieur Darzac knocked at the door of the pavilion. I must confess to feeling a strong impatience to reach the spot where the crime had been committed. It was some time before the door was opened by a man whom I at once recognised as Daddy Jacques.

He appeared to be well over sixty years of age. He had a long white beard and white hair, on which he wore a flat Basque cap. He was dressed in a complete suit of chestnut-coloured velveteen, worn at the sides; sabots were on his feet. He had rather a waspish-looking face, the expression of which lightened, however, as soon as he saw Monsieur Darzac.

"Friends," said our guide. "Nobody in the pavilion, Daddy Jacques?"

"I ought not to allow anybody to enter, Monsieur Robert, but of course the order does not apply to you. These gentlemen of justice have seen everything there is to be seen, and made enough drawings, and drawn up enough reports—"

"Excuse me, Monsieur Jacques, one question before anything else," said Rouletabille.

"What is it, young man? If I can answer it—"

"Did your mistress wear her hair in bands, that evening? You know what I mean—over her forehead?"

"No, young man. My mistress never wore her hair in the way you suggest, neither on that day nor on any other. She had her hair drawn up, as usual, so that her beautiful forehead could be seen, pure as that of an unborn child!"

Rouletabille grunted and set to work examining the door, finding that it fastened itself automatically. He satisfied himself that it could never remain open and needed a key to open it. Then we entered the vestibule, a small, well-lit room paved with square red tiles.

"Ah! This is the window by which the murderer escaped!" said Rouletabille.

"So they keep on saying, monsieur, so they keep on saying! But if he had gone off that way, we should have been sure to have seen him. We are not blind, neither Monsieur Stangerson nor me, nor the concierges who are in prison. Why have they not put me in prison, too, on account of my revolver?"

Rouletabille had already opened the window and was examining the shutters.

"Were these closed at the time of the crime?"

"And fastened with the iron catch inside," said Daddy Jacques, "and I am quite sure that the murderer did not get out that way."

"Are there any blood stains?"

"Yes, on the stones outside; but blood of what?"

"Ah!" said Rouletabille, "there are footmarks visible on the path—the ground was very moist. I will look into that presently."

"Nonsense!" interrupted Daddy Jacques; "the murderer did not go that way."

"Which way did he go, then?"

"How do I know?"

Rouletabille looked at everything, smelled everything. He went down on his knees and rapidly examined every one of the paving tiles. Daddy Jacques went on:

"Ah!—you can't find anything, monsieur. Nothing has been found. And now it is all dirty; too many persons have tramped over it. They wouldn't let me wash it, but on the day of the crime I had washed the floor thoroughly, and if the murderer had crossed it with his hobnailed boots, I should not have failed to see where he had been; he has left marks enough in Mademoiselle's chamber."

Rouletabille rose.

"When was the last time you washed these tiles?" he asked, and he fixed on Daddy Jacques a most searching look.

"Why—as I told you—on the day of the crime, towards half-past five—while Mademoiselle and her father were taking a little walk before dinner, here in this room: they had dined in the laboratory. The next day, the examining magistrate came and saw all the marks there were on the floor as plainly as if they had been made with ink on white paper. Well, neither in the laboratory nor in the vestibule, which were both as clean as a new pin, were there any traces of a man's footmarks. Since they have been found near this window outside, he must have made his way through the ceiling of the 'Yellow Room' into the attic, then cut his way through the roof and dropped to the ground outside the vestibule window. But—there's no hole, neither in the ceiling of the 'Yellow Room' nor in the roof of my attic—that's absolutely certain! So you see we know nothing—nothing! And nothing will ever be known! It's a mystery of the Devil's own making."

Rouletabille went down upon his knees again almost in front of a small lavatory at the back of the vestibule. In that position he remained for about a minute.

"Well?" I asked him when he got up.

"Oh! nothing very important,—a drop of blood," he replied, turning towards Daddy Jacques as he spoke. "While you were washing the laboratory and this vestibule, was the vestibule window open?" he asked.

"No, Monsieur, it was closed; but after I had done washing the floor, I lit some charcoal for Monsieur in the laboratory furnace, and, as I lit it with old newspapers, it smoked, so I opened both the windows in the laboratory and this one, to make a current of air; then I shut those in the laboratory and left this one open when I went out. When I returned to the pavilion, this window had been closed and Monsieur and Mademoiselle were already at work in the laboratory."

"Monsieur or Mademoiselle Stangerson had, no doubt, shut it?"

"No doubt."

"You did not ask them?"

After a close scrutiny of the little lavatory and of the staircase leading up to the attic, Rouletabille—to whom we seemed no longer to exist—entered the laboratory. I followed him. It was, I confess, in a state of great excitement. Robert Darzac lost none of my friend's movements. As for me, my eyes were drawn at once to the door of the "Yellow Room". It was closed and, as I immediately saw, partially shattered and out of commission.

My friend, who went about his work methodically, silently studied the room in which we were. It was large and well-lighted. Two big windows—almost bays—were protected by strong iron bars and looked out upon a wide extent of country. Through an opening in the forest, they commanded a wonderful view through the length of the valley and across the plain to the large town which could be clearly seen in fair weather. Today, however, a mist hung over the ground—and blood in that room!

The whole of one side of the laboratory was taken up with a large chimney, crucibles, ovens, and such implements as are needed for chemical experiments; tables, loaded with phials, papers, reports, an electrical machine,—an apparatus, as Monsieur Darzac informed me, employeeed by Professor Stangerson to demonstrate the Dissociation of Matter under the action of solar light—and other scientific implements.

Along the walls were cabinets, plain or glass-fronted, through which were visible microscopes, special photographic apparatus, and a large quantity of crystals.

Rouletabille, who was ferreting in the chimney, put his fingers into one of the crucibles. Suddenly he drew himself up, and held up a piece of half-consumed paper in his hand. He stepped up to where we were talking by one of the windows.

"Keep that for us, Monsieur Darzac," he said.

I bent over the piece of scorched paper which Monsieur Darzac took from the hand of Rouletabille, and read distinctly the only words that remained legible:

"Presbytery—lost nothing—charm, nor the gar—its brightness."

Twice since the morning these same meaningless words had struck me, and, for the second time, I saw that they produced on the Sorbonne professor the same paralysing effect. Monsieur Darzac's first anxiety showed itself when he turned his eyes in the direction of Daddy Jacques. But, occupied as he was at another window, he had seen nothing. Then tremblingly opening his pocket-book he put the piece of paper into it, sighing: "My God!"

During this time, Rouletabille had mounted into the opening of the fire-grate—that is to say, he had got upon the bricks of a furnace—and was attentively examining the chimney, which grew narrower towards the top, the outlet from it being closed with sheets of iron, fastened into the brickwork, through which passed three small chimneys.

"Impossible to get out that way," he said, jumping back into the laboratory. "Besides, even if he had tried to do it, he would have brought all that ironwork down to the ground. No, no; it is not on that side we have to search."

Rouletabille next examined the furniture and opened the doors of the cabinet. Then he came to the windows, through which he declared no one could possibly have passed. At the second window he found Daddy Jacques in contemplation.

"Well, Daddy Jacques," he said, "what are you looking at?"

"That policeman who is always going round and round the lake. Another of those fellows who think they can see better than anybody else!"

"You don't know Frederic Larsan, Daddy Jacques, or you wouldn't speak of him in that way," said Rouletabille in a melancholy tone. "If there is anyone who will find the murderer, it will be he." And Rouletabille heaved a deep sigh.

"Before they find him, they will have to learn how they lost him," said Daddy Jacques, stolidly.

At length we reached the door of the "Yellow Room" itself.

"There is the door behind which some terrible scene took place," said Rouletabille, with a solemnity which, under any other circumstances, would have been comical.

# VII

## In Which Rouletabille Sets Out on an Expedition Under the Bed

Rouletabille having pushed open the door of the "Yellow Room" paused on the threshold saying, with an emotion which I only later understood, "Ah, the perfume of the lady in black!"

The chamber was dark. Daddy Jacques was about to open the blinds when Rouletabille stopped him.

"Did not the tragedy take place in complete darkness?" he asked.

"No, young man, I don't think so. Mademoiselle always had a nightlight on her table, and I lit it every evening before she went to bed. I was a sort of chambermaid, you must understand, when the evening came. The real chambermaid did not come here much before the morning. Mademoiselle worked late—far into the night."

"Where did the table with the night-light stand,—far from the bed?"

"Some way from the bed."

"Can you light the burner now?"

"The lamp is broken and the oil that was in it was spilled when the table was upset. All the rest of the things in the room remain just as they were. I have only to open the blinds for you to see."

"Wait."

Rouletabille went back into the laboratory, closed the shutters of the two windows and the door of the vestibule.

When we were in complete darkness, he lit a wax vesta, and asked Daddy Jacques to move to the middle of the chamber with it to the place where the night-light was burning that night.

Daddy Jacques who was in his stockings—he usually left his sabots in the vestibule—entered the "Yellow Room" with his bit of a vesta. We vaguely distinguished objects overthrown on the floor, a bed in one corner, and, in front of us, to the left, the gleam of a looking-glass hanging on the wall, near to the bed.

"That will do!—you may now open the blinds," said Rouletabille.

"Don't come any further," Daddy Jacques begged, "you may make marks with your boots, and nothing must be deranged; it's an idea of the magistrate's—though he has nothing more to do here."

And he pushed open the shutter. The pale daylight entered from without, throwing a sinister light on the saffron-coloured walls. The floor—for though the laboratory and the vestibule were tiled, the "Yellow Room" had a flooring of wood—was covered with a single yellow mat which was large enough to cover nearly the whole room, under the bed and under the dressing-table—the only piece of furniture that remained upright. The centre round table, the night-table and two chairs had been overturned. These did not prevent a large stain of blood being visible on the mat, made, as Daddy Jacques informed us, by the blood which had flowed from the wound on Mademoiselle Stangerson's forehead. Besides these stains, drops of blood had fallen in all directions, in line with the visible traces of the footsteps—large and black—of the murderer. Everything led to the presumption that these drops of blood had fallen from the wound of the man who had, for a moment, placed his red hand on the wall. There were other traces of the same hand on the wall, but much less distinct.

"See!—see this blood on the wall!" I could not help exclaiming. "The man who pressed his hand so heavily upon it in the darkness must certainly have thought that he was pushing at a door! That's why he pressed on it so hard, leaving on the yellow paper the terrible evidence. I don't think there are many hands in the world of that sort. It is big and strong and the fingers are nearly all one as long as the other! The thumb is wanting and we have only the mark of the palm; but if we follow the trace of the hand," I continued, "we see that, after leaving its imprint on the wall, the touch sought the door, found it, and then felt for the lock—"

"No doubt," interrupted Rouletabille, chuckling,—"only there is no blood, either on the lock or on the bolt!"

"What does that prove?" I rejoined with a good sense of which I was proud; "he might have opened the lock with his left hand, which would have been quite natural, his right hand being wounded."

"He didn't open it at all!" Daddy Jacques again exclaimed. "We are not fools; and there were four of us when we burst open the door!"

"What a queer hand!—Look what a queer hand it is!" I said.

"It is a very natural hand," said Rouletabille, "of which the shape has been deformed by its having slipped on the wall. The man dried his hand on the wall. He must be a man about five feet eight in height."

"How do you come at that?"

"By the height of the marks on the wall."

My friend next occupied himself with the mark of the bullet in the wall. It was a round hole.

"This ball was fired straight, not from above, and consequently, not from below."

Rouletabille went back to the door and carefully examined the lock and the bolt, satisfying himself that the door had certainly been burst open from the outside, and, further, that the key had been found in the lock on the inside of the chamber. He finally satisfied himself that with the key in the lock, the door could not possibly be opened from without with another key. Having made sure of all these details, he let fall these words: "That's better!"—Then sitting down on the ground, he hastily took off his boots and, in his socks, went into the room.

The first thing he did was to examine minutely the overturned furniture. We watched him in silence.

"Young fellow, you are giving yourself a great deal of trouble," said Daddy Jacques ironically.

Rouletabille raised his head and said:

"You have spoken the simple truth, Daddy Jacques; your mistress did not have her hair in bands that evening. I was a donkey to have believed she did."

Then, with the suppleness of a serpent, he slipped under the bed. Presently we heard him ask:

"At what time, Monsieur Jacques, did Monsieur and Mademoiselle Stangerson arrive at the laboratory?"

"At six o'clock."

The voice of Rouletabille continued:

"Yes,—he's been under here,—that's certain; in fact, there was no where else where he could have hidden himself. Here, too, are the marks of his hobnails. When you entered—all four of you—did you look under the bed?"

"At once,—we drew it right out of its place—"

"And between the mattresses?"

"There was only one on the bed, and on that Mademoiselle was placed; and Monsieur Stangerson and the concierge immediately carried it into the laboratory. Under the mattress there was nothing but the metal netting, which could not conceal anything or anybody. Remember, monsieur, that there were four of us and we couldn't fail to see everything—the chamber is so small and scantily furnished, and all was locked behind in the pavilion."

I ventured on a hypothesis:

"Perhaps he got away with the mattress—in the mattress!—Anything is possible, in the face of such a mystery! In their distress of mind Monsieur Stangerson and the concierge may not have noticed they were bearing a double weight; especially if the concierge were an accomplice! I throw out this hypothesis for what it is worth, but it explains many things,—and particularly the fact that neither the laboratory nor the vestibule bear any traces of the footmarks found in the room. If, in carrying Mademoiselle on the mattress from the laboratory of the chateau, they rested for a moment, there might have been an opportunity for the man in it to escape.

"And then?" asked Rouletabille, deliberately laughing under the bed.

I felt rather vexed and replied:

"I don't know,—but anything appears possible"—

"The examining magistrate had the same idea, monsieur," said Daddy Jacques, "and he carefully examined the mattress. He was obliged to laugh at the idea, monsieur, as your friend is doing now,—for whoever heard of a mattress having a double bottom?"

I was myself obliged to laugh, on seeing that what I had said was absurd; but in an affair like this one hardly knows where an absurdity begins or ends.

My friend alone seemed able to talk intelligently. He called out from under the bed.

"The mat here has been moved out of place,—who did it?"

"We did, monsieur," explained Daddy Jacques. "When we could not find the assassin, we asked ourselves whether there was not some hole in the floor—"

"There is not," replied Rouletabille. "Is there a cellar?"

"No, there's no cellar. But that has not stopped our searching, and has not prevented the examining magistrate and his Registrar from studying the floor plank by plank, as if there had been a cellar under it."

The reporter then reappeared. His eyes were sparkling and his nostrils quivered. He remained on his hands and knees. He could not be better likened than to an admirable sporting dog on the scent of some unusual game. And, indeed, he was scenting the steps of a man,—the man whom he has sworn to report to his master, the manager of the "Epoque." It must not be forgotten that Rouletabille was first and last a journalist.

Thus, on his hands and knees, he made his way to the four corners of the room, so to speak, sniffing and going round everything—everything that we could see, which was not much, and everything that we could not see, which must have been infinite.

The toilette table was a simple table standing on four legs; there was nothing about it by which it could possibly be changed into a temporary hiding-place. There was not a closet or cupboard. Mademoiselle Stangerson kept her wardrobe at the chateau.

Rouletabille literally passed his nose and hands along the walls, constructed of solid brickwork. When he had finished with the walls, and passed his agile fingers over every portion of the yellow paper covering them, he reached to the ceiling, which he was able to touch by mounting on a chair placed on the toilette table, and by moving this ingeniously constructed stage from place to place he examined every foot of it. When he had finished his scrutiny of the ceiling, where he carefully examined the hole made by the second bullet, he approached the window, and, once more, examined the iron bars and blinds, all of which were solid and intact. At last, he gave a grunt of satisfaction and declared "Now I am at ease!"

"Well,—do you believe that the poor dear young lady was shut up when she was being murdered—when she cried out for help?" wailed Daddy Jacques.

"Yes," said the young reporter, drying his forehead, "the 'Yellow Room' was as tightly shut as an iron safe."

"That," I said, "is why this mystery is the most surprising I know. Edgar Allan Poe, in 'The Murders in the Rue Morgue,' invented nothing like it. The place of that crime was sufficiently closed to prevent the escape of a man; but there was that window through which the monkey, the perpetrator of the murder, could slip away! But here, there can be no question of an opening of any sort. The door was fastened, and through the window blinds, secure as they were, not even a fly could enter or get out."

"True, true," assented Rouletabille as he kept on drying his forehead, which seemed to be perspiring less from his recent bodily exertion than from his mental agitation. "Indeed, it's a great, a beautiful, and a very curious mystery."

"The Bete du bon Dieu," muttered Daddy Jacques, "the Bete du bon Dieu herself, if she had committed the crime, could not have escaped. Listen! Do you hear it? Hush!"

Daddy Jacques made us a sign to keep quiet and, stretching his arm towards the wall nearest the forest, listened to something which we could not hear.

"It's answering," he said at length. "I must kill it. It is too wicked, but it's the Bete du bon Dieu, and, every night, it goes to pray on the tomb of Sainte-Genevieve and nobody dares to touch her, for fear that Mother Angenoux should cast an evil spell on them."

"How big is the Bete du bon Dieu?"

"Nearly as big as a small retriever,—a monster, I tell you. Ah!—I have asked myself more than once whether it was not her that took our poor Mademoiselle by the throat with her claws. But the Bete du bon Dieu does not wear hobnailed boots, nor fire revolvers, nor has she a hand like that!" exclaimed Daddy Jacques, again pointing out to us the red mark on the wall. "Besides, we should have seen her as well as we would have seen a man—"

"Evidently," I said. "Before we had seen this 'Yellow Room', I had also asked myself whether the cat of Mother Angenoux—"

"You also!" cried Rouletabille.

"Didn't you?" I asked.

"Not for a moment. After reading the article in the 'Matin,' I knew that a cat had nothing to do with the matter. But I swear now that a frightful tragedy has been enacted here. You say nothing about the Basque cap, or the handkerchief, found here, Daddy Jacques?"

"Of course, the magistrate has taken them," the old man answered, hesitatingly.

"I haven't seen either the handkerchief or the cap, yet I can tell you how they are made," the reporter said to him gravely.

"Oh, you are very clever," said Daddy Jacques, coughing and embarrassed.

"The handkerchief is a large one, blue with red stripes and the cap is an old Basque cap, like the one you are wearing now."

"You are a wizard!" said Daddy Jacques, trying to laugh and not quite succeeding. "How do you know that the handkerchief is blue with red stripes?"

"Because, if it had not been blue with red stripes, it would not have been found at all."

Without giving any further attention to Daddy Jacques, my friend took a piece of paper from his pocket, and taking out a pair of scissors, bent over the footprints. Placing the paper over one of them he began to cut. In a short time he had made a perfect pattern which he handed to me, begging me not to lose it.

He then returned to the window and, pointing to the figure of Frederic Larsan, who had not quitted the side of the lake, asked Daddy Jacques whether the detective had, like himself, been working in the "Yellow Room"?

"No," replied Robert Darzac, who, since Rouletabille had handed him the piece of scorched paper, had not uttered a word, "He pretends that he does not need to examine the 'Yellow Room'. He says that the murderer made his escape from it in quite a natural way, and that he will, this evening, explain how he did it."

As he listened to what Monsieur Darzac had to say, Rouletabille turned pale.

"Has Frederic Larsan found out the truth, which I can only guess at?" he murmured. "He is very clever—very clever—and I admire him. But what we have to do today is something more than the work of a policeman, something quite different from the teachings of experience. We have to take hold of our reason by the right end."

The reporter rushed into the open air, agitated by the thought that the great and famous Fred might anticipate him in the solution of the problem of the "Yellow Room".

I managed to reach him on the threshold of the pavilion. "Calm yourself, my dear fellow," I said. "Aren't you satisfied?"

"Yes," he confessed to me, with a deep sigh. "I am quite satisfied. I have discovered many things."

"Moral or material?"

"Several moral,—one material. This, for example."

And rapidly he drew from his waistcoat pocket a piece of paper in which he had placed a light-coloured hair from a woman's head.

# VIII

## The Examining Magistrate Questions Mademoiselle Stangerson

Two minutes later, as Rouletabille was bending over the footprints discovered in the park, under the window of the vestibule, a man, evidently a servant at the chateau, came towards us rapidly and called out to Monsieur Darzac then coming out of the pavilion:

"Monsieur Robert, the magistrate, you know, is questioning Mademoiselle."

Monsieur Darzac uttered a muttered excuse to us and set off running towards the chateau, the man running after him.

"If the corpse can speak," I said, "it would be interesting to be there."

"We must know," said my friend. "Let's go to the chateau." And he drew me with him. But, at the chateau, a gendarme placed in the vestibule denied us admission up the staircase of the first floor. We were obliged to wait down stairs.

This is what passed in the chamber of the victim while we were waiting below.

The family doctor, finding that Mademoiselle Stangerson was much better, but fearing a relapse which would no longer permit of her being questioned, had thought it his duty to inform the examining magistrate of this, who decided to proceed immediately with a brief examination. At this examination, the Registrar, Monsieur Stangerson, and the doctor were present. Later, I obtained the text of the report of the examination, and I give it here, in all its legal dryness:

QUESTION: Are you able, mademoiselle, without too much fatiguing yourself, to give some necessary details of the frightful attack of which you have been the victim?

ANSWER: I feel much better, monsieur, and I will tell you all I know. When I entered my chamber I did not notice anything unusual there.

Q: Excuse me, mademoiselle,—if you will allow me, I will ask you some questions and you will answer them. That will fatigue you less than making a long recital.

A: Do so, monsieur.

Q: What did you do on that day?—I want you to be as minute and precise as possible. I wish to know all you did that day, if it is not asking too much of you.

A: I rose late, at ten o'clock, for my father and I had returned home late on the night previously, having been to dinner at the reception given by the President of the Republic, in honour of the Academy of Science of Philadelphia. When I left my chamber, at half-past ten, my father was already at work in the laboratory. We worked together till midday. We then took half-an-hour's walk in the park, as we were accustomed to do, before breakfasting at the chateau. After breakfast, we took another walk for half an hour, and then returned to the laboratory. There we found my chambermaid, who had come to set my room in order. I went into the "Yellow Room" to give her some slight orders and she directly afterwards left the pavilion, and I resumed my work with my father. At five o'clock, we again went for a walk in the park and afterward had tea.

Q: Before leaving the pavilion at five o'clock, did you go into your chamber?

A: No, monsieur, my father went into it, at my request to bring me my hat.

Q: And he found nothing suspicious there?

A: Evidently no, monsieur.

Q: It is, then, almost certain that the murderer was not yet concealed under the bed. When you went out, was the door of the room locked?

A: No, there was no reason for locking it.

Q: You were absent from the pavilion some length of time, Monsieur Stangerson and you?

A: About an hour.

Q: It was during that hour, no doubt, that the murderer got into the pavilion. But how? Nobody knows. Footmarks have been found in the park, leading away from the window of the vestibule, but none has been found going towards it. Did you notice whether the vestibule window was open when you went out?

A: I don't remember.

Monsieur Stangerson: It was closed.

Q: And when you returned?

Mademoiselle Stangerson: I did not notice.

M: Stangerson. It was still closed. I remember remarking aloud: 'Daddy Jacques must surely have opened it while we were away.'

Q: Strange!—Do you recollect, Monsieur Stangerson, if during your absence, and before going out, he had opened it? You returned to the laboratory at six o'clock and resumed work?

Mademoiselle Stangerson: Yes, monsieur.

Q: And you did not leave the laboratory from that hour up to the moment when you entered your chamber?

M: Stangerson. Neither my daughter nor I, monsieur. We were engaged on work that was pressing, and we lost not a moment,—neglecting everything else on that account.

Q: Did you dine in the laboratory?

A: For that reason.

Q: Are you accustomed to dine in the laboratory?

A: We rarely dine there.

Q: Could the murderer have known that you would dine there that evening?

M: Stangerson. Good Heavens!—I think not. It was only when we returned to the pavilion at six o'clock, that we decided, my daughter and I, to dine there. At that moment I was spoken to by my gamekeeper, who detained me a moment, to ask me to accompany him on an urgent tour of inspection in a part of the woods which I had decided to thin. I put this off until the next day, and begged him, as he was going by the chateau, to tell the steward that we should dine in the laboratory. He left me, to execute the errand and I rejoined my daughter, who was already at work.

Q: At what hour, mademoiselle, did you go to your chamber while your father continued to work there?

A: At midnight.

Q: Did Daddy Jacques enter the "Yellow Room" in the course of the evening?

A: To shut the blinds and light the night-light.

Q: He saw nothing suspicious?

A: He would have told us if he had seen. Daddy Jacques is an honest man and very attached to me.

Q: You affirm, Monsieur Stangerson, that Daddy Jacques remained with you all the time you were in the laboratory?

M: Stangerson. I am sure of it. I have no doubt of that.

Q: When you entered your chamber, mademoiselle, you immediately shut the door and locked and bolted it? That was taking unusual precautions, knowing that your father and your servant were there? Were you in fear of something, then?

A: My father would be returning to the chateau and Daddy Jacques would be going to his bed. And, in fact, I did fear something.

Q: You were so much in fear of something that you borrowed Daddy Jacques's revolver without telling him you had done so?

A: That is true. I did not wish to alarm anybody,—the more, because my fears might have proved to have been foolish.

Q: What was it you feared?

A: I hardly know how to tell you. For several nights, I seemed to hear, both in the park and out of the park, round the pavilion, unusual sounds, sometimes footsteps, at other times the cracking of branches. The night before the attack on me, when I did not get to bed before three o'clock in the morning, on our return from the Elysee, I stood for a moment before my window, and I felt sure I saw shadows.

Q: How many?

A: Two. They moved round the lake,—then the moon became clouded and I lost sight of them. At this time of the season, every year, I have generally returned to my apartment in the chateau for the winter; but this year I said to myself that I would not quit the pavilion before my father had finished the resume of his works on the 'Dissociation of Matter' for the Academy. I did not wish that that important work, which was to have been finished in the course of a few days, should be delayed by a change in our daily habit. You can well understand that I did not wish to speak of my childish fears to my father, nor did I say anything to Daddy Jacques who, I knew, would not have been able to hold his tongue. Knowing that he had a revolver in his room, I took advantage of his absence and borrowed it, placing it in the drawer of my night-table.

Q: You know of no enemies you have?

A: None.

Q: You understand, mademoiselle, that these precautions are calculated to cause surprise?

M: Stangerson. Evidently, my child, such precautions are very surprising.

A: No;—because I have told you that I had been uneasy for two nights.

M: Stangerson. You ought to have told me of that! This misfortune would have been avoided.

Q: The door of the "Yellow Room" locked, did you go to bed?

A: Yes, and, being very tired, I at once went to sleep.

Q: The night-light was still burning?

A: Yes, but it gave a very feeble light.

Q: Then, mademoiselle, tell us what happened.

A: I do not know whether I had been long asleep, but suddenly I awoke—and uttered a loud cry.

M: Stangerson. Yes—a horrible cry—'Murder!'—It still rings in my ears.

Q: You uttered a loud cry?

A: A man was in my chamber. He sprang at me and tried to strangle me. I was nearly stifled when suddenly I was able to reach the drawer of my night-table and grasp the revolver which I had placed in it. At that moment the man had forced me to the foot of my bed and brandished in over my head a sort of mace. But I had fired. He immediately struck a terrible blow at my head. All that, monsieur, passed more rapidly than I can tell it, and I know nothing more.

Q: Nothing?—Have you no idea as to how the assassin could escape from your chamber?

A: None whatever—I know nothing more. One does not know what is passing around one, when one is unconscious.

Q: Was the man you saw tall or short, little or big?

A: I only saw a shadow which appeared to me formidable.

Q: You cannot give us any indication?

A: I know nothing more, monsieur, than that a man threw himself upon me and that I fired at him. I know nothing more."

Here the interrogation of Mademoiselle Stangerson concluded.

Rouletabille waited patiently for Monsieur Robert Darzac, who soon appeared.

From a room near the chamber of Mademoiselle Stangerson, he had heard the interrogatory and now came to recount it to my friend with great exactitude, aided by an excellent memory. His docility still surprised me. Thanks to hasty pencil-notes, he was able to reproduce, almost textually, the questions and the answers given.

It looked as if Monsieur Darzac were being employeeed as the secretary of my young friend and acted as if he could refuse him nothing; nay, more, as if under a compulsion to do so.

The fact of the closed window struck the reporter as it had struck the magistrate. Rouletabille asked Darzac to repeat once more Mademoiselle Stangerson's account of how she and her father had spent their time on the day of the tragedy, as she had stated it to the magistrate. The circumstance of the dinner in the laboratory seemed to interest him in the highest degree; and he had it repeated to him three times. He also wanted to be sure that the forest-keeper knew that the professor and his daughter were going to dine in the laboratory, and how he had come to know it.

When Monsieur Darzac had finished, I said: "The examination has not advanced the problem much."

"It has put it back," said Monsieur Darzac.

"It has thrown light upon it," said Rouletabille, thoughtfully.

# IX

## REPORTER AND DETECTIVE

The three of us went back towards the pavilion. At some distance from the building the reporter made us stop and, pointing to a small clump of trees to the right of us, said:

"That's where the murderer came from to get into the pavilion."

As there were other patches of trees of the same sort between the great oaks, I asked why the murderer had chosen that one, rather than any of the others. Rouletabille answered me by pointing to the path which ran quite close to the thicket to the door of the pavilion.

"That path is as you see, topped with gravel," he said; "the man must have passed along it going to the pavilion, since no traces of his steps have been found on the soft ground. The man didn't have wings; he walked; but he walked on the gravel which left no impression of his tread. The gravel has, in fact, been trodden by many other feet, since the path is the most direct way between the pavilion and the chateau. As to the thicket, made of the sort of shrubs that don't flourish in the rough season—laurels and fuchsias—it offered the murderer a sufficient hiding-place until it was time for him to make his way to the pavilion. It was while hiding in that clump of trees that he saw Monsieur and Mademoiselle Stangerson, and then Daddy Jacques, leave the pavilion. Gravel has been spread nearly, very nearly, up to the windows of the pavilion. The footprints of a man, parallel with the wall—marks which we will examine presently, and which I have already seen—prove that he only needed to make one stride to find himself in front of the vestibule window, left open by Daddy Jacques. The man drew himself up by his hands and entered the vestibule."

"After all it is very possible," I said.

"After all what? After all what?" cried Rouletabille.

I begged of him not to be angry; but he was too much irritated to listen to me and declared, ironically, that he admired the prudent doubt with which certain people approached the most simple problems, risking nothing by saying "that is so, or 'that is not so." Their intelligence would have produced about the same result if nature had forgotten to furnish their brain-pan with a little grey matter. As I appeared vexed, my young friend took me by the arm and admitted that he had not meant that for me; he thought more of me than that.

"If I did not reason as I do in regard to this gravel," he went on, "I should have to assume a balloon!—My dear fellow, the science of the aerostation of dirigible balloons is not yet developed enough for me to consider it and suppose that a murderer would drop from the clouds! So don't say a thing is possible, when it could not be otherwise. We know now how the man entered by the window, and we also know the moment at which he entered,—during the five o'clock walk of the professor and his daughter. The fact of the presence of the chambermaid—who had come to clean up the 'Yellow Room'—in the laboratory, when Monsieur Stangerson and his daughter returned from their walk, at half-past one, permits us to affirm that at half-past one the murderer was not in the chamber under the bed, unless he was in collusion with the chambermaid. What do you say, Monsieur Darzac?"

Monsieur Darzac shook his head and said he was sure of the chambermaid's fidelity, and that she was a thoroughly honest and devoted servant.

"Besides," he added, "at five o'clock Monsieur Stangerson went into the room to fetch his daughter's hat."

"There is that also," said Rouletabille.

"That the man entered by the window at the time you say, I admit," I said; "but why did he shut the window? It was an act which would necessarily draw the attention of those who had left it open."

"It may be the window was not shut at once," replied the young reporter. "But if he did shut the window, it was because of the bend in the gravel path, a dozen yards from the pavilion, and on account of the three oaks that are growing at that spot."

"What do you mean by that?" asked Monsieur Darzac, who had followed us and listened with almost breathless attention to all that Rouletabille had said.

"I'll explain all to you later on, Monsieur, when I think the moment to be ripe for doing so; but I don't think I have anything of more importance to say on this affair, if my hypothesis is justified."

"And what is your hypothesis?"

"You will never know if it does not turn out to be the truth. It is of much too grave a nature to speak of it, so long as it continues to be only a hypothesis."

"Have you, at least, some idea as to who the murderer is?"

"No, monsieur, I don't know who the murderer is; but don't be afraid, Monsieur Robert Darzac—I shall know."

I could not but observe that Monsieur Darzac was deeply moved; and I suspected that Rouletabille's confident assertion was not pleasing to him. Why, I asked myself, if he was really afraid that the murderer should be discovered, was he helping the reporter to find him? My young friend seemed to have received the same impression, for he said, bluntly:

"Monsieur Darzac, don't you want me to find out who the murderer was?"

"Oh!—I should like to kill him with my own hand!" cried Mademoiselle Stangerson's fiancé, with a vehemence that amazed me.

"I believe you," said Rouletabille gravely; "but you have not answered my question."

We were passing by the thicket, of which the young reporter had spoken to us a minute before. I entered it and pointed out evident traces of a man who had been hidden there. Rouletabille, once more, was right.

"You, fool!" he said. "We have to do with a thing of flesh and blood, who uses the same means that we do. It'll all come out on those lines."

Having said this, he asked me for the paper pattern of the footprint which he had given me to take care of, and applied it to a very clear footmark behind the thicket. "Aha!" he said, rising.

I thought he was now going to trace back the track of the murderer's footmarks to the vestibule window; but he led us instead, far to the left, saying that it was useless ferreting in the mud, and that he was sure, now, of the road taken by the murderer.

"He went along the wall to the hedge and dry ditch, over which he jumped. See, just in front of the little path leading to the lake, that was his nearest way to get out."

"How do you know he went to the lake?"—

"Because Frederic Larsan has not quitted the borders of it since this morning. There must be some important marks there."

A few minutes later we reached the lake.

It was a little sheet of marshy water, surrounded by reeds, on which floated some dead water-lily leaves. The great Fred may have seen us approaching, but we probably interested him very little, for he took hardly any notice of us and continued to be stirring with his cane something which we could not see.

"Look!" said Rouletabille, "here again are the footmarks of the escaping man; they skirt the lake here and finally disappear just before this path, which leads to the high road to Epinay. The man continued his flight to Paris."

"What makes you think that?" I asked, "since these footmarks are not continued on the path?"

"What makes me think that?—Why these footprints, which I expected to find!" he cried, pointing to the sharply outlined imprint of a neat boot. "See!"—and he called to Frederic Larsan.

"Monsieur Fred, these neat footprints seem to have been made since the discovery of the crime."

"Yes, young man, yes, they have been carefully made," replied Fred without raising his head. "You see, there are steps that come, and steps that go back."

"And the man had a bicycle!" cried the reporter.

Here, after looking at the marks of the bicycle, which followed, going and coming, the neat footprints, I thought I might intervene.

"The bicycle explains the disappearance of the murderer's big footprints," I said. "The murderer, with his rough boots, mounted a bicycle. His accomplice, the wearer of the neat boots, had come to wait for him on the edge of the lake with the bicycle. It might be supposed that the murderer was working for the other."

"No, no!" replied Rouletabille with a strange smile. "I have expected to find these footmarks from the very beginning. These are not the footmarks of the murderer!"

"Then there were two?"

"No—there was but one, and he had no accomplice."

"Very good!—Very good!" cried Frederic Larsan.

"Look!" continued the young reporter, showing us the ground where it had been disturbed by big and heavy heels; "the man seated himself there, and took off his hobnailed boots, which he had worn only for the purpose of misleading detection, and then no doubt, taking them away with him, he stood up in his own boots, and quietly and slowly regained the high road, holding his bicycle in his hand, for he could not venture to ride it on this rough path. That accounts for the lightness of the impression made by the wheels along it, in spite of the softness of the ground. If there had been a man on the bicycle, the wheels would have sunk deeply into the soil. No, no; there was but one man there, the murderer on foot."

"Bravo!—bravo!" cried Fred again, and coming suddenly towards us and, planting himself in front of Monsieur Robert Darzac, he said to him:

"If we had a bicycle here, we might demonstrate the correctness of the young man's reasoning, Monsieur Robert Darzac. Do you know whether there is one at the chateau?"

"No!" replied Monsieur Darzac. "There is not. I took mine, four days ago, to Paris, the last time I came to the chateau before the crime."

"That's a pity!" replied Fred, very coldly. Then, turning to Rouletabille, he said: "If we go on at this rate, we'll both come to the same conclusion. Have you any idea, as to how the murderer got away from the 'Yellow Room'?"

"Yes," said my young friend; "I have an idea."

"So have I," said Fred, "and it must be the same as yours. There are no two ways of reasoning in this affair. I am waiting for the arrival of my chief before offering any explanation to the examining magistrate."

"Ah! Is the Chief of the Surete coming?"

"Yes, this afternoon. He is going to summon, before the magistrate, in the laboratory, all those who have played any part in this tragedy. It will be very interesting. It is a pity you won't be able to be present."

"I shall be present," said Rouletabille confidently.

"Really—you are an extraordinary fellow—for your age!" replied the detective in a tone not wholly free from irony. "You'd make a wonderful detective—if you had a little more method—if you didn't follow your instincts and that bump on your forehead. As I have already several times observed, Monsieur Rouletabille, you reason too much; you do not allow yourself to be guided by what you have seen. What do you say to the handkerchief full of blood, and the red mark of the hand on the wall? You have seen the stain on the wall, but I have only seen the handkerchief."

"Bah!" cried Rouletabille, "the murderer was wounded in the hand by Mademoiselle Stangerson's revolver!"

"Ah!—a simply instinctive observation! Take care!—You are becoming too strictly logical, Monsieur Rouletabille; logic will upset you if you use it indiscriminately. You are right, when you say that Mademoiselle Stangerson fired her revolver, but you are wrong when you say that she wounded the murderer in the hand."

"I am sure of it," cried Rouletabille.

Fred, imperturbable, interrupted him:

"Defective observation—defective observation!—the examination of the handkerchief, the numberless little round scarlet stains, the impression of drops which I found in the tracks of the footprints, at the moment when they were made on the floor, prove to me that the murderer was not wounded at all. Monsieur Rouletabille, the murderer bled at the nose!"

The great Fred spoke quite seriously. However, I could not refrain from uttering an exclamation.

The reporter looked gravely at Fred, who looked gravely at him. And Fred immediately concluded:

"The man allowed the blood to flow into his hand and handkerchief, and dried his hand on the wall. The fact is highly important," he added, "because there is no need of his being wounded in the hand for him to be the murderer."

Rouletabille seemed to be thinking deeply. After a moment he said:

"There is something—a something, Monsieur Frederic Larsan, much graver than the misuse of logic the disposition of mind in some detectives which makes them, in perfect good faith, twist logic to the necessities of their preconceived ideas. You, already, have your idea about the murderer, Monsieur Fred. Don't deny it; and your theory demands that the murderer should not have been wounded in the hand, otherwise it comes to nothing. And you have searched, and have found something else. It's dangerous, very dangerous, Monsieur Fred, to go from a preconceived idea to find the proofs to fit it. That method may lead you far astray. Beware of judicial error, Monsieur Fred, it will trip you up!"

And laughing a little, in a slightly bantering tone, his hands in his pockets, Rouletabille fixed his cunning eyes on the great Fred.

Frederic Larsan silently contemplated the young reporter who pretended to be as wise as himself. Shrugging his shoulders, he bowed to us and moved quickly away, hitting the stones on his path with his stout cane.

Rouletabille watched his retreat, and then turned toward us, his face joyous and triumphant.

"I shall beat him!" he cried. "I shall beat the great Fred, clever as he is; I shall beat them all!"

And he danced a double shuffle. Suddenly he stopped. My eyes followed his gaze; they were fixed on Monsieur Robert Darzac, who was looking anxiously at the impression left by his feet side by side with the elegant footmarks. There was not a particle of difference between them!

We thought he was about to faint. His eyes, bulging with terror, avoided us, while his right hand, with a spasmodic movement, twitched at the beard that covered his honest, gentle, and now despairing face. At length regaining his self-possession, he bowed to us, and remarking, in a changed voice, that he was obliged to return to the chateau, left us.

"The deuce!" exclaimed Rouletabille.

He, also, appeared to be deeply concerned. From his pocket-book he took a piece of white paper as I had seen him do before, and with his scissors, cut out the shape of the neat bootmarks that were on the ground. Then he fitted the new paper pattern with the one he had previously made—the two were exactly alike. Rising, Rouletabille exclaimed again: "The deuce!" Presently he added: "Yet I believe Monsieur Robert Darzac to be an honest man." He then led me on the road to the Donjon Inn, which we could see on the highway, by the side of a small clump of trees.

# X

## "We Shall Have to Eat Red Meat—Now"

The Donjon Inn was of no imposing appearance; but I like these buildings with their rafters blackened with age and the smoke of their hearths—these inns of the coaching-days, crumbling erections that will soon exist in the memory only. They belong to the bygone days, they are linked with history. They make us think of the Road, of those days when highwaymen rode.

I saw at once that the Donjon Inn was at least two centuries old—perhaps older. Under its sign-board, over the threshold, a man with a crabbed-looking face was standing, seemingly plunged in unpleasant thought, if the wrinkles on his forehead and the knitting of his brows were any indication.

When we were close to him, he deigned to see us and asked us, in a tone anything but engaging, whether we wanted anything. He was, no doubt, the not very amiable landlord of this charming dwelling-place. As we expressed a hope that he would be good enough to furnish us with a breakfast, he assured us that he had no provisions, regarding us, as he said this, with a look that was unmistakably suspicious.

"You may take us in," Rouletabille said to him, "we are not policemen."

"I'm not afraid of the police—I'm not afraid of anyone!" replied the man.

I had made my friend understand by a sign that we should do better not to insist; but, being determined to enter the inn, he slipped by the man on the doorstep and was in the common room.

"Come on," he said, "it is very comfortable here."

A good fire was blazing in the chimney, and we held our hands to the warmth it sent out; it was a morning in which the approach of winter was unmistakable. The room was a tolerably large one, furnished with two heavy tables, some stools, a counter decorated with rows of bottles of syrup and alcohol. Three windows looked out on to the road. A coloured advertisement lauded the many merits of a new vermouth. On the mantelpiece was arrayed the innkeeper's collection of figured earthenware pots and stone jugs.

"That's a fine fire for roasting a chicken," said Rouletabille. "We have no chicken—not even a wretched rabbit," said the landlord.

"I know," said my friend slowly; "I know—We shall have to eat red meat—now."

I confess I did not in the least understand what Rouletabille meant by what he had said; but the landlord, as soon as he heard the words, uttered an oath, which he at once stifled, and placed himself at our orders as obediently as Monsieur Robert Darzac had done, when he heard Rouletabille's prophetic sentence—"The presbytery has lost nothing of its charm, nor the garden its brightness." Certainly my friend knew how to make people understand him by the use of wholly incomprehensible phrases. I observed as much to him, but he merely smiled. I should have proposed that he give me some explanation; but he put a finger to his lips, which evidently signified that he had not only determined not to speak, but also enjoined silence on my part.

Meantime the man had pushed open a little side door and called to somebody to bring him half a dozen eggs and a piece of beefsteak. The commission was quickly executed by a strongly-built young woman with beautiful blonde hair and large, handsome eyes, who regarded us with curiosity.

The innkeeper said to her roughly:

"Get out!—and if the Green Man comes, don't let me see him."

She disappeared. Rouletabille took the eggs, which had been brought to him in a bowl, and the meat which was on a dish, placed all carefully beside him in the chimney, unhooked a frying-pan and a gridiron, and began to beat up our omelette before proceeding to grill our beefsteak. He then ordered two bottles of cider, and seemed to take as little notice of our host as our host did of him. The landlord let us do our own cooking and set our table near one of the windows.

Suddenly I heard him mutter:

"Ah!—there he is."

His face had changed, expressing fierce hatred. He went and glued himself to one of the windows, watching the road. There was no need for me to draw Rouletabille's attention; he had already left our omelette and had joined the landlord at the window. I went with him.

A man dressed entirely in green velvet, his head covered with a huntsman's cap of the same colour, was advancing leisurely, lighting a pipe as he walked. He carried a fowling-piece slung at his back. His movements displayed an almost aristocratic ease. He wore eye-glasses and appeared to be about five and forty years of age. His hair as well as his moustache were salt grey. He was remarkably handsome. As he passed near the inn, he hesitated, as if asking himself whether or no he should enter it; gave a glance towards us, took a few whiffs at his pipe, and then resumed his walk at the same nonchalant pace.

Rouletabille and I looked at our host. His flashing eyes, his clenched hands, his trembling lips, told us of the tumultuous feelings by which he was being agitated.

"He has done well not to come in here today!" he hissed.

"Who is that man?" asked Rouletabille, returning to his omelette.

"The Green Man," growled the innkeeper. "Don't you know him? Then all the better for you. He is not an acquaintance to make.—Well, he is Monsieur Stangerson's forest-keeper."

"You don't appear to like him very much?" asked the reporter, pouring his omelette into the frying-pan.

"Nobody likes him, monsieur. He's an upstart who must once have had a fortune of his own; and he forgives nobody because, in order to live, he has been compelled to become a servant. A keeper is as much a servant as any other, isn't he? Upon my word, one would say that he is the master of the Glandier, and that all the land and woods belong to him. He'll not let a poor creature eat a morsel of bread on the grass—his grass!"

"Does he often come here?"

"Too often. But I've made him understand that his face doesn't please me, and, for a month past, he hasn't been here. The Donjon Inn has never existed for him!—he hasn't had time!—been too much engaged in paying court to the landlady of the Three Lilies at Saint-Michel. A bad fellow!—There isn't an honest man who can bear him. Why, the concierges of the chateau would turn their eyes away from a picture of him!"

"The concierges of the chateau are honest people, then?"

"Yes, they are, as true as my name's Mathieu, monsieur. I believe them to be honest."

"Yet they've been arrested?"

"What does that prove?—But I don't want to mix myself up in other people's affairs."

"And what do you think of the murder?"

"Of the murder of poor Mademoiselle Stangerson?—A good girl much loved everywhere in the country. That's what I think of it—and many things besides; but that's nobody's business."

"Not even mine?" insisted Rouletabille.

The innkeeper looked at him sideways and said gruffly:

"Not even yours."

The omelette ready, we sat down at table and were silently eating, when the door was pushed open and an old woman, dressed in rags, leaning on a stick, her head doddering, her white hair hanging loosely over her wrinkled forehead, appeared on the threshold.

"Ah!—there you are, Mother Angenoux!—It's long since we saw you last," said our host.

"I have been very ill, very nearly dying," said the old woman. "If ever you should have any scraps for the Bete du Bon Dieu—?"

And she entered, followed by a cat, larger than any I had ever believed could exist. The beast looked at us and gave so hopeless a miau that I shuddered. I had never heard so lugubrious a cry.

As if drawn by the cat's cry a man followed the old woman in. It was the Green Man. He saluted by raising his hand to his cap and seated himself at a table near to ours.

"A glass of cider, Daddy Mathieu," he said.

As the Green Man entered, Daddy Mathieu had started violently; but visibly mastering himself he said.

"I've no more cider; I served the last bottles to these gentlemen."

"Then give me a glass of white wine," said the Green Man, without showing the least surprise.

"I've no more white wine—no more anything," said Daddy Mathieu, surlily.

"How is Madame Mathieu?"

"Quite well, thank you."

So the young Woman with the large, tender eyes, whom we had just seen, was the wife of this repugnant and brutal rustic, whose jealousy seemed to emphasise his physical ugliness.

Slamming the door behind him, the innkeeper left the room. Mother Angenoux was still standing, leaning on her stick, the cat at her feet.

"You've been ill, Mother Angenoux?—Is that why we have not seen you for the last week?" asked the Green Man.

"Yes, Monsieur keeper. I have been able to get up but three times, to go to pray to Sainte-Genevieve, our good patroness, and the rest of the time I have been lying on my bed. There was no one to care for me but the Bete du bon Dieu!"

"Did she not leave you?"

"Neither by day nor by night."

"Are you sure of that?"

"As I am of Paradise."

"Then how was it, Madame Angenoux, that all through the night of the murder nothing but the cry of the Bete du bon Dieu was heard?"

Mother Angenoux planted herself in front of the forest-keeper and struck the floor with her stick.

"I don't know anything about it," she said. "But shall I tell you something? There are no two cats in the world that cry like that. Well, on the night of the murder I also heard the cry of the Bete du bon Dieu outside; and yet she was on my knees, and did not mew once, I swear. I crossed myself when I heard that, as if I had heard the devil."

I looked at the keeper when he put the last question, and I am much mistaken if I did not detect an evil smile on his lips. At that moment, the noise of loud quarrelling reached us. We even thought we heard a dull sound of blows, as if some one was being beaten. The Green Man quickly rose and hurried to the door by the side of the fireplace; but it was opened by the landlord who appeared, and said to the keeper:

"Don't alarm yourself, Monsieur—it is my wife; she has the toothache." And he laughed. "Here, Mother Angenoux, here are some scraps for your cat."

He held out a packet to the old woman, who took it eagerly and went out by the door, closely followed by her cat.

"Then you won't serve me?" asked the Green Man.

Daddy Mathieu's face was placid and no longer retained its expression of hatred.

"I've nothing for you—nothing for you. Take yourself off."

The Green Man quietly refilled his pipe, lit it, bowed to us, and went out. No sooner was he over the threshold than Daddy Mathieu slammed the door after him and, turning towards us, with eyes bloodshot, and frothing at the mouth, he hissed to us, shaking his clenched fist at the door he had just shut on the man he evidently hated:

"I don't know who you are who tell me 'We shall have to eat red meat—now'; but if it will interest you to know it—that man is the murderer!"

With which words Daddy Mathieu immediately left us. Rouletabille returned towards the fireplace and said:

"Now we'll grill our steak. How do you like the cider?—It's a little tart, but I like it."

We saw no more of Daddy Mathieu that day, and absolute silence reigned in the inn when we left it, after placing five francs on the table in payment for our feast.

Rouletabille at once set off on a three mile walk round Professor Stangerson's estate. He halted for some ten minutes at the corner of a narrow road black with soot, near to some charcoal-burners' huts in the forest of Sainte-Genevieve, which touches on the road from Epinay to Corbeil, to tell me that the murderer had certainly passed that way, before entering the grounds and concealing himself in the little clump of trees.

"You don't think, then, that the keeper knows anything of it?" I asked.

"We shall see that, later," he replied. "For the present I'm not interested in what the landlord said about the man. The landlord hates him. I didn't take you to breakfast at the Donjon Inn for the sake of the Green Man."

Then Rouletabille, with great precaution glided, followed by me, towards the little building which, standing near the park gate, served for the home of the concierges, who had been arrested that morning. With the skill of an acrobat, he got into the lodge by an upper window which had been left open, and returned ten minutes later. He said only, "Ah!"—a word which, in his mouth, signified many things.

We were about to take the road leading to the chateau, when a considerable stir at the park gate attracted our attention. A carriage had arrived and some people had come from the chateau to meet it. Rouletabille pointed out to me a gentleman who descended from it.

"That's the Chief of the Surete" he said. "Now we shall see what Frederic Larsan has up his sleeve, and whether he is so much cleverer than anybody else."

The carriage of the Chief of the Surete was followed by three other vehicles containing reporters, who were also desirous of entering the park. But two gendarmes stationed at the gate had evidently received orders to refuse admission to anybody. The Chief of the Surete calmed their impatience by undertaking to furnish to the press, that evening, all the information he could give that would not interfere with the judicial inquiry.

## XI

## In Which Frederic Larsan Explains How the Murderer Was Able to Get Out of the "Yellow Room"

Among the mass of papers, legal documents, memoirs, and extracts from newspapers, which I have collected, relating to the mystery of the "Yellow Room", there is one very interesting piece; it is a detail of the famous examination which took place that afternoon, in the laboratory of Professor Stangerson, before the Chief of the Surete. This narrative is from the pen of Monsieur Maleine, the Registrar, who, like the examining magistrate, had spent some of his leisure time in the pursuit of literature. The piece was to have made part of a book which, however, has never been published, and which was to have been entitled: "My Examinations." It was given to me by the Registrar himself, some time after the astonishing denouement to this case, and is unique in judicial chronicles.

Here it is. It is not a mere dry transcription of questions and answers, because the Registrar often intersperses his story with his own personal comments.

### The Registrar's Narrative

The examining magistrate and I (the writer relates) found ourselves in the "Yellow Room" in the company of the builder who had constructed the pavilion after Professor Stangerson's designs. He had a workman with him. Monsieur de Marquet had had the walls laid entirely bare; that is to say, he had had them stripped of the paper which had decorated them. Blows with a pick, here and there, satisfied us of the absence of any sort of opening. The floor and the ceiling were thoroughly sounded. We found nothing. There was nothing to be found. Monsieur de Marquet appeared to be delighted and never ceased repeating:

"What a case! What a case! We shall never know, you'll see, how the murderer was able to get out of this room!"

Then suddenly, with a radiant face, he called to the officer in charge of the gendarmes.

"Go to the chateau," he said, "and request Monsieur Stangerson and

Monsieur Robert Darzac to come to me in the laboratory, also Daddy Jacques; and let your men bring here the two concierges."

Five minutes later all were assembled in the laboratory. The Chief of the Surete, who had arrived at the Glandier, joined us at that moment. I was seated at Monsieur Stangerson's desk ready for work, when Monsieur de Marquet made us the following little speech—as original as it was unexpected:

"With your permission, gentlemen—as examinations lead to nothing—we will, for once, abandon the old system of interrogation. I will not have you brought before me one by one, but we will all remain here as we are,—Monsieur Stangerson, Monsieur Robert Darzac, Daddy Jacques and the two concierges, the Chief of the Surete, the Registrar, and myself. We shall all be on the same footing. The concierges may, for the moment, forget that they have been arrested. We are going to confer together. We are on the spot where the crime was committed. We have nothing else to discuss but the crime. So let us discuss it freely—intelligently or otherwise, so long as we speak just what is in our minds. There need be no formality or method since this won't help us in any way."

Then, passing before me, he said in a low voice:

"What do you think of that, eh? What a scene! Could you have thought of that? I'll make a little piece out of it for the Vaudeville." And he rubbed his hands with glee.

I turned my eyes on Monsieur Stangerson. The hope he had received from the doctor's latest reports, which stated that Mademoiselle Stangerson might recover from her wounds, had not been able to efface from his noble features the marks of the great sorrow that was upon him. He had believed his daughter to be dead, and he was still broken by that belief. His clear, soft, blue eyes expressed infinite sorrow. I had had occasion, many times, to see Monsieur Stangerson at public ceremonies, and from the first had been struck by his countenance, which seemed as pure as that of a child—the dreamy gaze with the sublime and mystical expression of the inventor and thinker.

On those occasions his daughter was always to be seen either following him or by his side; for they never quitted each other, it was said, and had shared the same labours for many years. The young lady, who was then five and thirty, though she looked no more than thirty, had devoted herself entirely to science. She still won admiration for her imperial beauty which had remained intact, without a wrinkle, withstanding time and love. Who would have dreamed that I should one day be seated by her pillow with my papers, and that I should see her, on the point of death, painfully recounting to us the most monstrous and most mysterious crime I have heard of in my career? Who would have thought that I should be, that afternoon, listening to the despairing father vainly trying to explain how his daughter's assailant had been able to escape from him? Why bury ourselves with our work in obscure retreats in the depths of woods, if it may not protect us against those dangerous threats to life which meet us in the busy cities?

"Now, Monsieur Stangerson," said Monsieur de Marquet, with somewhat of an important air, "place yourself exactly where you were when Mademoiselle Stangerson left you to go to her chamber."

Monsieur Stangerson rose and, standing at a certain distance from the door of the "Yellow Room", said, in an even voice and without the least trace of emphasis—a voice which I can only describe as a dead voice:

"I was here. About eleven o'clock, after I had made a brief chemical experiment at the furnaces of the laboratory, needing all the space behind me, I had my desk moved here by Daddy Jacques, who spent the evening in cleaning some of my apparatus. My daughter had been working at the same desk with me. When it was her time to leave she rose, kissed me, and bade Daddy Jacques goodnight. She had to pass behind my desk and the door to enter her chamber, and she could do this only with some difficulty. That is to say, I was very near the place where the crime occurred later."

"And the desk?" I asked, obeying, in thus mixing myself in the conversation, the express orders of my chief, "as soon as you heard the cry of 'murder' followed by the revolver shots, what became of the desk?"

Daddy Jacques answered.

"We pushed it back against the wall, here—close to where it is at the present moment—so as to be able to get at the door at once."

I followed up my reasoning, to which, however, I attached but little importance, regarding it as only a weak hypothesis, with another question.

"Might not a man in the room, the desk being so near to the door, by stooping and slipping under the desk, have left it unobserved?"

"You are forgetting," interrupted Monsieur Stangerson wearily, "that my daughter had locked and bolted her door, that the door had remained fastened, that we vainly tried to force it open when we heard the noise, and that we were at the door while the struggle between the murderer and my poor child was going on—immediately after we heard her stifled cries as she was being held by the fingers that have left their red mark upon her throat. Rapid as the attack was, we were no less rapid in our endeavors to get into the room where the tragedy was taking place."

I rose from my seat and once more examined the door with the greatest care. Then I returned to my place with a despairing gesture.

"If the lower panel of the door," I said, "could be removed without the whole door being necessarily opened, the problem would be solved. But, unfortunately, that last hypothesis is untenable after an examination of the door—it's of oak, solid and massive. You can see that quite plainly, in spite of the injury done in the attempt to burst it open."

"Ah!" cried Daddy Jacques, "it is an old and solid door that was brought from the chateau—they don't make such doors now. We had to use this bar of iron to get it open, all four of us—for the concierge, brave woman she is, helped us. It pains me to find them both in prison now."

Daddy Jacques had no sooner uttered these words of pity and protestation than tears and lamentations broke out from the concierges. I never saw two accused people crying more bitterly. I was extremely disgusted. Even if they were innocent, I could not understand how they could behave like that in the face of misfortune. A dignified bearing at such times is better than tears and groans, which, most often, are feigned.

"Now then, enough of that sniveling," cried Monsieur de Marquet; "and, in your interest, tell us what you were doing under the windows of the pavilion at the time your mistress was being attacked; for you were close to the pavilion when Daddy Jacques met you."

"We were coming to help!" they whined.

"If we could only lay hands on the murderer, he'd never taste bread again!" the woman gurgled between her sobs.

As before we were unable to get two connecting thoughts out of them. They persisted in their denials and swore, by heaven and all the saints, that they were in bed when they heard the sound of the revolver shot.

"It was not one, but two shots that were fired!—You see, you are lying. If you had heard one, you would have heard the other."

"Mon Dieu! Monsieur—it was the second shot we heard. We were asleep when the first shot was fired."

"Two shots were fired," said Daddy Jacques. "I am certain that all the cartridges were in my revolver. We found afterward that two had been exploded, and we heard two shots behind the door. Was not that so, Monsieur Stangerson?"

"Yes," replied the Professor, "there were two shots, one dull, and the other sharp and ringing."

"Why do you persist in lying?" cried Monsieur de Marquet, turning to the concierges. "Do you think the police are the fools you are? Everything points to the fact that you were out of doors and near the pavilion at the time of the tragedy. What were you doing there? So far as I am concerned," he said, turning to Monsieur Stangerson, "I can only explain the escape of the murderer on the assumption of help from these two accomplices. As soon as the door was forced open, and while you, Monsieur Stangerson, were occupied with your unfortunate child, the concierge and his wife facilitated the flight of the murderer, who, screening himself behind them, reached the window in the vestibule, and sprang out of it into the park. The concierge closed the window after him and fastened the blinds, which certainly could not have closed and fastened of themselves. That is the conclusion I have arrived at. If anyone here has any other idea, let him state it."

Monsieur Stangerson intervened:

"What you say was impossible. I do not believe either in the guilt or in the connivance of my concierges, though I cannot understand what they were doing in the park at that late hour of the night. I say it was impossible, because Madame Bernier held the lamp and did not move from the threshold of the room; because I, as soon as the door was forced open, threw myself on my knees beside my daughter, and no one could have left or entered the room by the door, without passing over her body and forcing his way by me! Daddy Jacques and the concierge had but to cast a glance round the chamber and under the bed, as I had done on entering, to see that there was nobody in it but my daughter lying on the floor."

"What do you think, Monsieur Darzac?" asked the magistrate.

Monsieur Darzac replied that he had no opinion to express. Monsieur Dax, the Chief of the Surete who, so far, had been listening and examining the room, at length deigned to open his lips:

"While search is being made for the criminal, we had better try to find out the motive for the crime; that will advance us a little," he said. Turning towards Monsieur Stangerson, he continued, in the even, intelligent tone indicative of a strong character, "I understand that Mademoiselle was shortly to have been married?"

The professor looked sadly at Monsieur Robert Darzac.

"To my friend here, whom I should have been happy to call my son—to Monsieur Robert Darzac."

"Mademoiselle Stangerson is much better and is rapidly recovering from her wounds. The marriage is simply delayed, is it not, Monsieur?" insisted the Chief of the Surete.

"I hope so.

"What! Is there any doubt about that?"

Monsieur Stangerson did not answer. Monsieur Robert Darzac seemed agitated. I saw that his hand trembled as it fingered his watchchain. Monsieur Dax coughed, as did Monsieur de Marquet. Both were evidently embarrassed.

"You understand, Monsieur Stangerson," he said, "that in an affair so perplexing as this, we cannot neglect anything; we must know all, even the smallest and seemingly most futile thing concerning the victim—information apparently the most insignificant. Why do you doubt that this marriage will take place? You expressed a hope; but the hope implies a doubt. Why do you doubt?"

Monsieur Stangerson made a visible effort to recover himself.

"Yes, Monsieur," he said at length, "you are right. It will be best that you should know something which, if I concealed it, might appear to be of importance; Monsieur Darzac agrees with me in this."

Monsieur Darzac, whose pallor at that moment seemed to me to be altogether abnormal, made a sign of assent. I gathered he was unable to speak.

"I want you to know then," continued Monsieur Stangerson, "that my daughter has sworn never to leave me, and adheres firmly to her oath, in spite of all my prayers and all that I have argued to induce her to marry. We have known Monsieur Robert Darzac many years. He loves my child; and I believed that she loved him; because she only recently consented to this marriage which I desire with all my heart. I am an old man, Monsieur, and it was a happy hour to me when I knew that, after I had gone, she would have at her side, one who loved her and who would help her in continuing our common labours. I love and esteem Monsieur Darzac both for his greatness of heart and for his devotion to science. But, two days before the tragedy, for I know not what reason, my daughter declared to me that she would never marry Monsieur Darzac."

A dead silence followed Monsieur Stangerson's words. It was a moment fraught with suspense.

"Did Mademoiselle give you any explanation,—did she tell you what her motive was?" asked Monsieur Dax.

"She told me she was too old to marry—that she had waited too long. She said she had given much thought to the matter and while she had a great esteem, even affection, for Monsieur Darzac, she felt it would be better if things remained as they were. She would be happy, she said, to see the relations between ourselves and Monsieur Darzac become closer, but only on the understanding that there would be no more talk of marriage."

"That is very strange!" muttered Monsieur Dax.

"Strange!" repeated Monsieur de Marquet.

"You'll certainly not find the motive there, Monsieur Dax," Monsieur Stangerson said with a cold smile.

"In any case, the motive was not theft!" said the Chief impatiently.

"Oh! we are quite convinced of that!" cried the examining magistrate.

At that moment the door of the laboratory opened and the officer in charge of the gendarmes entered and handed a card to the examining magistrate. Monsieur de Marquet read it and uttered a half angry exclamation:

"This is really too much!" he cried.

"What is it?" asked the Chief.

"It's the card of a young reporter engaged on the 'Epoque,' a Monsieur Joseph Rouletabille. It has these words written on it: 'One of the motives of the crime was robbery.'"

The Chief smiled.

"Ah,—young Rouletabille—I've heard of him he is considered rather clever. Let him come in."

Monsieur Joseph Rouletabille was allowed to enter. I had made his acquaintance in the train that morning on the way to Epinay-sur-Orge. He had introduced himself almost against my wish into our compartment. I had better say at once that his manners, and the arrogance with which he assumed to know what was incomprehensible even to us, impressed him unfavourably on my mind. I do not like journalists. They are a class of writers to be avoided as the pest. They think that everything is permissible and they respect nothing. Grant them the least favour, allow them even to approach you, and you never can tell what annoyance they may give you. This one appears to be scarcely twenty years old, and the effrontery with which he dared to question us and discuss the matter with us made him particularly obnoxious to me. Besides, he had a way of expressing himself that left us guessing as to whether he was mocking us or not. I know quite well that the 'Epoque' is an influential paper with which it is well to be on good terms, but the paper ought not to allow itself to be represented by sneaking reporters.

Monsieur Joseph Rouletabille entered the laboratory, bowed to us, and waited for Monsieur de Marquet to ask him to explain his presence.

"You pretend, Monsieur, that you know the motive for the crime, and that that motive—in the face of all the evidence that has been forthcoming—was robbery?"

"No, Monsieur, I do not pretend that. I do not say that robbery was the motive for the crime, and I don't believe it was."

"Then, what is the meaning of this card?"

"It means that robbery was one of the motives for the crime."

"What leads you to think that?"

"If you will be good enough to accompany me, I will show you."

The young man asked us to follow him into the vestibule, and we did. He led us towards the lavatory and begged Monsieur de Marquet to kneel beside him. This lavatory is lit by the glass door, and, when the door was open, the light which penetrated was sufficient to light it perfectly. Monsieur de Marquet and Monsieur Joseph Rouletabille knelt down on the threshold, and the young man pointed to a spot on the pavement.

"The stones of the lavatory have not been washed by Daddy Jacques for some time," he said; "that can be seen by the layer of dust that covers them. Now, notice here, the marks of two large footprints and the black ash they left where they have been. That ash is nothing else than the charcoal dust that covers the path along which you must pass through the forest, in order to get directly from Epinay to the Glandier. You know there is a little village of charcoal-burners at that place, who make large quantities of charcoal. What the murderer did was to come here at midday, when there was nobody at the pavilion, and attempt his robbery."

"But what robbery?—Where do you see any signs of robbery? What proves to you that a robbery has been committed?" we all cried at once.

"What put me on the trace of it," continued the journalist. . .

"Was this?" interrupted Monsieur de Marquet, still on his knees.

"Evidently," said Rouletabille.

And Monsieur de Marquet explained that there were on the dust of the pavement marks of two footsteps, as well as the impression, freshly-made, of a heavy rectangular parcel, the marks of the cord with which it had been fastened being easily distinguished.

"You have been here, then, Monsieur Rouletabille? I thought I had given orders to Daddy Jacques, who was left in charge of the pavilion, not to allow anybody to enter."

"Don't scold Daddy Jacques, I came here with Monsieur Robert Darzac."

"Ah,—Indeed!" exclaimed Monsieur de Marquet, disagreeably, casting a side-glance at Monsieur Darzac, who remained perfectly silent.

"When I saw the mark of the parcel by the side of the footprints, I had no doubt as to the robbery," replied Monsieur Rouletabille. "The thief had not brought a parcel with him; he had made one here—a parcel with the stolen objects, no doubt; and he put it in this corner intending to take it away when the moment came for him to make his escape. He had also placed his heavy boots beside the parcel,—for, see—there are no marks of steps leading to the marks left by the boots, which were placed side by side. That accounts for the fact that the murderer left no trace of his steps when he fled from the 'Yellow Room', nor any in the laboratory, nor in the vestibule. After entering the 'Yellow Room' in his boots, he took them off, finding them troublesome, or because he wished to make as little noise as possible. The marks made by him in going through the vestibule and the laboratory were subsequently washed out by Daddy Jacques. Having, for some reason or other, taken off his boots, the murderer carried them in his hand and placed them by the side of the parcel he had made,—by that time the robbery had been accomplished. The man then returned to the 'Yellow Room' and slipped under the bed, where the mark of his body is perfectly visible on the floor and even on the mat, which has been slightly moved from its place and creased. Fragments of straw also, recently torn, bear witness to the murderer's movements under the bed."

"Yes, yes,—we know all about that," said Monsieur de Marquet.

"The robber had another motive for returning to hide under the bed," continued the astonishing boy-journalist. "You might think that he was trying to hide himself quickly on seeing, through the vestibule window,

Monsieur and Mademoiselle Stangerson about to enter the pavilion. It would have been much easier for him to have climbed up to the attic and hidden there, waiting for an opportunity to get away, if his purpose had been only flight.—No! No!—he had to be in the 'Yellow Room'."

Here the Chief intervened.

"That's not at all bad, young man. I compliment you. If we do not know yet how the murderer succeeded in getting away, we can at any rate see how he came in and committed the robbery. But what did he steal?"

"Something very valuable," replied the young reporter.

At that moment we heard a cry from the laboratory. We rushed in and found Monsieur Stangerson, his eyes haggard, his limbs trembling, pointing to a sort of bookcase which he had opened, and which, we saw, was empty. At the same instant he sank into the large armchair that was placed before the desk and groaned, the tears rolling down his cheeks, "I have been robbed again! For God's sake, do not say a word of this to my daughter. She would be more pained than I am." He heaved a deep sigh and added, in a tone I shall never forget: "After all, what does it matter,— so long as she lives!"

"She will live!" said Monsieur Darzac, in a voice strangely touching.

"And we will find the stolen articles," said Monsieur Dax. "But what was in the cabinet?"

"Twenty years of my life," replied the illustrious professor sadly, "or rather of our lives—the lives of myself and my daughter! Yes, our most precious documents, the records of our secret experiments and our labours of twenty years were in that cabinet. It is an irreparable loss to us and, I venture to say, to science. All the processes by which I had been able to arrive at the precious proof of the destructibility of matter were there—all. The man who came wished to take all from me,—my daughter and my work—my heart and my soul."

And the great scientist wept like a child.

We stood around him in silence, deeply affected by his great distress. Monsieur Darzac pressed closely to his side, and tried in vain to restrain his tears—a sight which, for the moment, almost made me like him, in spite of an instinctive repulsion which his strange demeanour and his inexplicable anxiety had inspired me.

Monsieur Rouletabille alone,—as if his precious time and mission on earth did not permit him to dwell in the contemplation on human suffering—had, very calmly, stepped up to the empty cabinet and, pointing at it, broke the almost solemn silence. He entered into explanations, for which there was no need, as to why he had been led to believe that a robbery had been committed, which included the simultaneous discovery he had made in the lavatory, and the empty precious cabinet in the laboratory. The first thing that had struck him, he said, was the unusual form of that piece of furniture. It was very strongly built of fire-proof iron, clearly showing that it was intended for the keeping of most valuable objects. Then he noticed that the key had been left in the lock. "One does not ordinarily have a safe and leave it open!" he had said to himself. This little key, with its brass head and complicated wards, had strongly attracted him,—its presence had suggested robbery.

Monsieur de Marquet appeared to be greatly perplexed, as if he did not know whether he ought to be glad of the new direction given to the inquiry by the young reporter, or sorry that it had not been done by himself. In our profession and for the general welfare, we have to put up with such mortifications and bury selfish feelings. That was why Monsieur de Marquet controlled himself and joined his compliments with those of Monsieur Dax. As for Monsieur Rouletabille, he simply shrugged his shoulders and said: "There's nothing at all in that!" I should have liked to box his ears, especially when he added: "You will do well, Monsieur, to ask Monsieur Stangerson who usually kept that key?"

"My daughter," replied Monsieur Stangerson, "she was never without it."

"Ah! then that changes the aspect of things which no longer corresponds with Monsieur Rouletabille's ideas!" cried Monsieur de Marquet. "If that key never left Mademoiselle Stangerson, the murderer must have waited for her in her room for the purpose of stealing it; and the robbery could not have been committed until after the attack had been made on her. But after the attack four persons were in the laboratory! I can't make it out!"

"The robbery," said the reporter, "could only have been committed before the attack upon Mademoiselle Stangerson in her room. When the murderer entered the pavilion he already possessed the brass-headed key."

"That is impossible," said Monsieur Stangerson in a low voice.

"It is quite possible, Monsieur, as this proves."

And the young rascal drew a copy of the "Epoque" from his pocket, dated the 21st of October (I recall the fact that the crime was committed on the night between the 24th and 25th), and showing us an advertisement, he read:

"'Yesterday a black satin reticule was lost in the Grands Magasins de la Louvre. It contained, amongst other things, a small key with a brass head. A handsome reward will be given to the person who has found it. This person must write, poste restante, bureau 40, to this address: M. A. T. H. S. N.' Do not these letters suggest Mademoiselle Stangerson?" continued the reporter. "The 'key with a brass head'—is not this the key? I always read advertisements. In my business, as in yours, Monsieur, one should always read the personals.' They are often the keys to intrigues, that are not always brass-headed, but which are none the less interesting. This advertisement interested me specially; the woman of the key surrounded it with a kind of mystery. Evidently she valued the key, since she promised a big reward for its restoration! And I thought on these six letters: M. A. T. H. S. N. The first four at once pointed to a Christian name; evidently I said Math is Mathilde. But I could make nothing of the two last letters. So I threw the journal aside and occupied myself with other matters. Four days later, when the evening paper appeared with enormous head-lines announcing the murder of Mademoiselle Stangerson, the letters in the advertisement mechanically recurred to me. I had forgotten the two last letters, S. N. When I saw them again I could not help exclaiming, 'Stangerson!' I jumped into a cab and rushed into the bureau No. 40, asking: 'Have you a letter addressed to M. A. T. H. S. N.?' The clerk replied that he had not. I insisted, begged and entreated him to search. He wanted to know if I were playing a joke on him, and then told me that he had had a letter with the initials M. A. T. H. S. N, but he had given it up three days ago, to a lady who came for it. 'You come today to claim the letter, and the day before yesterday another gentleman claimed it! I've had enough of this,' he concluded angrily. I tried to question him as to the two persons who had already claimed the letter; but whether he wished to entrench himself behind professional secrecy,—he may have thought that he had already said too much,—or whether he was disgusted at the joke that had been played on him—he would not answer any of my questions."

Rouletabille paused. We all remained silent. Each drew his own conclusions from the strange story of the poste restante letter. It seemed, indeed, that we now had a thread by means of which we should be able to follow up this extraordinary mystery.

"Then it is almost certain," said Monsieur Stangerson, "that my daughter did lose the key, and that she did not tell me of it, wishing to spare any anxiety, and that she begged whoever had found it to write to the poste restante. She evidently feared that, by giving our address, inquiries would have resulted that would have apprised me of the loss of the key. It was quite logical, quite natural for her to have taken that course—for I have been robbed once before."

"Where was that, and when?" asked the Chief of the Surete.

"Oh! many years ago, in America, in Philadelphia. There were stolen from my laboratory the drawings of two inventions that might have made the fortune of a man. Not only have I never learnt who the thief was, but I have never heard even a word of the object of the robbery, doubtless because, in order to defeat the plans of the person who had robbed me, I myself brought these two inventions before the public, and so rendered the robbery of no avail. From that time on I have been very careful to shut myself in when I am at work. The bars to these windows, the lonely situation of this pavilion, this cabinet, which I had specially constructed, this special lock, this unique key, all are precautions against fears inspired by a sad experience."

"Most interesting!" remarked Monsieur Dax.

Monsieur Rouletabille asked about the reticule. Neither Monsieur Stangerson nor Daddy Jacques had seen it for several days, but a few hours later we learned from Mademoiselle Stangerson herself that the reticule had either been stolen from her, or she had lost it. She further corroborated all that had passed just as her father had stated. She had gone to the poste restante and, on the 23rd of October, had received a letter which, she affirmed, contained nothing but a vulgar pleasantry, which she had immediately burned.

To return to our examination, or rather to our conversation. I must state that the Chief of the Surete having inquired of Monsieur Stangerson under what conditions his daughter had gone to Paris on the 20th of October, we learned that Monsieur Robert Darzac had accompanied her, and Darzac had not been again seen at the chateau from that time to the day after the crime had been committed. The fact that Monsieur Darzac was with her in the Grands Magasins de la Louvre when the reticule disappeared could not pass unnoticed, and, it must be said, strongly awakened our interest.

This conversation between magistrates, accused, victim, witnesses and journalist, was coming to a close when quite a theatrical sensation— an incident of a kind displeasing to Monsieur de Marquet—was produced. The officer of the gendarmes came to announce that Frederic Larsan requested to be admitted,—a request that was at once complied with. He held in his hand a heavy pair of muddy boots, which he threw on the pavement of the laboratory.

"Here," he said, "are the boots worn by the murderer. Do you recognise them, Daddy Jacques?"

Daddy Jacques bent over them and, stupefied, recognised a pair of old boots which he had, some time back, thrown into a corner of his attic. He was so taken aback that he could not hide his agitation.

Then pointing to the handkerchief in the old man's hand, Frederic Larsan said:

"That's a handkerchief astonishingly like the one found in the "Yellow Room."

"I know," said Daddy Jacques, trembling, "they are almost alike."

"And then," continued Frederic Larsan, "the old Basque cap also found in the 'Yellow Room' might at one time have been worn by Daddy Jacques himself. All this, gentlemen, proves, I think, that the murderer wished to disguise his real personality. He did it in a very clumsy way—or, at least, so it appears to us. Don't be alarmed, Daddy Jacques; we are quite sure that you were not the murderer; you never left the side of Monsieur Stangerson. But if Monsieur Stangerson had not been working that night and had gone back to the chateau after parting with his daughter, and Daddy Jacques had gone to sleep in his attic, no one would have doubted that he was the murderer. He owes his safety, therefore, to the tragedy having been enacted too soon,—the murderer, no doubt, from the silence in the laboratory, imagined that it was empty, and that the moment for action had come. The man who had been able to introduce himself here so mysteriously and to leave so many evidences against Daddy Jacques, was, there can be no doubt, familiar with the house. At what hour exactly he entered, whether in the afternoon or in the evening, I cannot say. One familiar with the proceedings and persons of this pavilion could choose his own time for entering the 'Yellow Room'."

"He could not have entered it if anybody had been in the laboratory," said Monsieur de Marquet.

"How do we know that?" replied Larsan. "There was the dinner in the laboratory, the coming and going of the servants in attendance. There was a chemical experiment being carried on between ten and eleven o'clock, with Monsieur Stangerson, his daughter, and Daddy Jacques engaged at the furnace in a corner of the high chimney. Who can say that the murderer—an intimate!—a friend!—did not take advantage of that moment to slip into the 'Yellow Room', after having taken off his boots in the lavatory?"

"It is very improbable," said Monsieur Stangerson.

"Doubtless—but it is not impossible. I assert nothing. As to the escape from the pavilion—that's another thing, the most natural thing in the world."

For a moment Frederic Larsan paused,—a moment that appeared to us a very long time. The eagerness with which we awaited what he was going to tell us may be imagined.

"I have not been in the 'Yellow Room'," he continued, "but I take it for granted that you have satisfied yourselves that he could have left the room only by way of the door; it is by the door, then, that the murderer made his way out. At what time? At the moment when it was most easy for him to do so; at the moment when it became most explainable—so completely explainable that there can be no other explanation. Let us go over the moments which followed after the crime had been committed. There was the first moment, when Monsieur Stangerson and Daddy Jacques were close to the door, ready to bar the way. There was the second moment, during which Daddy Jacques was absent and Monsieur Stangerson was left alone before the door. There was a third moment, when Monsieur Stangerson was joined by the concierge. There was a fourth moment, during which Monsieur Stangerson, the concierge and his wife and Daddy Jacques were before the door. There was a fifth moment, during which the door was burst open and the 'Yellow Room' entered. The moment at which the flight is explainable is the very moment when there was the least number of persons before the door. There was one moment when there was but one person,—Monsieur Stangerson. Unless a complicity of silence on the part of Daddy Jacques is admitted—in which I do not believe—the door was opened in the presence of Monsieur Stangerson alone and the man escaped.

"Here we must admit that Monsieur Stangerson had powerful reasons for not arresting, or not causing the arrest of the murderer, since he allowed him to reach the window in the vestibule and closed it after him!—That done, Mademoiselle Stangerson, though horribly wounded, had still strength enough, and no doubt in obedience to the entreaties of her father, to refasten the door of her chamber, with both the bolt and the lock, before sinking on the floor. We do not know who committed the crime; we do not know of what wretch Monsieur and Mademoiselle

Stangerson are the victims, but there is no doubt that they both know! The secret must be a terrible one, for the father had not hesitated to leave his daughter to die behind a door which she had shut upon herself,— terrible for him to have allowed the assassin to escape. For there is no other way in the world to explain the murderer's flight from the 'Yellow Room'!"

The silence which followed this dramatic and lucid explanation was appalling. We all of us felt grieved for the illustrious professor, driven into a corner by the pitiless logic of Frederic Larsan, forced to confess the whole truth of his martyrdom or to keep silent, and thus make a yet more terrible admission. The man himself, a veritable statue of sorrow, raised his hand with a gesture so solemn that we bowed our heads to it as before something sacred. He then pronounced these words, in a voice so loud that it seemed to exhaust him:

"I swear by the head of my suffering child that I never for an instant left the door of her chamber after hearing her cries for help; that that door was not opened while I was alone in the laboratory; and that, finally, when we entered the 'Yellow Room', my three domestics and I, the murderer was no longer there! I swear I do not know the murderer!"

Must I say it,—in spite of the solemnity of Monsieur Stangerson's words, we did not believe in his denial. Frederic Larsan had shown us the truth and it was not so easily given up.

Monsieur de Marquet announced that the conversation was at an end, and as we were about to leave the laboratory, Joseph Rouletabille approached Monsieur Stangerson, took him by the hand with the greatest respect, and I heard him say:

"I believe you, Monsieur."

I here close the citation which I have thought it my duty to make from Monsieur Maleine's narrative. I need not tell the reader that all that passed in the laboratory was immediately and faithfully reported to me by Rouletabille.

# XII

## FREDERIC LARSAN'S CANE

It was not till six o'clock that I left the chateau, taking with me the article hastily written by my friend in the little sitting-room which Monsieur Robert Darzac had placed at our disposal. The reporter was to sleep at the chateau, taking advantage of the to me inexplicable hospitality offered him by Monsieur Robert Darzac, to whom Monsieur Stangerson, in that sad time, left the care of all his domestic affairs. Nevertheless he insisted on accompanying me to the station at Epinay. In crossing the park, he said to me:

"Frederic is really very clever and has not belied his reputation. Do you know how he came to find Daddy Jacques's boots?—Near the spot where we noticed the traces of the neat boots and the disappearance of the rough ones, there was a square hole, freshly made in the moist ground, where a stone had evidently been removed. Larsan searched for that stone without finding it, and at once imagined that it had been used by the murderer with which to sink the boots in the lake. Fred's calculation was an excellent one, as the success of his search proves. That escaped me; but my mind was turned in another direction by the large number of false indications of his track which the murderer left, and by the measure of the black foot-marks corresponding with that of Daddy Jacques's boots, which I had established without his suspecting it, on the floor of the 'Yellow Room'. All which was a proof, in my eyes, that the murderer had sought to turn suspicion on to the old servant. Up to that point, Larsan and I are in accord; but no further. It is going to be a terrible matter; for I tell you he is working on wrong lines, and I—I, must fight him with nothing!"

I was surprised at the profoundly grave accent with which my young friend pronounced the last words.

He repeated:

"Yes—terrible!—terrible! For it is fighting with nothing, when you have only an idea to fight with."

At that moment we passed by the back of the chateau. Night had come. A window on the first floor was partly open. A feeble light came from it as well as some sounds which drew our attention. We approached until we had reached the side of a door that was situated just under the window. Rouletabille, in a low tone, made me understand, that this was the window of Mademoiselle Stangerson's chamber. The sounds which had attracted our attention ceased, then were renewed for a moment, and then we heard stifled sobs. We were only able to catch these words, which reached us distinctly: "My poor Robert!"— Rouletabille whispered in my ear:

"If we only knew what was being said in that chamber, my inquiry would soon be finished."

He looked about him. The darkness of the evening enveloped us; we could not see much beyond the narrow path bordered by trees, which ran behind the chateau. The sobs had ceased.

"If we can't hear we may at least try to see," said Rouletabille.

And, making a sign to me to deaden the sound of my steps, he led me across the path to the trunk of a tall beech tree, the white bole of which was visible in the darkness. This tree grew exactly in front of the window in which we were so much interested, its lower branches being on a level with the first floor of the chateau. From the height of those branches one might certainly see what was passing in Mademoiselle Stangerson's chamber. Evidently that was what Rouletabille thought, for, enjoining me to remain hidden, he clasped the trunk with his vigorous arms and climbed up. I soon lost sight of him amid the branches, and then followed a deep silence. In front of me, the open window remained lighted, and I saw no shadow move across it. I listened, and presently from above me these words reached my ears:

"After you!"

"After you, pray!"

Somebody was overhead, speaking,—exchanging courtesies. What was my astonishment to see on the slippery column of the tree two human forms appear and quietly slip down to the ground. Rouletabille had mounted alone, and had returned with another.

"Good evening, Monsieur Sainclair!"

It was Frederic Larsan. The detective had already occupied the post of observation when my young friend had thought to reach it alone. Neither noticed my astonishment. I explained that to myself by the fact that they must have been witnesses of some tender and despairing scene between Mademoiselle Stangerson, lying in her bed, and Monsieur Darzac on his knees by her pillow. I guessed that each had drawn different conclusions from what they had seen. It was easy to see that the scene had strongly impressed Rouletabille in favour of Monsieur Robert Darzac; while, to Larsan, it showed nothing but consummate hypocrisy, acted with finished art by Mademoiselle Stangerson's fiance.

As we reached the park gate, Larsan stopped us.

"My cane!" he cried. "I left it near the tree."

He left us, saying he would rejoin us presently.

"Have you noticed Frederic Larsan's cane?" asked the young reporter, as soon as we were alone. "It is quite a new one, which I have never seen him use before. He seems to take great care of it—it never leaves him. One would think he was afraid it might fall into the hands of strangers. I never saw it before today. Where did he find it? It isn't natural that a man who had never before used a walking-stick should, the day after the Glandier crime, never move a step without one. On the day of our arrival at the chateau, as soon as he saw us, he put his watch in his pocket and picked up his cane from the ground—a proceeding to which I was perhaps wrong not to attach some importance."

We were now out of the park. Rouletabille had dropped into silence. His thoughts were certainly still occupied with Frederic Larsan's new cane. I had proof of that when, as we came near to Epinay, he said:

"Frederic Larsan arrived at the Glandier before me; he began his inquiry before me; he has had time to find out things about which I know nothing. Where did he find that cane?" Then he added: "It is probable that his suspicion—more than that, his reasoning—has led him to lay his hand on something tangible. Has this cane anything to do with it? Where the deuce could he have found it?"

As I had to wait twenty minutes for the train at Epinay, we entered a wine shop. Almost immediately the door opened and Frederic Larsan made his appearance, brandishing his famous cane.

"I found it!" he said laughingly.

The three of us seated ourselves at a table. Rouletabille never took his eyes off the cane; he was so absorbed that he did not notice a sign Larsan made to a railway employeee, a young man with a chin decorated by a tiny blond and ill-kept beard. On the sign he rose, paid for his drink, bowed, and went out. I should not myself have attached any importance to the circumstance, if it had not been recalled to my mind, some months later, by the reappearance of the man with the beard at one of the most tragic moments of this case. I then learned that the youth was one of Larsan's assistants and had been charged by him to watch the going and coming of travellers at the station of Epinay-sur-Orge. Larsan neglected nothing in any case on which he was engaged.

I turned my eyes again on Rouletabille.

"Ah,—Monsieur Fred!" he said, "when did you begin to use a walking-stick? I have always seen you walking with your hands in your pockets!"

"It is a present," replied the detective.

"Recent?" insisted Rouletabille.

"No, it was given to me in London."

"Ah, yes, I remember—you have just come from London. May I look at it?"

"Oh!—certainly!"

Fred passed the cane to Rouletabille. It was a large yellow bamboo with a crutch handle and ornamented with a gold ring. Rouletabille, after examining it minutely, returned it to Larsan, with a bantering expression on his face, saying:

"You were given a French cane in London!"

"Possibly," said Fred, imperturbably.

"Read the mark there, in tiny letters: Cassette, 6a, Opera."

"Cannot English people buy canes in Paris?"

When Rouletabille had seen me into the train, he said:

"You'll remember the address?"

"Yes,—Cassette, 6a, Opera. Rely on me; you shall have word tomorrow morning."

That evening, on reaching Paris, I saw Monsieur Cassette, dealer in walking-sticks and umbrellas, and wrote to my friend:

"A man unmistakably answering to the description of Monsieur Robert Darzac—same height, slightly stooping, putty-coloured overcoat, bowler hat—purchased a cane similar to the one in which we are interested, on the evening of the crime, about eight o'clock. Monsieur Cassette had not sold another such cane during the last two years. Fred's cane is new. It is quite clear that it's the same cane. Fred did not buy it, since he was in London. Like you, I think that he found it somewhere near Monsieur Robert Darzac. But if, as you suppose, the murderer was in the 'Yellow Room' for five, or even six hours, and the crime was not committed until towards midnight, the purchase of this cane proves an incontestable alibi for Darzac."

# XIII

## "The Presbytery Has Lost Nothing of Its Charm, Nor the Garden Its Brightness"

A week after the occurrence of the events I have just recounted—on the 2nd of November, to be exact—I received at my home in Paris the following telegraphic message: "Come to the Glandier by the earliest train. Bring revolvers. Friendly greetings. Rouletabille."

I have already said, I think, that at that period, being a young barrister with but few briefs, I frequented the Palais de Justice rather for the purpose of familiarising myself with my professional duties than for the defence of the widow and orphan. I could, therefore, feel no surprise at Rouletabille disposing of my time. Moreover, he knew how keenly interested I was in his journalistic adventures in general and, above all, in the murder at the Glandier. I had not heard from him for a week, nor of the progress made with that mysterious case, except by the innumerable paragraphs in the newspapers and by the very brief notes of Rouletabille in the "Epoque." Those notes had divulged the fact that traces of human blood had been found on the mutton-bone, as well as fresh traces of the blood of Mademoiselle Stangerson—the old stains belonged to other crimes, probably dating years back.

It may be easily imagined that the crime engaged the attention of the press throughout the world. No crime known had more absorbed the minds of people. It appeared to me, however, that the judicial inquiry was making but very little progress; and I should have been very glad, if, on the receipt of my friend's invitation to rejoin him at the Glandier, the despatch had not contained the words, "Bring revolvers."

That puzzled me greatly. Rouletabille telegraphing for revolvers meant that there might be occasion to use them. Now, I confess it without shame, I am not a hero. But here was a friend, evidently in danger, calling on me to go to his aid. I did not hesitate long; and after assuring myself that the only revolver I possessed was properly loaded, I hurried towards the Orleans station. On the way I remembered that Rouletabille had asked for two revolvers; I therefore entered a gunsmith's shop and bought an excellent weapon for my friend.

I had hoped to find him at the station at Epinay; but he was not there. However, a cab was waiting for me and I was soon at the Glandier. Nobody was at the gate, and it was only on the threshold of the chateau that I met the young man. He saluted me with a friendly gesture and threw his arms about me, inquiring warmly as to the state of my health.

When we were in the little sitting-room of which I have spoken, Rouletabille made me sit down.

"It's going badly," he said.

"What's going badly?" I asked.

"Everything."

He came nearer to me and whispered:

"Frederic Larsan is working with might and main against Darzac."

This did not astonish me. I had seen the poor show Mademoiselle Stangerson's fiance had made at the time of the examination of the footprints. However, I immediately asked:

"What about that cane?"

"It is still in the hands of Frederic Larsan. He never lets go of it."

"But doesn't it prove the alibi for Monsieur Darzac?"

"Not at all. Gently questioned by me, Darzac denied having, on that evening, or on any other, purchased a cane at Cassette's. However," said Rouletabille, "I'll not swear to anything; Monsieur Darzac has such strange fits of silence that one does not know exactly what to think of what he says."

"To Frederic Larsan this cane must mean a piece of very damaging evidence. But in what way? The time when it was bought shows it could not have been in the murderer's possession."

"The time doesn't worry Larsan. He is not obliged to adopt my theory which assumes that the murderer got into the 'Yellow Room' between five and six o'clock. But there's nothing to prevent him assuming that the murderer got in between ten and eleven o'clock at night. At that hour Monsieur and Mademoiselle Stangerson, assisted by Daddy Jacques, were engaged in making an interesting chemical experiment in the part of the laboratory taken up by the furnaces. Larsan says, unlikely as that may seem, that the murderer may have slipped behind them. He has already got the examining magistrate to listen to him. When one looks closely into it, the reasoning is absurd, seeing that the 'intimate'—if there is one—must have known that the professor would shortly leave the pavilion, and that the 'friend' had only to put off operating till after the professor's departure. Why should he have risked crossing the laboratory while the professor was in it? And then, when he had got into the 'Yellow Room'?

"There are many points to be cleared up before Larsan's theory can be admitted. I sha'n't waste my time over it, for my theory won't allow me to occupy myself with mere imagination. Only, as I am obliged for the moment to keep silent, and Larsan sometimes talks, he may finish by coming out openly against Monsieur Darzac,—if I'm not there," added the young reporter proudly. "For there are surface evidences against Darzac, much more convincing than that cane, which remains incomprehensible to me, all the more so as Larsan does not in the least hesitate to let Darzac see him with it!—I understand many things in Larsan's theory, but I can't make anything of that cane.

"Is he still at the chateau?"

"Yes; he hardly ever leaves it!—He sleeps there, as I do, at the request of Monsieur Stangerson, who has done for him what Monsieur Robert Darzac has done for me. In spite of the accusation made by Larsan that Monsieur Stangerson knows who the murderer is he yet affords him every facility for arriving at the truth,—just as Darzac is doing for me."

"But you are convinced of Darzac's innocence?"

"At one time I did believe in the possibility of his guilt. That was when we arrived here for the first time. The time has come for me to tell you what has passed between Monsieur Darzac and myself."

Here Rouletabille interrupted himself and asked me if I had brought the revolvers. I showed him them. Having examined both, he pronounced them excellent, and handed them back to me.

"Shall we have any use for them?" I asked.

"No doubt; this evening. We shall pass the night here—if that won't tire you?"

"On the contrary," I said with an expression that made Rouletabille laugh.

"No, no," he said, "this is no time for laughing. You remember the phrase which was the 'open sesame' of this chateau full of mystery?"

"Yes," I said, "perfectly,—'The presbytery has lost nothing of its charm, nor the garden its brightness.' It was the phrase which you found on the half-burned piece of paper amongst the ashes in the laboratory."

"Yes; at the bottom of the paper, where the flame had not reached, was this date: 23rd of October. Remember this date, it is highly important. I am now going to tell you about that curious phrase. On the evening before the crime, that is to say, on the 23rd, Monsieur and Mademoiselle Stangerson were at a reception at the Elysee. I know that, because I was there on duty, having to interview one of the savants of the Academy of Philadelphia, who was being feted there. I had never before seen either Monsieur or Mademoiselle Stangerson. I was seated in the room which precedes the Salon des Ambassadeurs, and, tired of being jostled by so many noble personages, I had fallen into a vague reverie, when I scented near me the perfume of the lady in black.

"Do you ask me what is the 'perfume of the lady in black'? It must suffice for you to know that it is a perfume of which I am very fond, because it was that of a lady who had been very kind to me in my childhood,—a lady whom I had always seen dressed in black. The lady who, that evening, was scented with the perfume of the lady in black, was dressed in white. She was wonderfully beautiful. I could not help rising and following her. An old man gave her his arm and, as they passed, I heard voices say: 'Professor Stangerson and his daughter.' It was in that way I learned who it was I was following.

"They met Monsieur Robert Darzac, whom I knew by sight. Professor Stangerson, accosted by Mr. Arthur William Rance, one of the American savants, seated himself in the great gallery, and Monsieur Robert Darzac led Mademoiselle Stangerson into the conservatory. I followed. The weather was very mild that evening; the garden doors were open. Mademoiselle Stangerson threw a fichu shawl over her shoulders and I plainly saw that it was she who was begging Monsieur Darzac to go with her into the garden. I continued to follow, interested by the agitation plainly exhibited by the bearing of Monsieur Darzac. They slowly passed along the wall abutting on the Avenue Marigny. I took the central alley, walking parallel with them, and then crossed over for the purpose of getting nearer to them. The night was dark, and the grass deadened the sound of my steps. They had stopped under the vacillating light of a gas jet and appeared to be both bending over a paper held by Mademoiselle Stangerson, reading something which deeply interested them. I stopped in the darkness and silence.

"Neither of them saw me, and I distinctly heard Mademoiselle Stangerson repeat, as she was refolding the paper: 'The presbytery has lost nothing of its charm, nor the garden its brightness!'—It was said in a tone at once mocking and despairing, and was followed by a burst of such nervous laughter that I think her words will never cease to sound in my ears. But another phrase was uttered by Monsieur Robert Darzac:

'Must I commit a crime, then, to win you?' He was in an extraordinarily agitated state. He took the hand of Mademoiselle Stangerson and held it for a long time to his lips, and I thought, from the movement of his shoulders, that he was crying. Then they went away.

"When I returned to the great gallery," continued Rouletabille, "I saw no more of Monsieur Robert Darzac, and I was not to see him again until after the tragedy at the Glandier. Mademoiselle was near Mr. Rance, who was talking with much animation, his eyes, during the conversation, glowing with a singular brightness. Mademoiselle Stangerson, I thought, was not even listening to what he was saying, her face expressing perfect indifference. His face was the red face of a drunkard. When Monsieur and Mademoiselle Stangerson left, he went to the bar and remained there. I joined him, and rendered him some little service in the midst of the pressing crowd. He thanked me and told me he was returning to America three days later, that is to say, on the 26th (the day after the crime). I talked with him about Philadelphia; he told me he had lived there for five-and-twenty years, and that it was there he had met the illustrious Professor Stangerson and his daughter. He drank a great deal of champagne, and when I left him he was very nearly drunk.

"Such were my experiences on that evening, and I leave you to imagine what effect the news of the attempted murder of Mademoiselle Stangerson produced on me,—with what force those words pronounced by Monsieur Robert Darzac, 'Must I commit a crime, then, to win you?' recurred to me. It was not this phrase, however, that I repeated to him, when we met here at Glandier. The sentence of the presbytery and the bright garden sufficed to open the gate of the chateau. If you ask me if I believe now that Monsieur Darzac is the murderer, I must say I do not. I do not think I ever quite thought that. At the time I could not really think seriously of anything. I had so little evidence to go on. But I needed to have at once the proof that he had not been wounded in the hand.

"When we were alone together, I told him how I had chanced to overhear a part of his conversation with Mademoiselle Stangerson in the garden of the Elysee; and when I repeated to him the words, 'Must I commit a crime, then, to win you?' he was greatly troubled, though much less so than he had been by hearing me repeat the phrase about the presbytery. What threw him into a state of real consternation was to learn from me that the day on which he had gone to meet Mademoiselle

Stangerson at the Elysee, was the very day on which she had gone to the Post Office for the letter. It was that letter, perhaps, which ended with the words: 'The presbytery has lost nothing of its charm, nor the garden its brightness.' My surmise was confirmed by my finding, if you remember, in the ashes of the laboratory, the fragment of paper dated October the 23rd. The letter had been written and withdrawn from the Post Office on the same day.

"There can be no doubt that, on returning from the Elysee that night, Mademoiselle Stangerson had tried to destroy that compromising paper. It was in vain that Monsieur Darzac denied that that letter had anything whatever to do with the crime. I told him that in an affair so filled with mystery as this, he had no right to hide this letter; that I was persuaded it was of considerable importance; that the desperate tone in which Mademoiselle Stangerson had pronounced the prophetic phrase,—that his own tears, and the threat of a crime which he had professed after the letter was read—all these facts tended to leave no room for me to doubt. Monsieur Darzac became more and more agitated, and I determined to take advantage of the effect I had produced on him. 'You were on the point of being married, Monsieur,' I said negligently and without looking at him, 'and suddenly your marriage becomes impossible because of the writer of that letter; because as soon as his letter was read, you spoke of the necessity for a crime to win Mademoiselle Stangerson. Therefore there is someone between you and her—someone who is preventing your marriage with her—someone who has attempted to kill her, so that she should not be able to marry!' And I concluded with these words: 'Now, monsieur, you have only to tell me in confidence the name of the murderer!'—The words I had uttered must have struck him ominously, for when I turned my eyes on him, I saw that his face was haggard, the perspiration standing on his forehead, and terror showing in his eyes.

"'Monsieur,' he said to me, 'I am going to ask of you something which may appear insane, but in exchange for which I place my life in your hands. You must not tell the magistrates of what you saw and heard in the garden of the Elysee,—neither to them nor to anybody. I swear to you, that I am innocent, and I know, I feel, that you believe me; but I would rather be taken for the guilty man than see justice go astray on that phrase, "The presbytery has lost nothing of its charm, nor the garden its brightness." The judges must know nothing about that phrase. All this matter is in your hands. Monsieur, I leave it there; but forget the evening at the Elysee. A hundred other roads are open to you in your search for the criminal. I will open them for you myself. I will help you. Will you take up your quarters here?—You may remain here to do as you please.—Eat—sleep here—watch my actions—the actions of all here. You shall be master of the Glandier, Monsieur; but forget the evening at the Elysee.'"

Rouletabille here paused to take breath. I now understood what had appeared so unexplainable in the demeanour of Monsieur Robert Darzac towards my friend, and the facility with which the young reporter had been able to install himself on the scene of the crime. My curiosity could not fail to be excited by all I had heard. I asked Rouletabille to satisfy it still further. What had happened at the Glandier during the past week?—Had he not told me that there were surface indications against Monsieur Darzac much more terrible than that of the cane found by Larsan?

"Everything seems to be pointing against him," replied my friend, "and the situation is becoming exceedingly grave. Monsieur Darzac appears not to mind it much; but in that he is wrong. I was interested only in the health of Mademoiselle Stangerson, which was daily improving, when something occurred that is even more mysterious than—than the mystery of the 'Yellow Room'!"

"Impossible!" I cried, "What could be more mysterious than that?"

"Let us first go back to Monsieur Robert Darzac," said Rouletabille, calming me. "I have said that everything seems to be pointing against him. The marks of the neat boots found by Frederic Larsan appear to be really the footprints of Mademoiselle Stangerson's fiance. The marks made by the bicycle may have been made by his bicycle. He had usually left it at the chateau; why did he take it to Paris on that particular occasion? Was it because he was not going to return again to the chateau? Was it because, owing to the breaking off of his marriage, his relations with the Stangersons were to cease? All who are interested in the matter affirm that those relations were to continue unchanged.

"Frederic Larsan, however, believes that all relations were at an end. From the day when Monsieur Darzac accompanied Mademoiselle Stangerson to the Grands Magasins de la Louvre until the day after the crime, he had not been at the Glandier. Remember that Mademoiselle Stangerson lost her reticule containing the key with the brass head while she was in his company. From that day to the evening at the Elysee, the Sorbonne professor and Mademoiselle Stangerson did not see one another; but they may have written to each other. Mademoiselle Stangerson went to the Post Office to get a letter, which Larsan says was written by Robert Darzac; for knowing nothing of what had passed at the Elysee, Larsan believes that it was Monsieur Darzac himself who stole the reticule with the key, with the design of forcing her consent, by getting possession of the precious papers of her father—papers which he would have restored to him on condition that the marriage engagement was to be fulfilled.

"All that would have been a very doubtful and almost absurd hypothesis, as Larsan admitted to me, but for another and much graver circumstance. In the first place here is something which I have not been able to explain—Monsieur Darzac had himself, on the 24th, gone to the Post Office to ask for the letter which Mademoiselle had called for and received on the previous evening. The description of the man who made application tallies in every respect with the appearance of Monsieur Darzac, who, in answer to the questions put to him by the examining magistrate, denies that he went to the Post Office. Now even admitting that the letter was written by him—which I do not believe—he knew that Mademoiselle Stangerson had received it, since he had seen it in her hands in the garden at the Elysee. It could not have been he, then, who had gone to the Post Office, the day after the 24th, to ask for a letter which he knew was no longer there.

"To me it appears clear that somebody, strongly resembling him, stole Mademoiselle Stangerson's reticule and in that letter, had demanded of her something which she had not sent him. He must have been surprised at the failure of his demand, hence his application at the Post Office, to learn whether his letter had been delivered to the person to whom it had been addressed. Finding that it had been claimed, he had become furious. What had he demanded? Nobody but Mademoiselle Stangerson knows. Then, on the day following, it is reported that she had been attacked during the night, and, the next day, I discovered that the Professor had, at the same time, been robbed by means of the key referred to in the poste restante letter. It would seem, then, that the man who went to the Post Office to inquire for the letter must have been the murderer. All these arguments Larsan applies as against Monsieur Darzac. You may be sure that the examining magistrate, Larsan, and myself, have done our best to get from the Post Office precise details relative to the singular personage who applied there on the 24th of October. But nothing has been learned. We don't know where he came from—or where he went.

Beyond the description which makes him resemble Monsieur Darzac, we know nothing.

"I have announced in the leading journals that a handsome reward will be given to a driver of any public conveyance who drove a fare to No. 40, Post Office, about ten o'clock on the morning of the 24th of October. Information to be addressed to 'M. R.,' at the office of the 'Epoque'; but no answer has resulted. The man may have walked; but, as he was most likely in a hurry, there was a chance that he might have gone in a cab. Who, I keep asking myself night and day, is the man who so strongly resembles Monsieur Robert Darzac, and who is also known to have bought the cane which has fallen into Larsan's hands?

"The most serious fact is that Monsieur Darzac was, at the very same time that his double presented himself at the Post Office, scheduled for a lecture at the Sorbonne. He had not delivered that lecture, and one of his friends took his place. When I questioned him as to how he had employeeed the time, he told me that he had gone for a stroll in the Bois de Boulogne. What do you think of a professor who, instead of giving his lecture, obtains a substitute to go for a stroll in the Bois de Boulogne? When Frederic Larsan asked him for information on this point, he quietly replied that it was no business of his how he spent his time in Paris. On which Fred swore aloud that he would find out, without anybody's help.

"All this seems to fit in with Fred's hypothesis, namely, that Monsieur Stangerson allowed the murderer to escape in order to avoid a scandal. The hypothesis is further substantiated by the fact that Darzac was in the 'Yellow Room' and was permitted to get away. That hypothesis I believe to be a false one.—Larsan is being misled by it, though that would not displease me, did it not affect an innocent person. Now does that hypothesis really mislead Frederic Larsan? That is the question— that is the question."

"Perhaps he is right," I cried, interrupting Rouletabille. "Are you sure that Monsieur Darzac is innocent?—It seems to me that these are extraordinary coincidences—"

"Coincidences," replied my friend, "are the worst enemies to truth."

"What does the examining magistrate think now of the matter?"

"Monsieur de Marquet hesitates to accuse Monsieur Darzac, in the absence of absolute proofs. Not only would he have public opinion wholly against him, to say nothing of the Sorbonne, but Monsieur and Mademoiselle Stangerson. She adores Monsieur Robert Darzac.

Indistinctly as she saw the murderer, it would be hard to make the public believe that she could not have recognised him, if Darzac had been the criminal. No doubt the 'Yellow Room' was very dimly lit; but a night-light, however small, gives some light. Here, my boy, is how things stood when, three days, or rather three nights ago, an extraordinarily strange incident occurred."

# XIV

## "I Expect the Assassin This Evening"

I must take you," said Rouletabille, "so as to enable you to understand, to the various scenes. I myself believe that I have discovered what everybody else is searching for, namely, how the murderer escaped from the 'Yellow Room', without any accomplice, and without Mademoiselle Stangerson having had anything to do with it. But so long as I am not sure of the real murderer, I cannot state the theory on which I am working. I can only say that I believe it to be correct and, in any case, a quite natural and simple one. As to what happened in this place three nights ago, I must say it kept me wondering for a whole day and a night. It passes all belief. The theory I have formed from the incident is so absurd that I would rather matters remained as yet unexplained."

Saying which the young reporter invited me to go and make the tour of the chateau with him. The only sound to be heard was the crunching of the dead leaves beneath our feet. The silence was so intense that one might have thought the chateau had been abandoned. The old stones, the stagnant water of the ditch surrounding the donjon, the bleak ground strewn with the dead leaves, the dark, skeleton-like outlines of the trees, all contributed to give to the desolate place, now filled with its awful mystery, a most funereal aspect. As we passed round the donjon, we met the Green Man, the forest-keeper, who did not greet us, but walked by as if we had not existed. He was looking just as I had formerly seen him through the window of the Donjon Inn. He had still his fowling-piece slung at his back, his pipe was in his mouth, and his eye-glasses on his nose.

"An odd kind of fish!" Rouletabille said to me, in a low tone.

"Have you spoken to him?" I asked.

"Yes, but I could get nothing out of him. His only answers are grunts and shrugs of the shoulders. He generally lives on the first floor of the donjon, a big room that once served for an oratory. He lives like a bear, never goes out without his gun, and is only pleasant with the girls. The women, for twelve miles round, are all setting their caps for him. For the present, he is paying attention to Madame Mathieu, whose husband is keeping a lynx eye upon her in consequence."

After passing the donjon, which is situated at the extreme end of the left wing, we went to the back of the chateau. Rouletabille, pointing to a window which I recognised as the only one belonging to Mademoiselle Stangerson's apartment, said to me:

"If you had been here, two nights ago, you would have seen your humble servant at the top of a ladder, about to enter the chateau by that window."

As I expressed some surprise at this piece of nocturnal gymnastics, he begged me to notice carefully the exterior disposition of the chateau. We then went back into the building.

"I must now show you the first floor of the chateau, where I am living," said my friend.

To enable the reader the better to understand the disposition of these parts of the dwelling, I annex a plan of the first floor of the right wing, drawn by Rouletabille the day after the extraordinary phenomenon occurred, the details of which I am about to relate.

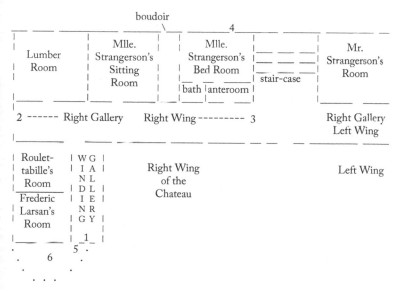

Rouletabille motioned me to follow him up a magnificent flight of stairs ending in a landing on the first floor. From this landing one could pass to the right or left wing of the chateau by a gallery opening from it. This gallery, high and wide, extended along the whole length of the building and was lit from the front of the chateau facing the north. The rooms, the windows of which looked to the south, opened out of the gallery. Professor Stangerson inhabited the left wing of the building. Mademoiselle Stangerson had her apartment in the right wing.

We entered the gallery to the right. A narrow carpet, laid on the waxed oaken floor, which shone like glass, deadened the sound of our footsteps. Rouletabille asked me, in a low tone, to walk carefully, as we were passing the door of Mademoiselle Stangerson's apartment. This consisted of a bed-room, an ante-room, a small bath-room, a boudoir, and a drawing-room. One could pass from one to another of these rooms without having to go by way of the gallery. The gallery continued straight to the western end of the building, where it was lit by a high window (window 2 on the plan). At about two-thirds of its length this gallery, at a right angle, joined another gallery following the course of the right wing.

The better to follow this narrative, we shall call the gallery leading from the stairs to the eastern window, the "right" gallery and the gallery quitting it at a right angle, the "off-turning" gallery (winding gallery in the plan). It was at the meeting point of the two galleries that Rouletabille had his chamber, adjoining that of Frederic Larsan, the door of each opening on to the "off-turning" gallery, while the doors of Mademoiselle Stangerson's apartment opened into the "right" gallery. (See the plan.)

Rouletabille opened the door of his room and after we had passed in, carefully drew the bolt. I had not had time to glance round the place in which he had been installed, when he uttered a cry of surprise and pointed to a pair of eye-glasses on a side-table.

"What are these doing here?" he asked.

I should have been puzzled to answer him.

"I wonder," he said, "I wonder if this is what I have been searching for. I wonder if these are the eye-glasses from the presbytery!"

He seized them eagerly, his fingers caressing the glass. Then looking at me, with an expression of terror on his face, he murmured, "Oh!—Oh!"

He repeated the exclamation again and again, as if his thoughts had suddenly turned his brain.

He rose and, putting his hand on my shoulder, laughed like one demented as he said:

"Those glasses will drive me silly! Mathematically speaking the thing is possible; but humanly speaking it is impossible—or afterwards—or afterwards—"

Two light knocks struck the door. Rouletabille opened it. A figure entered. I recognised the concierge, whom I had seen when she was being taken to the pavilion for examination. I was surprised, thinking she was still under lock and key. This woman said in a very low tone:

"In the grove of the parquet."

Rouletabille replied: "Thanks."—The woman then left. He again turned to me, his look haggard, after having carefully refastened the door, muttering some incomprehensible phrases.

"If the thing is mathematically possible, why should it not be humanly!—And if it is humanly possible, the matter is simply awful." I interrupted him in his soliloquy:

"Have they set the concierges at liberty, then?" I asked.

"Yes," he replied, "I had them liberated, I needed people I could trust. The woman is thoroughly devoted to me, and her husband would lay down his life for me."

"Oho!" I said, "when will he have occasion to do it?"

"This evening,—for this evening I expect the murderer."

"You expect the murderer this evening? Then you know him?"

"I shall know him; but I should be mad to affirm, categorically, at this moment that I do know him. The mathematical idea I have of the murderer gives results so frightful, so monstrous, that I hope it is still possible that I am mistaken. I hope so, with all my heart!"

"Five minutes ago, you did not know the murderer; how can you say that you expect this evening?"

"Because I know that he must come."

Rouletabille very slowly filled his pipe and lit it. That meant an interesting story. At that moment we heard some one walking in the gallery and passing before our door. Rouletabille listened. The sound of the footstep died away in the distance.

"Is Frederic Larsan in his room?" I asked, pointing to the partition.

"No," my friend answered. "He went to Paris this morning,—still on the scent of Darzac, who also left for Paris. That matter will turn out badly. I expect that Monsieur Darzac will be arrested in the course of the next week. The worst of it is that everything seems to be in league against him,—circumstances, things, people. Not an hour passes without bringing some new evidence against him. The examining magistrate is overwhelmed by it—and blind."

"Frederic Larsan, however, is not a novice," I said.

"I thought so," said Rouletabille, with a slightly contemptuous turn of his lips, "I fancied he was a much abler man. I had, indeed, a great admiration for him, before I got to know his method of working. It's deplorable. He owes his reputation solely to his ability; but he lacks reasoning power,—the mathematics of his ideas are very poor."

I looked closely at Rouletabille and could not help smiling, on hearing this boy of eighteen talking of a man who had proved to the world that he was the finest police sleuth in Europe.

"You smile," he said? "you are wrong! I swear I will outwit him—and in a striking way! But I must make haste about it, for he has an enormous start on me—given him by Monsieur Robert Darzac, who is this evening going to increase it still more. Think of it!—every time the murderer comes to the chateau, Monsieur Darzac, by a strange fatality, absents himself and refuses to give any account of how he employs his time."

"Every time the assassin comes to the chateau!" I cried. "Has he returned then—?"

"Yes, during that famous night when the strange phenomenon occurred."

I was now going to learn about the astonishing phenomenon to which Rouletabille had made allusion half an hour earlier without giving me any explanation of it. But I had learned never to press Rouletabille in his narratives. He spoke when the fancy took him and when he judged it to be right. He was less concerned about my curiosity than he was for making a complete summing up for himself of any important matter in which he was interested.

At last, in short rapid phrases, he acquainted me with things which plunged me into a state bordering on complete bewilderment. Indeed, the results of that still unknown science known as hypnotism, for example, were not more inexplicable than the disappearance of the "matter" of the murderer at the moment when four persons were within touch of him. I speak of hypnotism as I would of electricity, for of the nature of both we are ignorant and we know little of their laws. I cite these examples because, at the time, the case appeared to me to be only explicable by the inexplicable,—that is to say, by an event outside of known natural laws. And yet, if I had had Rouletabille's brain, I should, like him, have had a presentiment of the natural explanation; for the most curious thing about all the mysteries of the Glandier case was the natural manner in which he explained them.

I have among the papers that were sent me by the young man, after the affair was over, a note-book of his, in which a complete account is given of the phenomenon of the disappearance of the "matter" of the assassin, and the thoughts to which it gave rise in the mind of my young friend. It is preferable, I think, to give the reader this account, rather than continue to reproduce my conversation with Rouletabille; for I should be afraid, in a history of this nature, to add a word that was not in accordance with the strictest truth.

# XV

## THE TRAP

### (Extract from the Note-Book of Joseph Rouletabille)

L ast night—the night between the 29th and 30th of October—" wrote Joseph Rouletabille, "I woke up towards one o'clock in the morning. Was it sleeplessness, or noise without?—The cry of the Bete du Bon Dieu rang out with sinister loudness from the end of the park. I rose and opened the window. Cold wind and rain; opaque darkness; silence. I reclosed my window. Again the sound of the cat's weird cry in the distance. I partly dressed in haste. The weather was too bad for even a cat to be turned out in it. What did it mean, then—that imitating of the mewing of Mother Angenoux' cat so near the chateau? I seized a good-sized stick, the only weapon I had, and, without making any noise, opened the door.

"The gallery into which I went was well lit by a lamp with a reflector. I felt a keen current of air and, on turning, found the window open, at the extreme end of the gallery, which I call the 'off-turning' gallery, to distinguish it from the 'right' gallery, on to which the apartment of Mademoiselle Stangerson opened. These two galleries cross each other at right angles. Who had left that window open? Or, who had come to open it? I went to the window and leaned out. Five feet below me there was a sort of terrace over the semi-circular projection of a room on the ground-floor. One could, if one wanted, jump from the window on to the terrace, and allow oneself to drop from it into the court of the chateau. Whoever had entered by this road had, evidently, not had a key to the vestibule door. But why should I be thinking of my previous night's attempt with the ladder?—Because of the open window—left open, perhaps, by the negligence of a servant? I reclosed it, smiling at the ease with which I built a drama on the mere suggestion of an open window.

"Again the cry of the Bete du Bon Dieu!—and then silence. The rain ceased to beat on the window. All in the chateau slept. I walked with infinite precaution on the carpet of the gallery. On reaching the corner of the 'right' gallery, I peered round it cautiously. There was another lamp there with a reflector which quite lit up the several objects in it,—three chairs and some pictures hanging on the wall. What was I doing there? Perfect silence reigned throughout. Everything was sunk in repose. What was the instinct that urged me towards Mademoiselle Stangerson's chamber? Why did a voice within me cry: 'Go on, to the chamber of Mademoiselle Stangerson!' I cast my eyes down upon the carpet on which I was treading and saw that my steps were being directed towards Mademoiselle Stangerson's chamber by the marks of steps that had already been made there. Yes, on the carpet were traces of footsteps stained with mud leading to the chamber of Mademoiselle Stangerson. Horror! Horror!—I recognised in those footprints the impression of the neat boots of the murderer! He had come, then, from without in this wretched night. If you could descend from the gallery by way of the window, by means of the terrace, then you could get into the chateau by the same means.

"The murderer was still in the chateau, for here were marks as of returning footsteps. He had entered by the open window at the extremity of the 'off-turning' gallery; he had passed Frederic Larsan's door and mine, had turned to the right, and had entered Mademoiselle Stangerson's room. I am before the door of her ante-room—it is open. I push it, without making the least noise. Under the door of the room itself I see a streak of light. I listen—no sound—not even of breathing! Ah!—if I only knew what was passing in the silence that is behind that door! I find the door locked and the key turned on the inner side. And the murderer is there, perhaps. He must be there! Will he escape this time?—All depends on me!—I must be calm, and above all, I must make no false steps. I must see into that room. I can enter it by Mademoiselle Stangerson's drawing-room; but, to do that I should have to cross her boudoir; and while I am there, the murderer may escape by the gallery door—the door in front of which I am now standing.

"I am sure that no other crime is being committed, on this night; for there is complete silence in the boudoir, where two nurses are taking care of Mademoiselle Stangerson until she is restored to health.

"As I am almost sure that the murderer is there, why do I not at once give the alarm? The murderer may, perhaps, escape; but, perhaps, I may be able to save Mademoiselle Stangerson's life. Suppose the murderer on this occasion is not here to murder? The door has been opened to allow him to enter; by whom?—And it has been refastened—by whom?—Mademoiselle Stangerson shuts herself up in her apartment with her nurses every night. Who turned the key of that chamber to allow the murderer to enter?—The nurses,—two faithful domestics? The old chambermaid, Sylvia? It is very improbable. Besides, they slept in the boudoir, and Mademoiselle Stangerson, very nervous and careful, Monsieur Robert Darzac told me, sees to her own safety since she has been well enough to move about in her room, which I have not yet seen her leave. This nervousness and sudden care on her part, which had struck Monsieur Darzac, had given me, also, food for thought. At the time of the crime in the 'Yellow Room', there can be no doubt that she expected the murderer. Was he expected this night?—Was it she herself who had opened her door to him? Had she some reason for doing so? Was she obliged to do it?—Was it a meeting for purposes of crime?— Certainly it was not a lover's meeting, for I believe Mademoiselle Stangerson adores Monsieur Darzac.

"All these reflections ran through my brain like a flash of lightning. What would I not give to know!

"It is possible that there was some reason for the awful silence. My intervention might do more harm than good. How could I tell? How could I know I might not any moment cause another crime? If I could only see and know, without breaking that silence!

"I left the ante-room and descended the central stairs to the vestibule and, as silently as possible, made my way to the little room on the ground-floor where Daddy Jacques had been sleeping since the attack made at the pavilion.

"I found him dressed, his eyes wide open, almost haggard. He did not seem surprised to see me. He told me that he had got up because he had heard the cry of the Bete du bon Dieu, and because he had heard footsteps in the park, close to his window, out of which he had looked and, just then, had seen a black shadow pass by. I asked him whether he had a firearm of any kind. No, he no longer kept one, since the examining magistrate had taken his revolver from him. We went out together, by a little back door, into the park, and stole along the chateau to the point which is just below Mademoiselle Stangerson's window.

"I placed Daddy Jacques against the wall, ordering him not to stir from the spot, while I, taking advantage of a moment when the moon was hidden by a cloud, moved to the front of the window, out of the patch of light which came from it,—for the window was half-open! If I could only know what was passing in that silent chamber! I returned to

Daddy Jacques and whispered the word 'ladder' in his ear. At first I had thought of the tree which, a week ago, served me for an observatory; but I immediately saw that, from the way the window was half-opened, I should not be able to see from that point of view anything that was passing in the room; and I wanted, not only to see, but to hear, and—to act.

"Greatly agitated, almost trembling, Daddy Jacques disappeared for a moment and returned without the ladder, but making signs to me with his arms, as signals to me to come quickly to him. When I got near him he gasped: 'Come!'

"He led me round the château, past the don-jon. Arrived there, he said:

"'I went to the donjon in search of my ladder, and in the lower part of the donjon which serves me and the gardener for a lumber room, I found the door open and the ladder gone. On coming out, that's what I caught sight of by the light of the moon.

"And he pointed to the further end of the chateau, where a ladder stood resting against the stone brackets supporting the terrace, under the window which I had found open. The projection of the terrace had prevented my seeing it. Thanks to that ladder, it was quite easy to get into the 'off-turning' gallery of the first floor, and I had no doubt of it having been the road taken by the unknown.

"We ran to the ladder, but at the moment of reaching it, Daddy Jacques drew my attention to the half-open door of the little semi-circular room, situated under the terrace, at the extremity of the right wing of the chateau, having the terrace for its roof. Daddy Jacques pushed the door open a little further and looked in.

"'He's not there!" he whispered.

"Who is not there?"

"'The forest—keeper."

With his lips once more to my ear, he added:

"'Do you know that he has slept in the upper room of the donjon ever since it was restored?' And with the same gesture he pointed to the half-open door, the ladder, the terrace, and the windows in the 'off-turning' gallery which, a little while before, I had re-closed.

"What were my thoughts then? I had no time to think. I felt more than I thought.

"Evidently, I felt, if the forest-keeper is up there in the chamber (I say, if, because at this moment, apart from the presence of the ladder and his vacant room, there are no evidences which permit me even to suspect him)—if he is there, he has been obliged to pass by the ladder, and the rooms which lie behind his, in his new lodging, are occupied by the family of the steward and by the cook, and by the kitchens, which bar the way by the vestibule to the interior of the chateau. And if he had been there during the evening on any pretext, it would have been easy for him to go into the gallery and see that the window could be simply pushed open from the outside. This question of the unfastened window easily narrowed the field of search for the murderer. He must belong to the house, unless he had an accomplice, which I do not believe he had; unless—unless Mademoiselle Stangerson herself had seen that that window was not fastened from the inside. But, then,—what could be the frightful secret which put her under the necessity of doing away with obstacles that separated her from the murderer?

"I seized hold of the ladder, and we returned to the back of the chateau to see if the window of the chamber was still half-open. The blind was drawn but did not join and allowed a bright stream of light to escape and fall upon the path at our feet. I planted the ladder under the window. I am almost sure that I made no noise; and while Daddy Jacques remained at the foot of the ladder, I mounted it, very quietly, my stout stick in my hand. I held my breath and lifted my feet with the greatest care. Suddenly a heavy cloud discharged itself at that moment in a fresh downpour of rain.

"At the same instant the sinister cry of the Bete du bon Dieu arrested me in my ascent. It seemed to me to have come from close by me— only a few yards away. Was the cry a signal?—Had some accomplice of the man seen me on the ladder!—Would the cry bring the man to the window?—Perhaps! Ah, there he was at the window! I felt his head above me. I heard the sound of his breath! I could not look up towards him; the least movement of my head, and—I might be lost. Would he see me?—Would he peer into the darkness? No; he went away. He had seen nothing. I felt, rather than heard, him moving on tip-toe in the room; and I mounted a few steps higher. My head reached to the level of the window-sill; my forehead rose above it; my eyes looked between the opening in the blinds—and I saw—A man seated at Mademoiselle Stangerson's little desk, writing. His back was turned toward me. A candle was lit before him, and he bent over the flame, the light from it projecting shapeless shadows. I saw nothing but a monstrous, stooping back.

"Mademoiselle Stangerson herself was not there!—Her bed had not been lain on! Where, then, was she sleeping that night? Doubtless in the side-room with her women. Perhaps this was but a guess. I must content myself with the joy of finding the man alone. I must be calm to prepare my trap.

"But who, then, is this man writing there before my eyes, seated at the desk, as if he were in his own home? If there had not been that ladder under the window; if there had not been those footprints on the carpet in the gallery; if there had not been that open window, I might have been led to think that this man had a right to be there, and that he was there as a matter of course and for reasons about which as yet I knew nothing. But there was no doubt that this mysterious unknown was the man of the 'Yellow Room',—the man to whose murderous assault Mademoiselle Stangerson—without denouncing him—had had to submit. If I could but see his face! Surprise and capture him!

"If I spring into the room at this moment, he will escape by the right-hand door opening into the boudoir,—or crossing the drawing-room, he will reach the gallery and I shall lose him. I have him now and in five minutes more he'll be safer than if I had him in a cage.—What is he doing there, alone in Mademoiselle Stangerson's room?—What is he writing? I descend and place the ladder on the ground. Daddy Jacques follows me. We re-enter the chateau. I send Daddy Jacques to wake Monsieur Stangerson, and instruct him to await my coming in Mademoiselle Stangerson's room and to say nothing definite to him before my arrival. I will go and awaken Frederic Larsan. It's a bore to have to do it, for I should have liked to work alone and to have carried off all the honors of this affair myself, right under the very nose of the sleeping detective. But Daddy Jacques and Monsieur Stangerson are old men, and I am not yet fully developed. I might not be strong enough. Larsan is used to wrestling and putting on the handcuffs. He opened his eyes swollen with sleep, ready to send me flying, without in the least believing in my reporter's fancies. I had to assure him that the man was there!

"'That's strange!' he said; 'I thought I left him this afternoon in Paris.'

"He dressed himself in haste and armed himself with a revolver. We stole quietly into the gallery.

"'Where is he?' Larsan asked.

"'In Mademoiselle Stangerson's room.

"'And—Mademoiselle Stangerson?'

"'She is not in there.'

"'Let's go in.'

"'Don't go there! On the least alarm the man will escape. He has four ways by which to do it—the door, the window, the boudoir, or the room in which the women are sleeping.'

"'I'll draw him from below.'

"'And if you fail?—If you only succeed in wounding him—he'll escape again, without reckoning that he is certainly armed. No, let me direct the expedition, and I'll answer for everything.'

"'As you like,' he replied, with fairly good grace.

"Then, after satisfying myself that all the windows of the two galleries were thoroughly secure, I placed Frederic Larsan at the end of the 'off-turning' gallery, before the window which I had found open and had reclosed.

"'Under no consideration,' I said to him, 'must you stir from this post till I call you. The chances are even that the man, when he is pursued, will return to this window and try to save himself that way; for it is by that way he came in and made a way ready for his flight. You have a dangerous post.'

"'What will be yours?' asked Fred.

"'I shall spring into the room and knock him over for you.'

"'Take my revolver,' said Fred, 'and I'll take your stick.'

"'Thanks,' I said; 'You are a brave man.'

"I accepted his offer. I was going to be alone with the man in the room writing and was really thankful to have the weapon.

"I left Fred, having posted him at the window (No. 5 on the plan), and, with the greatest precaution, went towards Monsieur Stangerson's apartment in the left wing of the chateau. I found him with Daddy Jacques, who had faithfully obeyed my directions, confining himself to asking his master to dress as quickly as possible. In a few words I explained to Monsieur Stangerson what was passing. He armed himself with a revolver, followed me, and we were all three speedily in the gallery. Since I had seen the murderer seated at the desk ten minutes had elapsed. Monsieur Stangerson wished to spring upon the assassin at once and kill him. I made him understand that, above all, he must not, in his desire to kill him, miss him.

"When I had sworn to him that his daughter was not in the room, and in no danger, he conquered his impatience and left me to direct the operations. I told them that they must come to me the moment I called to them, or when I fired my revolver. I then sent Daddy Jacques to place himself before the window at the end of the 'right' gallery. (No. 2 on my plan.) I chose that position 'for Daddy Jacques because I believed that the murderer, tracked, on leaving the room, would run through the gallery towards the window which he had left open, and, instantly seeing that it was guarded by Larsan, would pursue his course along the 'right' gallery. There he would encounter Daddy Jacques, who would prevent his springing out of the window into the park. Under that window there was a sort of buttress, while all the other windows in the galleries were at such a height from the ground that it was almost impossible to jump from them without breaking one's neck. All the doors and windows, including those of the lumber-room at the end of the 'right' gallery—as I had rapidly assured myself—were strongly secured.

"Having indicated to Daddy Jacques the post he was to occupy, and having seen him take up his position, I placed Monsieur Stangerson on the landing at the head of the stairs not far from the door of his daughter's ante-room, rather than the boudoir, where the women were, and the door of which must have been locked by Mademoiselle Stangerson herself if, as I thought, she had taken refuge in the boudoir for the purpose of avoiding the murderer who was coming to see her. In any case, he must return to the gallery where my people were awaiting him at every possible exit.

"On coming there, he would see on his left, Monsieur Stangerson; he would turn to the right, towards the 'off-turning' gallery—the way he had pre-arranged for flight, where, at the intersection of the two galleries, he would see at once, as I have explained, on his left, Frederic Larsan at the end of the 'off-turning' gallery, and in front, Daddy Jacques, at the end of the 'right' gallery. Monsieur Stangerson and myself would arrive by way of the back of the chateau.—He is ours!—He can no longer escape us! I was sure of that.

"The plan I had formed seemed to me the best, the surest, and the most simple. It would, no doubt, have been simpler still, if we had been able to place some one directly behind the door of Mademoiselle's boudoir, which opened out of her bedchamber, and, in that way, had been in a position to besiege the two doors of the room in which the man was. But we could not penetrate the boudoir except by way of the drawing-room, the door of which had been locked on the inside by Mademoiselle Stangerson. But even if I had had the free disposition of the boudoir, I should have held to the plan I had formed; because any other plan of attack would have separated us at the moment of the struggle with the man, while my plan united us all for the attack, at a spot which I had selected with almost mathematical precision,—the intersection of the two galleries.

"Having so placed my people, I again left the chateau, hurried to my ladder, and, replacing it, climbed up, revolver in hand.

"If there be any inclined to smile at my taking so many precautionary measures, I refer them to the mystery of the 'Yellow Room', and to all the proofs we have of the weird cunning of the murderer. Further, if there be some who think my observations needlessly minute at a moment when they ought to be completely held by rapidity of movement and decision of action, I reply that I have wished to report here, at length and completely, all the details of a plan of attack conceived so rapidly that it is only the slowness of my pen that gives an appearance of slowness to the execution. I have wished, by this slowness and precision, to be certain that nothing should be omitted from the conditions under which the strange phenomenon was produced, which, until some natural explanation of it is forthcoming, seems to me to prove, even better than the theories of Professor Stangerson, the Dissociation of Matter—I will even say, the instantaneous Dissociation of Matter."

# XVI

## STRANGE PHENOMENON OF THE DISSOCIATION OF MATTER

### (Extract from the Note-Book of Joseph Rouletabille, Continued)

I am again at the window-sill," continues Rouletabille, "and once more I raise my head above it. Through an opening in the curtains, the arrangement of which has not been changed, I am ready to look, anxious to note the position in which I am going to find the murderer,—whether his back will still be turned towards me!—whether he is still seated at the desk writing! But perhaps—perhaps—he is no longer there!—Yet how could he have fled?—Was I not in possession of his ladder? I force myself to be cool. I raise my head yet higher. I look—he is still there. I see his monstrous back, deformed by the shadow thrown by the candle. He is no longer writing now, and the candle is on the parquet, over which he is bending—a position which serves my purpose.

"I hold my breath. I mount the ladder. I am on the uppermost rung of it, and with my left hand seize hold of the window-sill. In this moment of approaching success, I feel my heart beating wildly. I put my revolver between my teeth. A quick spring, and I shall be on the window-ledge. But—the ladder! I had been obliged to press on it heavily, and my foot had scarcely left it, when I felt it swaying beneath me. It grated on the wall and fell. But, already, my knees were touching the window-sill, and, by a movement quick as lightning, I got on to it.

"But the murderer had been even quicker than I had been. He had heard the grating of the ladder on the wall, and I saw the monstrous back of the man raise itself. I saw his head. Did I really see it?—The candle on the parquet lit up his legs only. Above the height of the table the chamber was in darkness. I saw a man with long hair, a full beard, wild-looking eyes, a pale face, framed in large whiskers,—as well as I could distinguish, and, as I think—red in colour. I did not know the face. That was, in brief, the chief sensation I received from that face in the dim half-light in which I saw it. I did not know it—or, at least, I did not recognise it.

"Now for quick action! It was indeed time for that, for as I was about to place my legs through the window, the man had seen me, had bounded to his feet, had sprung—as I foresaw he would—to the door of the ante-chamber, had time to open it, and fled. But I was already behind him, revolver in hand, shouting 'Help!'

"Like an arrow I crossed the room, but noticed a letter on the table as I rushed. I almost came up with the man in the ante-room, for he had lost time in opening the door to the gallery. I flew on wings, and in the gallery was but a few feet behind him. He had taken, as I supposed he would, the gallery on his right,—that is to say, the road he had prepared for his flight. 'Help, Jacques!—help, Larsan!' I cried. He could not escape us! I raised a shout of joy, of savage victory. The man reached the intersection of the two galleries hardly two seconds before me for the meeting which I had prepared—the fatal shock which must inevitably take place at that spot! We all rushed to the crossing-place—Monsieur Stangerson and I coming from one end of the right gallery, Daddy Jacques coming from the other end of the same gallery, and Frederic Larsan coming from the 'off-turning' gallery.

"The man was not there!

"We looked at each other stupidly and with eyes terrified. The man had vanished like a ghost. 'Where is he—where is he?' we all asked.

"'It is impossible he can have escaped!' I cried, my terror mastered by my anger.

"'I touched him!' exclaimed Frederic Larsan.

"'I felt his breath on my face!' cried Daddy Jacques.

"'Where is he?'—where is he?' we all cried.

"We raced like madmen along the two galleries; we visited doors and windows—they were closed, hermetically closed. They had not been opened. Besides, the opening of a door or window by this man whom we were hunting, without our having perceived it, would have been more inexplicable than his disappearance.

"'Where is he?—where is he?—He could not have got away by a door or a window, nor by any other way. He could not have passed through our bodies!

"I confess that, for the moment, I felt 'done for.' For the gallery was perfectly lighted, and there was neither trap, nor secret door in the walls, nor any sort of hiding-place. We moved the chairs and lifted the pictures. Nothing!—nothing! We would have looked into a flower-pot, if there had been one to look into!"

When this mystery, thanks to Rouletabille, was naturally explained, by the help alone of his masterful mind, we were able to realise that the murderer had got away neither by a door, a window, nor the stairs—a fact which the judges would not admit.

# XVII

## The Inexplicable Gallery

M ademoiselle Stangerson appeared at the door of her ante-room,"
continues Rouletabille's note-book. "We were near her door in
the gallery where this incredible phenomenon had taken place. There
are moments when one feels as if one's brain were about to burst. A
bullet in the head, a fracture of the skull, the seat of reason shattered—
with only these can I compare the sensation which exhausted and left
me void of sense.

"Happily, Mademoiselle Stangerson appeared on the threshold of
her ante-room. I saw her, and that helped to relieve my chaotic state
of mind. I breathed her—I inhaled the perfume of the lady in black,
whom I should never see again. I would have given ten years of my
life—half my life—to see once more the lady in black! Alas! I no more
meet her but from time to time,—and yet!—and yet! how the memory
of that perfume—felt by me alone—carries me back to the days of my
childhood.* It was this sharp reminder from my beloved perfume, of the
lady in black, which made me go to her—dressed wholly in white and
so pale—so pale and so beautiful!—on the threshold of the inexplicable
gallery. Her beautiful golden hair, gathered into a knot on the back of
her neck, left visible the red star on her temple which had so nearly
been the cause of her death. When I first got on the right track of the
mystery of this case I had imagined that, on the night of the tragedy
in the 'Yellow Room', Mademoiselle Stangerson had worn her hair in
bands. But then, how could I have imagined otherwise when I had not
been in the 'Yellow Room'!

"But now, since the occurrence of the inexplicable gallery, I did not
reason at all. I stood there, stupid, before the apparition—so pale and
so beautiful—of Mademoiselle Stangerson. She was clad in a dressing-
gown of dreamy white. One might have taken her to be a ghost—a lovely

---

* When I wrote these lines, Joseph Rouletabille was eighteen years of age,—and he spoke
of his "youth." I have kept the text of my friend, but I inform the reader here that the
episode of the mystery of the "Yellow Room" has no connection with that of the perfume
of the lady in black. It is not my fault if, in the document which I have cited, Rouletabille
thought fit to refer to his childhood.

phantom. Her father took her in his arms and kissed her passionately, as if he had recovered her after being long lost to him. I dared not question her. He drew her into the room and we followed them,—for we had to know!—The door of the boudoir was open. The terrified faces of the two nurses craned towards us. Mademoiselle Stangerson inquired the meaning of all the disturbance. That she was not in her own room was quite easily explained—quite easily. She had a fancy not to sleep that night in her chamber, but in the boudoir with her nurses, locking the door on them. Since the night of the crime she had experienced feelings of terror, and fears came over her that are easily to be comprehended.

"But who could imagine that on that particular night when he was to come, she would, by a mere chance, determine to shut herself in with her women? Who would think that she would act contrary to her father's wish to sleep in the drawing-room? Who could believe that the letter which had so recently been on the table in her room would no longer be there? He who could understand all this, would have to assume that Mademoiselle Stangerson knew that the murderer was coming—she could not prevent his coming again—unknown to her father, unknown to all but to Monsieur Robert Darzac. For he must know it now—perhaps he had known it before! Did he remember that phrase in the Elysee garden: 'Must I commit a crime, then, to win you?' Against whom the crime, if not against the obstacle, against the murderer? 'Ah, I would kill him with my own hand!' And I replied, 'You have not answered my question.' That was the very truth. In truth, in truth, Monsieur Darzac knew the murderer so well that—while wishing to kill him himself—he was afraid I should find him. There could be but two reasons why he had assisted me in my investigation. First, because I forced him to do it; and, second, because she would be the better protected.

"I am in the chamber—her room. I look at her, also at the place where the letter had just now been. She has possessed herself of it; it was evidently intended for her—evidently. How she trembles!— Trembles at the strange story her father is telling her, of the presence of the murderer in her chamber, and of the pursuit. But it is plainly to be seen that she is not wholly satisfied by the assurance given her until she had been told that the murderer, by some incomprehensible means, had been able to elude us.

"Then follows a silence. What a silence! We are all there—looking at her—her father, Larsan, Daddy Jacques and I. What were we all thinking of in the silence? After the events of that night, of the mystery of the inexplicable gallery, of the prodigious fact of the presence of the murderer in her room, it seemed to me that all our thoughts might have been translated into the words which were addressed to her. 'You who know of this mystery, explain it to us, and we shall perhaps be able to save you. How I longed to save her—for herself, and, from the other!— It brought the tears to my eyes.

"She is there, shedding about her the perfume of the lady in black. At last, I see her, in the silence of her chamber. Since the fatal hour of the mystery of the 'Yellow Room', we have hung about this invisible and silent woman to learn what she knows. Our desires, our wish to know must be a torment to her. Who can tell that, should we learn the secret of her mystery, it would not precipitate a tragedy more terrible than that which had already been enacted here? Who can tell if it might not mean her death? Yet it had brought her close to death,—and we still knew nothing. Or, rather, there are some of us who know nothing. But I—if I knew who, I should know all. Who?—Who?—Not knowing who, I must remain silent, out of pity for her. For there is no doubt that she knows how he escaped from the 'Yellow Room', and yet she keeps the secret. When I know who, I will speak to him—to him!"

"She looked at us now—with a far-away look in her eyes—as if we were not in the chamber. Monsieur Stangerson broke the silence. He declared that, henceforth, he would no more absent himself from his daughter's apartments. She tried to oppose him in vain. He adhered firmly to his purpose. He would install himself there this very night, he said. Solely concerned for the health of his daughter, he reproached her for having left her bed. Then he suddenly began talking to her as if she were a little child. He smiled at her and seemed not to know either what he said or what he did. The illustrious professor had lost his head. Mademoiselle Stangerson in a tone of tender distress said: 'Father!— father!' Daddy Jacques blows his nose, and Frederic Larsan himself is obliged to turn away to hide his emotion. For myself, I am able neither to think or feel. I felt an infinite contempt for myself.

"It was the first time that Frederic Larsan, like myself, found himself face to face with Mademoiselle Stangerson since the attack in the 'Yellow Room'. Like me, he had insisted on being allowed to question the unhappy lady; but he had not, any more than had I, been permitted. To him, as to me, the same answer had always been given: Mademoiselle Stangerson was too weak to receive us. The questionings of the examining magistrate had over-fatigued her. It was evidently intended not to give us any assistance in our researches. I was not surprised; but Frederic Larsan had always resented this conduct. It is true that he and I had a totally different theory of the crime.

"I still catch myself repeating from the depths of my heart: 'Save her!—save her without his speaking!' Who is he—the murderer? Take him and shut his mouth. But Monsieur Darzac made it clear that in order to shut his mouth he must be killed. Have I the right to kill Mademoiselle Stangerson's murderer? No, I had not. But let him only give me the chance! Let me find out whether he is really a creature of flesh and blood!—Let me see his dead body, since it cannot be taken alive.

"If I could but make this woman, who does not even look at us, understand! She is absorbed by her fears and by her father's distress of mind. And I can do nothing to save her. Yes, I will go to work once more and accomplish wonders.

"I move towards her. I would speak to her. I would entreat her to have confidence in me. I would, in a word, make her understand— she alone—that I know how the murderer escaped from the 'Yellow Room'—that I have guessed the motives for her secrecy—and that I pity her with all my heart. But by her gestures she begged us to leave her alone, expressing weariness and the need for immediate rest. Monsieur Stangerson asked us to go back to our rooms and thanked us. Frederic Larsan and I bowed to him and, followed by Daddy Jacques, we regained the gallery. I heard Larsan murmur: 'Strange! strange!' He made a sign to me to go with him into his room. On the threshold he turned towards Daddy Jacques.

"'Did you see him distinctly?' he asked.

"'Who?'

"'The man?'

"'Saw him!—why, he had a big red beard and red hair.'

"'That's how he appeared to me,' I said.

"'And to me,' said Larsan.

"The great Fred and I were alone in his chamber, now, to talk over this thing. We talked for an hour, turning the matter over and viewing it from every side. From the questions put by him, from the explanation which he gives me, it is clear to me that—in spite of all our senses—he is persuaded the man disappeared by some secret passage in the chateau known to him alone.

"'He knows the chateau,' he said to me; 'he knows it well.'

"'He is a rather tall man—well-built,' I suggested.

"'He is as tall as he wants to be,' murmured Fred.

"'I understand,' I said; 'but how do you account for his red hair and beard?'

"'Too much beard—too much hair—false,' says Fred.

"'That's easily said. You are always thinking of Robert Darzac. You can't get rid of that idea? I am certain that he is innocent.'

"'So much the better. I hope so; but everything condemns him. Did you notice the marks on the carpet?—Come and look at them.'

"'I have seen them; they are the marks of the neat boots, the same as those we saw on the border of the lake.'

"'Can you deny that they belong to Robert Darzac?'

"'Of course, one may be mistaken.'

"'Have you noticed that those footprints only go in one direction?—that there are no return marks? When the man came from the chamber, pursued by all of us, his footsteps left no traces behind them.'

"'He had, perhaps, been in the chamber for hours. The mud from his boots had dried, and he moved with such rapidity on the points of his toes—We saw him running, but we did not hear his steps.'

"I suddenly put an end to this idle chatter—void of any logic, and made a sign to Larsan to listen.

"'There—below; some one is shutting a door.'

"I rise; Larsan follows me; we descend to the ground-floor of the chateau. I lead him to the little semi-circular room under the terrace beneath the window of the 'off-turning' gallery. I point to the door, now closed, open a short time before, under which a shaft of light is visible.

"'The forest-keeper!' says Fred.

"'Come on!' I whisper.

"Prepared—I know not why—to believe that the keeper is the guilty man—I go to the door and rap smartly on it. Some might think that we were rather late in thinking of the keeper, since our first business, after having found that the murderer had escaped us in the gallery, ought to have been to search everywhere else,—around the chateau,—in the park—

"Had this criticism been made at the time, we could only have answered that the assassin had disappeared from the gallery in such a way that we thought he was no longer anywhere! He had eluded us when we all had our hands stretched out ready to seize him—when we were almost touching him. We had no longer any ground for hoping that we could clear up the mystery of that night.

"As soon as I rapped at the door it was opened, and the keeper asked us quietly what we wanted. He was undressed and preparing to go to bed. The bed had not yet been disturbed.

"We entered and I affected surprise.

"'Not gone to bed yet?'

"'No,' he replied roughly. 'I have been making a round of the park and in the woods. I am only just back—and sleepy. Good-night!'

"'Listen,' I said. 'An hour or so ago, there was a ladder close by your window.'

"'What ladder?—I did not see any ladder. Good-night!'

"And he simply put us out of the room. When we were outside I looked at Larsan. His face was impenetrable.

"'Well?' I said.

"'Well?' he repeated.

"'Does that open out any new view to you?'

"There was no mistaking Larsan's bad temper. On re-entering the chateau, I heard him mutter:

"'It would be strange—very strange—if I had deceived myself on that point!'

"He seemed to be talking to me rather than to himself. He added: 'In any case, we shall soon know what to think. The morning will bring light with it.'"

# XVIII

## Rouletabille Has Drawn a Circle Between the Two Bumps on His Forehead

### (Extract from the Note-Book of Joseph Rouletabille, Continued)

We separated on the thresholds of our rooms, with a melancholy shake of the hands. I was glad to have aroused in him a suspicion of error. His was an original brain, very intelligent but—without method. I did not go to bed. I awaited the coming of daylight and then went down to the front of the chateau, and made a detour, examining every trace of footsteps coming towards it or going from it. These, however, were so mixed and confusing that I could make nothing of them. Here I may make a remark,—I am not accustomed to attach an exaggerated importance to exterior signs left in the track of a crime.

"The method which traces the criminal by means of the tracks of his footsteps is altogether primitive. So many footprints are identical. However, in the disturbed state of my mind, I did go into the deserted court and did look at all the footprints I could find there, seeking for some indication, as a basis for reasoning.

"If I could but find a right starting-point! In despair I seated myself on a stone. For over an hour I busied myself with the common, ordinary work of a policeman. Like the least intelligent of detectives I went on blindly over the traces of footprints which told me just no more than they could.

"I came to the conclusion that I was a fool, lower in the scale of intelligence than even the police of the modern romancer. Novelists build mountains of stupidity out of a footprint on the sand, or from an impression of a hand on the wall. That's the way innocent men are brought to prison. It might convince an examining magistrate or the head of a detective department, but it's not proof. You writers forget that what the senses furnish is not proof. If I am taking cognisance of what is offered me by my senses I do so but to bring the results within the circle of my reason. That circle may be the most circumscribed, but if it is, it has this advantage—it holds nothing but the truth! Yes, I swear that I have never used the evidence of the senses but as servants to my reason. I have never permitted them to become my master. They have not made of me that monstrous thing,—worse than a blind man,—a man who sees falsely. And that is why I can triumph over your error and your merely animal intelligence, Frederic Larsan.

"Be of good courage, then, friend Rouletabille; it is impossible that the incident of the inexplicable gallery should be outside the circle of your reason. You know that! Then have faith and take thought with yourself and forget not that you took hold of the right end when you drew that circle in your brain within which to unravel this mysterious play of circumstance.

"To it, once again! Go—back to the gallery. Take your stand on your reason and rest there as Frederic Larsan rests on his cane. You will then soon prove that the great Fred is nothing but a fool.

30th October. Noon
JOSEPH ROULETABILLE

"I acted as I planned. With head on fire, I retraced my way to the gallery, and without having found anything more than I had seen on the previous night, the right hold I had taken of my reason drew me to something so important that I was obliged to cling to it to save myself from falling.

"Now for the strength and patience to find sensible traces to fit in with my thinking—and these must come within the circle I have drawn between the two bumps on my forehead!

30th of October. Midnight
JOSEPH ROULETABILLE

# XIX

## Rouletabille Invites Me to Breakfast at the Donjon Inn

It was not until later that Rouletabille sent me the note-book in which he had written at length the story of the phenomenon of the inexplicable gallery. On the day I arrived at the Glandier and joined him in his room, he recounted to me, with the greatest detail, all that I have now related, telling me also how he had spent several hours in Paris where he had learned nothing that could be of any help to him.

The event of the inexplicable gallery had occurred on the night between the 29th and 30th of October, that is to say, three days before my return to the chateau. It was on the 2nd of November, then, that I went back to the Glandier, summoned there by my friend's telegram, and taking the revolvers with me.

I am now in Rouletabille's room and he has finished his recital.

While he had been telling me the story I noticed him continually rubbing the glass of the eyeglasses he had found on the side table. From the evident pleasure he was taking in handling them I felt they must be one of those sensible evidences destined to enter what he had called the circle of the right end of his reason. That strange and unique way of his, to express himself in terms wonderfully adequate for his thoughts, no longer surprised me. It was often necessary to know his thought to understand the terms he used; and it was not easy to penetrate into Rouletabille's thinking.

This lad's brain was one of the most curious things I have ever observed. Rouletabille went on the even tenor of his way without suspecting the astonishment and even bewilderment he roused in others. I am sure he was not himself in the least conscious of the originality of his genius. He was himself and at ease wherever he happened to be.

When he had finished his recital he asked me what I thought of it. I replied that I was much puzzled by his question. Then he begged me to try, in my turn, to take my reason in hand "by the right end."

"Very well," I said. "It seems to me that the point of departure of my reason would be this—there can be no doubt that the murderer you pursued was in the gallery." I paused.

"After making so good a start, you ought not to stop so soon," he exclaimed. "Come, make another effort."

"I'll try. Since he disappeared from the gallery without passing through any door or window, he must have escaped by some other opening."

Rouletabille looked at me pityingly, smiled carelessly, and remarked that I was reasoning like a postman, or—like Frederic Larsan.

Rouletabille had alternate fits of admiration and disdain for the great Fred. It all depended as to whether Larsan's discoveries tallied with Rouletabille's reasoning or not. When they did he would exclaim: "He is really great!" When they did not he would grunt and mutter, "What an ass!" It was a petty side of the noble character of this strange youth.

We had risen, and he led me into the park. When we reached the court and were making towards the gate, the sound of blinds thrown back against the wall made us turn our heads, and we saw, at a window on the first floor of the chateau, the ruddy and clean shaven face of a person I did not recognise.

"Hullo!" muttered Rouletabille. "Arthur Rance!"—He lowered his head, quickened his pace, and I heard him ask himself between his teeth: "Was he in the chateau that night? What is he doing here?"

We had gone some distance from the chateau when I asked him who this Arthur Rance was, and how he had come to know him. He referred to his story of that morning and I remembered that Mr. Arthur W. Rance was the American from Philadelphia with whom he had had so many drinks at the Elysee reception.

"But was he not to have left France almost immediately?" I asked.

"No doubt; that's why I am surprised to find him here still, and not only in France, but above all, at the Glandier. He did not arrive this morning; and he did not get here last night. He must have got here before dinner, then. Why didn't the concierges tell me?"

I reminded my friend, apropos of the concierges, that he had not yet told me what had led him to get them set at liberty.

We were close to their lodge. Monsieur and Madame Bernier saw us coming. A frank smile lit up their happy faces. They seemed to harbour no ill-feeling because of their detention. My young friend asked them at what hour Mr. Arthur Rance had arrived. They answered that they did not know he was at the chateau. He must have come during the evening of the previous night, but they had not had to open the gate for him, because, being a great walker, and not wishing that a carriage should be sent to meet him, he was accustomed to get off at the little hamlet of Saint-Michel, from which he came to the chateau by way of the forest. He reached the park by the grotto of Sainte-Genevieve, over the little gate of which, giving on to the park, he climbed.

As the concierges spoke, I saw Rouletabille's face cloud over and exhibit disappointment—a disappointment, no doubt, with himself. Evidently he was a little vexed, after having worked so much on the spot, with so minute a study of the people and events at the Glandier, that he had to learn now that Arthur Rance was accustomed to visit the chateau.

"You say that Monsieur Arthur Rance is accustomed to come to the chateau. When did he come here last?"

"We can't tell you exactly," replied Madame Bernier—that was the name of the concierge—"we couldn't know while they were keeping us in prison. Besides, as the gentleman comes to the chateau without passing through our gate he goes away by the way he comes."

"Do you know when he came the first time?"

"Oh yes, Monsieur!—nine years ago."

"He was in France nine years ago, then," said Rouletabille, "and, since that time, as far as you know, how many times has he been at the Glandier?"

"Three times."

"When did he come the last time, as far as you know?"

"A week before the attempt in the 'Yellow Room'."

Rouletabille put another question—this time addressing himself particularly to the woman:

"In the grove of the parquet?"

"In the grove of the parquet," she replied.

"Thanks!" said Rouletabille. "Be ready for me this evening."

He spoke the last words with a finger on his lips as if to command silence and discretion.

We left the park and took the way to the Donjon Inn.

"Do you often eat here?"

"Sometimes."

"But you also take your meals at the chateau?"

"Yes, Larsan and I are sometimes served in one of our rooms."

"Hasn't Monsieur Stangerson ever invited you to his own table?"

"Never."

"Does your presence at the chateau displease him?"

"I don't know; but, in any case, he does not make us feel that we are in his way."

"Doesn't he question you?"

"Never. He is in the same state of mind as he was in at the door of the 'Yellow Room' when his daughter was being murdered, and when he broke open the door and did not find the murderer. He is persuaded, since he could discover nothing, that there's no reason why we should be able to discover more than he did. But he has made it his duty, since Larsan expressed his theory, not to oppose us."

Rouletabille buried himself in thought again for some time. He aroused himself later to tell me of how he came to set the two concierges free.

"I went recently to see Monsieur Stangerson, and took with me a piece of paper on which was written: 'I promise, whatever others may say, to keep in my service my two faithful servants, Bernier and his wife.' I explained to him that, by signing that document, he would enable me to compel those two people to speak out; and I declared my own assurance of their innocence of any part in the crime. That was also his opinion. The examining magistrate, after it was signed, presented the document to the Berniers, who then did speak. They said, what I was certain they would say, as soon as they were sure they would not lose their place.

"They confessed to poaching on Monsieur Stangerson's estates, and it was while they were poaching, on the night of the crime, that they were found not far from the pavilion at the moment when the outrage was being committed. Some rabbits they caught in that way were sold by them to the landlord of the Donjon Inn, who served them to his customers, or sent them to Paris. That was the truth, as I had guessed from the first. Do you remember what I said, on entering the Donjon Inn?—'We shall have to eat red meat—now!' I had heard the words on the same morning when we arrived at the park gate. You heard them also, but you did not attach any importance to them. You recollect, when we reached the park gate, that we stopped to look at a man who was running by the side of the wall, looking every minute at his watch. That was Larsan. Well, behind us the landlord of the Donjon Inn, standing on his doorstep, said to someone inside: 'We shall have to eat red meat—now.'

"Why that 'now'? When you are, as I am, in search of some hidden secret, you can't afford to have anything escape you. You've got to know the meaning of everything. We had come into a rather out-of-the-way part of the country which had been turned topsy-turvey by a crime, and my reason led me to suspect every phrase that could bear upon the event of the day. 'Now,' I took to mean, 'since the outrage.' In the course of my inquiry, therefore, I sought to find a relation between that phrase and the tragedy. We went to the Donjon Inn for breakfast; I repeated the phrase and saw, by the surprise and trouble on Daddy Mathieu's face, that I had not exaggerated its importance, so far as he was concerned.

"I had just learned that the concierges had been arrested. Daddy Mathieu spoke of them as of dear friends—people for whom one is sorry. That was a reckless conjunction of ideas, I said to myself. 'Now,' that the concierges are arrested, 'we shall have to eat red meat.' No more concierges, no more game! The hatred expressed by Daddy Mathieu for Monsieur Stangerson's forest-keeper—a hatred he pretended was shared by the concierges led me easily to think of poaching. Now as all the evidence showed the concierges had not been in bed at the time of the tragedy, why were they abroad that night? As participants in the crime? I was not disposed to think so. I had already arrived at the conclusion, by steps of which I will tell you later—that the assassin had had no accomplice, and that the tragedy held a mystery between Mademoiselle Stangerson and the murderer, a mystery with which the concierges had nothing to do.

"With that theory in my mind, I searched for proof in their lodge, which, as you know, I entered. I found there under their bed, some springs and brass wire. 'Ah!' I thought, 'these things explain why they were out in the park at night!' I was not surprised at the dogged silence they maintained before the examining magistrate, even under the accusation so grave as that of being accomplices in the crime. Poaching would save them from the Assize Court, but it would lose them their places; and, as they were perfectly sure of their innocence of the crime they hoped it would soon be established, and then their poaching might go on as usual. They could always confess later. I, however, hastened their confession by means of the document Monsieur Stangerson signed. They gave all the necessary 'proofs,' were set at liberty, and have now a lively gratitude for me. Why did I not get them released sooner? Because I was not sure that nothing more than poaching was against them. I wanted to study the ground. As the days went by, my conviction became more and more certain. The day after the events of the inexplicable gallery I had need of help I could rely on, so I resolved to have them released at once."

That was how Joseph Rouletabille explained himself. Once more I could not but be astonished at the simplicity of the reasoning which had brought him to the truth of the matter. Certainly this was no big thing; but I think, myself, that the young man will, one of these days, explain with the same simplicity, the fearful tragedy in the "Yellow Room" as well as the phenomenon of the inexplicable gallery.

We reached the Donjon Inn and entered it.

This time we did not see the landlord, but were received with a pleasant smile by the hostess. I have already described the room in which we found ourselves, and I have given a glimpse of the charming blonde woman with the gentle eyes who now immediately began to prepare our breakfast.

"How's Daddy Mathieu?" asked Rouletabille.

"Not much better—not much better; he is still confined to his bed."

"His rheumatism still sticks to him, then?"

"Yes. Last night I was again obliged to give him morphine—the only drug that gives him any relief.

She spoke in a soft voice. Everything about her expressed gentleness. She was, indeed, a beautiful woman; somewhat with an air of indolence, with great eyes seemingly black and blue—amorous eyes. Was she happy with her crabbed, rheumatic husband? The scene at which we had once been present did not lead us to believe that she was; yet there was something in her bearing that was not suggestive of despair. She disappeared into the kitchen to prepare our repast, leaving on the table a bottle of excellent cider. Rouletabille filled our earthenware mugs, loaded his pipe, and quietly explained to me his reason for asking me to come to the Glandier with revolvers.

"Yes," he said, contemplatively looking at the clouds of smoke he was puffing out, "yes, my dear boy, I expect the assassin tonight." A brief silence followed, which I took care not to interrupt, and then he went on:

"Last night, just as I was going to bed, Monsieur Robert Darzac knocked at my room. When he came in he confided to me that he was compelled to go to Paris the next day, that is, this morning. The reason which made this journey necessary was at once peremptory and mysterious; it was not possible for him to explain its object to me. 'I go, and yet,' he added, 'I would give my life not to leave Mademoiselle

Stangerson at this moment.' He did not try to hide that he believed her to be once more in danger. 'It will not greatly astonish me if something happens tomorrow night,' he avowed, 'and yet I must be absent. I cannot be back at the Glandier before the morning of the day after tomorrow.'

"I asked him to explain himself, and this is all he would tell me. His anticipation of coming danger had come to him solely from the coincidence that Mademoiselle Stangerson had been twice attacked, and both times when he had been absent. On the night of the incident of the inexplicable gallery he had been obliged to be away from the Glandier. On the night of the tragedy in the 'Yellow Room' he had also not been able to be at the Glandier, though this was the first time he had declared himself on the matter. Now a man so moved who would still go away must be acting under compulsion—must be obeying a will stronger than his own. That was how I reasoned, and I told him so. He replied 'Perhaps.'—I asked him if Mademoiselle Stangerson was compelling him. He protested that she was not. His determination to go to Paris had been taken without any conference with Mademoiselle Stangerson.

"To cut the story short, he repeated that his belief in the possibility of a fresh attack was founded entirely on the extraordinary coincidence. 'If anything happens to Mademoiselle Stangerson,' he said, 'it would be terrible for both of us. For her, because her life would be in danger; for me because I could neither defend her from the attack nor tell of where I had been. I am perfectly aware of the suspicions cast on me. The examining magistrate and Monsieur Larsan are both on the point of believing in my guilt. Larsan tracked me the last time I went to Paris, and I had all the trouble in the world to get rid of him.'

"'Why do you not tell me the name of the murderer now, if you know it?' I cried.

"Monsieur Darzac appeared extremely troubled by my question, and replied to me in a hesitating tone:

"'I?—I know the name of the murderer? Why, how could I know his name?'

"I at once replied: 'From Mademoiselle Stangerson.'

"He grew so pale that I thought he was about to faint, and I saw that I had hit the nail right on the head. Mademoiselle and he knew the name of the murderer! When he recovered himself, he said to me: 'I am going to leave you. Since you have been here I have appreciated your exceptional intelligence and your unequalled ingenuity. But I ask this service of you. Perhaps I am wrong to fear an attack during the coming night; but, as I must act with foresight, I count on you to frustrate any attempt that may be made. Take every step needful to protect Mademoiselle Stangerson. Keep a most careful watch of her room. Don't go to sleep, nor allow yourself one moment of repose. The man we dread is remarkably cunning—with a cunning that has never been equalled. If you keep watch his very cunning may save her; because it's impossible that he should not know that you are watching; and knowing it, he may not venture.'

"'Have you spoken of all this to Monsieur Stangerson?'

"'No. I do not wish him to ask me, as you just now did, for the name of the murderer. I tell you all this, Monsieur Rouletabille, because I have great, very great, confidence in you. I know that you do not suspect me.'

"The poor man spoke in jerks. He was evidently suffering. I pitied him, the more because I felt sure that he would rather allow himself to be killed than tell me who the murderer was. As for Mademoiselle Stangerson, I felt that she would rather allow herself to be murdered than denounce the man of the 'Yellow Room' and of the inexplicable gallery. The man must be dominating her, or both, by some inscrutable power. They were dreading nothing so much as the chance of Monsieur Stangerson knowing that his daughter was 'held' by her assailant. I made Monsieur Darzac understand that he had explained himself sufficiently, and that he might refrain from telling me any more than he had already told me. I promised him to watch through the night. He insisted that I should establish an absolutely impassable barrier around Mademoiselle Stangerson's chamber, around the boudoir where the nurses were sleeping, and around the drawing-room where, since the affair of the inexplicable gallery, Monsieur Stangerson had slept. In short, I was to put a cordon round the whole apartment.

"From his insistence I gathered that Monsieur Darzac intended not only to make it impossible for the expected man to reach the chamber of Mademoiselle Stangerson, but to make that impossibility so visibly clear that, seeing himself expected, he would at once go away. That was how I interpreted his final words when we parted: 'You may mention your suspicions of the expected attack to Monsieur Stangerson, to Daddy Jacques, to Frederic Larsan, and to anybody in the chateau.'

"The poor fellow left me hardly knowing what he was saying. My silence and my eyes told him that I had guessed a large part of his secret. And, indeed, he must have been at his wits' end, to have come to me at such a time, and to abandon Mademoiselle Stangerson in spite of his fixed idea as to the consequence.

"When he was gone, I began to think that I should have to use even a greater cunning than his so that if the man should come that night, he might not for a moment suspect that his coming had been expected. Certainly! I would allow him to get in far enough, so that, dead or alive, I might see his face clearly! He must be got rid of. Mademoiselle Stangerson must be freed from this continual impending danger.

"Yes, my boy," said Rouletabille, after placing his pipe on the table, and emptying his mug of cider, "I must see his face distinctly, so as to make sure to impress it on that part of my brain where I have drawn my circle of reasoning."

The landlady re-appeared at that moment, bringing in the traditional bacon omelette. Rouletabille chaffed her a little, and she took the chaff with the most charming good humour.

"She is much jollier when Daddy Mathieu is in bed with his rheumatism," Rouletabille said to me.

But I had eyes neither for Rouletabille nor for the landlady's smiles. I was entirely absorbed over the last words of my young friend and in thinking over Monsieur Robert Darzac's strange behaviour.

When he had finished his omelette and we were again alone, Rouletabille continued the tale of his confidences.

"When I sent you my telegram this morning," he said, "I had only the word of Monsieur Darzac, that 'perhaps' the assassin would come tonight. I can now say that he will certainly come. I expect him."

"What has made you feel this certainty?"

"I have been sure since half-past ten o'clock this morning that he would come. I knew that before we saw Arthur Rance at the window in the court."

"Ah!" I said, "But, again—what made you so sure? And why since half-past ten this morning?"

"Because, at half-past ten, I had proof that Mademoiselle Stangerson was making as many efforts to permit of the murderer's entrance as Monsieur Robert Darzac had taken precautions against it."

"Is that possible!" I cried. "Haven't you told me that Mademoiselle Stangerson loves Monsieur Robert Darzac?"

"I told you so because it is the truth."

"Then do you see nothing strange—"

"Everything in this business is strange, my friend; but take my word for it, the strangeness you now feel is nothing to the strangeness that's to come!"

"It must be admitted, then," I said, "that Mademoiselle Stangerson and her murderer are in communication—at any rate in writing?"

"Admit it, my friend, admit it! You don't risk anything! I told you about the letter left on her table, on the night of the inexplicable gallery affair,—the letter that disappeared into the pocket of Mademoiselle Stangerson. Why should it not have been a summons to a meeting? Might he not, as soon as he was sure of Darzac's absence, appoint the meeting for 'the coming night?"

And my friend laughed silently. There are moments when I ask myself if he is not laughing at me.

The door of the inn opened. Rouletabille was on his feet so suddenly that one might have thought he had received an electric shock.

"Mr. Arthur Rance!" he cried.

Mr. Arthur Rance stood before us calmly bowing.

# XX

## AN ACT OF MADEMOISELLE STANGERSON

Y<sup>ou</sup> remember me, Monsieur?" asked Rouletabille.

"Perfectly!" replied Arthur Rance. "I recognise you as the lad at the bar. (The face of Rouletabille crimsoned at being called a "lad.") I want to shake hands with you. You are a bright little fellow."

The American extended his hand and Rouletabille, relaxing his frown, shook it and introduced Mr. Arthur Rance to me. He invited him to share our meal.

"No thanks. I breakfasted with Monsieur Stangerson."

Arthur Rance spoke French perfectly,—almost without an accent.

"I did not expect to have the pleasure of seeing you again, Monsieur. I thought you were to have left France the day after the reception at the Elysee."

Rouletabille and I, outwardly indifferent, listened most intently for every word the American would say.

The man's purplish red face, his heavy eyelids, the nervous twitchings, all spoke of his addiction to drink. How came it that so sorry a specimen of a man should be so intimate with Monsieur Stangerson?

Some days later, I learned from Frederic Larsan—who, like ourselves, was surprised and mystified by his appearance and reception at the chateau—that Mr. Rance had been an inebriate for only about fifteen years; that is to say, since the professor and his daughter left Philadelphia. During the time the Stangersons lived in America they were very intimate with Arthur Rance, who was one of the most distinguished phrenologists of the new world. Owing to new experiments, he had made enormous strides beyond the science of Gall and Lavater. The friendliness with which he was received at the Glandier may be explained by the fact that he had once rendered Mademoiselle Stangerson a great service by stopping, at the peril of his own life, the runaway horses of her carriage. The immediate result of that could, however, have been no more than a mere friendly association with the Stangersons; certainly, not a love affair.

Frederic Larsan did not tell me where he had picked up this information; but he appeared to be quite sure of what he said.

Had we known these facts at the time Arthur Rance met us at the Donjon Inn, his presence at the chateau might not have puzzled us, but they could not have failed to increase our interest in the man himself. The American must have been at least forty-five years old. He spoke in a perfectly natural tone in reply to Rouletabille's question.

"I put off my return to America when I heard of the attack on Mademoiselle Stangerson. I wanted to be certain the lady had not been killed, and I shall not go away until she is perfectly recovered."

Arthur Rance then took the lead in talk, paying no heed to some of Rouletabille's questions. He gave us, without our inviting him, his personal views on the subject of the tragedy,—views which, as well as I could make out, were not far from those held by Frederic Larzan. The American also thought that Robert Darzac had something to do with the matter. He did not mention him by name, but there was no room to doubt whom he meant. He told us he was aware of the efforts young Rouletabille was making to unravel the tangled skein of the "Yellow Room" mystery. He explained that Monsieur Stangerson had related to him all that had taken place in the inexplicable gallery. He several times expressed his regret at Monsieur Darzac's absence from the chateau on all these occasions, and thought that Monsieur Darzac had done cleverly in allying himself with Monsieur Joseph Rouletabille, who could not fail, sooner or later, to discover the murderer. He spoke the last sentence with unconcealed irony. Then he rose, bowed to us, and left the inn.

Rouletabille watched him through the window.

"An odd fish, that!" he said.

"Do you think he'll pass the night at the Glandier?" I asked.

To my amazement the young reporter answered that it was a matter of entire indifference to him whether he did or not.

As to how we spent our time during the afternoon, all I need say is that Rouletabille led me to the grotto of Sainte-Genevieve, and, all the time, talked of every subject but the one in which we were most interested. Towards evening I was surprised to find Rouletabille making none of the preparations I had expected him to make. I spoke to him about it when night had come on, and we were once more in his room. He replied that all his arrangements had already been made, and this time the murderer would not get away from him.

I expressed some doubt on this, reminding him of his disappearance in the gallery, and suggested that the same phenomenon might occur again. He answered that he hoped it would. He desired nothing more. I did not insist, knowing by experience how useless that would have been. He told me that, with the help of the concierges, the chateau had since early dawn been watched in such a way that nobody could approach it without his knowing it, and that he had no concern for those who might have left it and remained without.

It was then six o'clock by his watch. Rising, he made a sign to me to follow him, and, without in the least trying to conceal his movements or the sound of his footsteps, he led me through the gallery. We reached the 'right' gallery and came to the landing-place which we crossed. We then continued our way in the gallery of the left wing, passing Professor Stangerson's apartment.

At the far end of the gallery, before coming to the donjon, is the room occupied by Arthur Rance. We knew that, because we had seen him at the window looking on to the court. The door of the room opens on to the end of the gallery, exactly facing the east window, at the extremity of the 'right' gallery, where Rouletabille had placed Daddy Jacques, and commands an uninterrupted view of the gallery from end to end of the chateau.

"That 'off-turning' gallery," said Rouletabille, "I reserve for myself; when I tell you you'll come and take your place here."

And he made me enter a little dark, triangular closet built in a bend of the wall, to the left of the door of Arthur Rance's room. From this recess I could see all that occurred in the gallery as well as if I had been standing in front of Arthur Rance's door, and I could watch that door, too. The door of the closet, which was to be my place of observation, was fitted with panels of transparent glass. In the gallery, where all the lamps had been lit, it was quite light. In the closet, however, it was quite dark. It was a splendid place from which to observe and remain unobserved.

I was soon to play the part of a spy—a common policeman. I wonder what my leader at the bar would have said had he known! I was not altogether pleased with my duties, but I could not refuse Rouletabille the assistance he had begged me to give him. I took care not to make him see that I in the least objected, and for several reasons. I wanted to oblige him; I did not wish him to think me a coward; I was filled with curiosity; and it was too late for me to draw back, even had I determined to do so. That I had not had these scruples sooner was because my curiosity had quite got the better of me. I might also urge that I was helping to save the life of a woman, and even a lawyer may do that conscientiously.

We returned along the gallery. On reaching the door of Mademoiselle Stangerson's apartment, it opened from a push given by the steward who was waiting at the dinner-table. (Monsieur Stangerson had, for the last three days, dined with his daughter in the drawing-room on the first floor.) As the door remained open, we distinctly saw Mademoiselle Stangerson, taking advantage of the steward's absence, and while her father was stooping to pick up something he had let fall, pour the contents of a phial into Monsieur Stangerson's glass.

# XXI

## ON THE WATCH

The act, which staggered me, did not appear to affect Rouletabille much. We returned to his room and, without even referring to what we had seen, he gave me his final instructions for the night. First we were to go to dinner; after dinner, I was to take my stand in the dark closet and wait there as long as it was necessary—to look out for what might happen.

"If you see anything before I do," he explained, "you must let me know. If the man gets into the 'right' gallery by any other way than the 'off-turning' gallery, you will see him before I shall, because you have a view along the whole length of the 'right' gallery, while I can only command a view of the 'off-turning' gallery. All you need do to let me know is to undo the cord holding the curtain of the 'right' gallery window, nearest to the dark closet. The curtain will fall of itself and immediately leave a square of shadow where previously there had been a square of light. To do this, you need but stretch your hand out of the closet, I shall understand your signal perfectly."

"And then?"

"Then you will see me coming round the corner of the 'off-turning' gallery."

"What am I to do then?"

"You will immediately come towards me, behind the man; but I shall already be upon him, and shall have seen his face."

I attempted a feeble smile.

"Why do you smile? Well, you may smile while you have the chance, but I swear you'll have no time for that a few hours from now."

"And if the man escapes?"

"So much the better," said Rouletabille, coolly, "I don't want to capture him. He may take himself off any way he can. I will let him go—after I have seen his face. That's all I want. I shall know afterwards what to do so that as far as Mademoiselle Stangerson is concerned he shall be dead to her even though he continues to live. If I took him alive, Mademoiselle Stangerson and Robert Darzac would, perhaps, never forgive me! And I wish to retain their good-will and respect.

"Seeing, as I have just now seen, Mademoiselle Stangerson pour a narcotic into her father's glass, so that he might not be awake to interrupt the conversation she is going to have with her murderer, you can imagine she would not be grateful to me if I brought the man of the 'Yellow Room' and the inexplicable gallery, bound and gagged, to her father. I realise now that if I am to save the unhappy lady, I must silence the man and not capture him. To kill a human being is no small thing. Besides, that's not my business, unless the man himself makes it my business. On the other hand, to render him forever silent without the lady's assent and confidence is to act on one's own initiative and assumes a knowledge of everything with nothing for a basis. Fortunately, my friend, I have guessed, no, I have reasoned it all out. All that I ask of the man who is coming tonight is to bring me his face, so that it may enter—"

"Into the circle?"

"Exactly! And his face won't surprise me!"

"But I thought you saw his face on the night when you sprang into the chamber?"

"Only imperfectly. The candle was on the floor; and, his beard—"

"Will he wear his beard this evening?"

"I think I can say for certain that he will. But the gallery is light and, now, I know—or—at least, my brain knows—and my eyes will see."

"If we are here only to see him and let him escape, why are we armed?"

"Because, if the man of the 'Yellow Room' and the inexplicable gallery knows that I know, he is capable of doing anything! We should then have to defend ourselves."

"And you are sure he will come tonight?"

"As sure as that you are standing there! This morning, at half-past ten o'clock, Mademoiselle Stangerson, in the cleverest way in the world, arranged to have no nurses tonight. She gave them leave of absence for twenty-four hours, under some plausible pretexts, and did not desire anybody to be with her but her father, while they are away. Her father, who is to sleep in the boudoir, has gladly consented to the arrangement. Darzac's departure and what he told me, as well as the extraordinary precautions Mademoiselle Stangerson is taking to be alone tonight leaves me no room for doubt. She has prepared the way for the coming of the man whom Darzac dreads."

"That's awful!"

"It is!"

"And what we saw her do was done to send her father to sleep?"

"Yes."

"Then there are but two of us for tonight's work?"

"Four; the concierge and his wife will watch at all hazards. I don't set much value on them before—but the concierge may be useful after—if there's to be any killing!"

"Then you think there may be?"

"If he wishes it."

"Why haven't you brought in Daddy Jacques?—Have you made no use of him today?"

"No," replied Rouletabille sharply.

I kept silence for awhile, then, anxious to know his thoughts, I asked him point blank:

"Why not tell Arthur Rance?—He may be of great assistance to us?"

"Oh!" said Rouletabille crossly, "then you want to let everybody into Mademoiselle Stangerson's secrets?—Come, let us go to dinner; it is time. This evening we dine in Frederic Larsan's room,—at least, if he is not on the heels of Darzac. He sticks to him like a leech. But, anyhow, if he is not there now, I am quite sure he will be, tonight! He's the one I am going to knock over!"

At this moment we heard a noise in the room near us.

"It must be he," said Rouletabille.

"I forgot to ask you," I said, "if we are to make any allusion to tonight's business when we are with this policeman. I take it we are not. Is that so?"

"Evidently. We are going to operate alone, on our own personal account."

"So that all the glory will be ours?"

Rouletabille laughed.

We dined with Frederic Larsan in his room. He told us he had just come in and invited us to be seated at table. We ate our dinner in the best of humours, and I had no difficulty in appreciating the feelings of certainty which both Rouletabille and Larsan felt. Rouletabille told the great Fred that I had come on a chance visit, and that he had asked me to stay and help him in the heavy batch of writing he had to get through for the "Epoque." I was going back to Paris, he said, by the eleven o'clock train, taking his "copy," which took a story form, recounting the principal episodes in the mysteries of the Glandier. Larsan smiled at the explanation like a man who was not fooled and politely refrains from making the slightest remark on matters which did not concern him.

With infinite precautions as to the words they used, and even as to the tones of their voices, Larsan and Rouletabille discussed, for a long time, Mr. Arthur Rance's appearance at the chateau, and his past in America, about which they expressed a desire to know more, at any rate, so far as his relations with the Stangersons. At one time, Larsan, who appeared to me to be unwell, said, with an effort:

"I think, Monsieur Rouletabille, that we've not much more to do at the Glandier, and that we sha'n't sleep here many more nights."

"I think so, too, Monsieur Fred."

"Then you think the conclusion of the matter has been reached?"

"I think, indeed, that we have nothing more to find out," replied Rouletabille.

"Have you found your criminal?" asked Larsan.

"Have you?"

"Yes."

"So have I," said Rouletabille.

"Can it be the same man?"

"I don't know if you have swerved from your original idea," said the young reporter. Then he added, with emphasis: "Monsieur Darzac is an honest man!"

"Are you sure of that?" asked Larsan. "Well, I am sure he is not. So it's a fight then?"

"Yes, it is a fight. But I shall beat you, Monsieur Frederic Larsan."

"Youth never doubts anything," said the great Fred laughingly, and held out his hand to me by way of conclusion.

Rouletabille's answer came like an echo:

"Not anything!"

Suddenly Larsan, who had risen to wish us goodnight, pressed both his hands to his chest and staggered. He was obliged to lean on Rouletabille for support, and to save himself from falling.

"Oh! Oh!" he cried. "What is the matter with me?—Have I been poisoned?"

He looked at us with haggard eyes. We questioned him vainly; he did not answer us. He had sunk into an armchair and we could get not a word from him. We were extremely distressed, both on his account and on our own, for we had partaken of all the dishes he had eaten. He seemed to be out of pain; but his heavy head had fallen on his shoulder and his eyelids were tightly closed. Rouletabille bent over him, listening for the beatings of the heart.

My friend's face, however, when he stood up, was as calm as it had been a moment before agitated.

"He is asleep," he said.

He led me to his chamber, after closing Larsan's room.

"The drug?" I asked. "Does Mademoiselle Stangerson wish to put everybody to sleep, tonight?"

"Perhaps," replied Rouletabille; but I could see he was thinking of something else.

"But what about us?" I exclaimed. "How do we know that we have not been drugged?"

"Do you feel indisposed?" Rouletabille asked me coolly.

"Not in the least."

"Do you feel any inclination to go to sleep?"

"None whatever."

"Well, then, my friend, smoke this excellent cigar."

And he handed me a choice Havana, one Monsieur Darzac had given him, while he lit his briarwood—his eternal briarwood.

We remained in his room until about ten o'clock without a word passing between us. Buried in an armchair Rouletabille sat and smoked steadily, his brow in thought and a far-away look in his eyes. On the stroke of ten he took off his boots and signalled to me to do the same. As we stood in our socks he said, in so low a tone that I guessed, rather than heard, the word:

"Revolver."

I drew my revolver from my jacket pocket.

"Cock it!" he said.

I did as he directed.

Then moving towards the door of his room, he opened it with infinite precaution; it made no sound. We were in the "off-turning" gallery. Rouletabille made another sign to me which I understood to mean that I was to take up my post in the dark closet.

When I was some distance from him, he rejoined me and embraced me; and then I saw him, with the same precaution, return to his room. Astonished by his embrace, and somewhat disquieted by it, I arrived at the right gallery without difficulty, crossing the landing-place, and reaching the dark closet.

Before entering it I examined the curtain-cord of the window and found that I had only to release it from its fastening with my fingers for the curtain to fall by its own weight and hide the square of light from Rouletabille—the signal agreed upon. The sound of a footstep made me halt before Arthur Rance's door. He was not yet in bed, then! How was it that, being in the chateau, he had not dined with Monsieur Stangerson and his daughter? I had not seen him at table with them, at the moment when we looked in.

I retired into the dark closet. I found myself perfectly situated. I could see along the whole length of the gallery. Nothing, absolutely nothing could pass there without my seeing it. But what was going to pass there? Rouletabille's embrace came back to my mind. I argued that people don't part from each, other in that way unless on an important or dangerous occasion. Was I then in danger?

My hand closed on the butt of my revolver and I waited. I am not a hero; but neither am I a coward.

I waited about an hour, and during all that time I saw nothing unusual. The rain, which had begun to come down strongly towards nine o'clock, had now ceased.

My friend had told me that, probably, nothing would occur before midnight or one o'clock in the morning. It was not more than half-past eleven, however, when I heard the door of Arthur Rance's room open very slowly. The door remained open for a minute, which seemed to me a long time. As it opened into the gallery, that is to say, outwards, I could not see what was passing in the room behind the door.

At that moment I noticed a strange sound, three times repeated, coming from the park. Ordinarily I should not have attached any more importance to it than I would to the noise of cats on the roof. But the third time, the mew was so sharp and penetrating that I remembered what I had heard about the cry of the Bete du bon Dieu. As the cry had accompanied all the events at the Glandier, I could not refrain from shuddering at the thought.

Directly afterwards I saw a man appear on the outside of the door, and close it after him. At first I could not recognise him, for his back was towards me and he was bending over a rather bulky package. When he had closed the door and picked up the package, he turned towards the dark closet, and then I saw who he was. He was the forest-keeper, the Green Man. He was wearing the same costume that he had worn when I first saw him on the road in front of the Donjon Inn. There was no doubt about his being the keeper. As the cry of the Bete du Bon Dieu came for the third time, he put down the package and went to the second window, counting from the dark closet. I dared not risk making any movement, fearing I might betray my presence.

Arriving at the window, he peered out on to the park. The night was now light, the moon showing at intervals. The Green Man raised his arms twice, making signs which I did not understand; then, leaving the window, he again took up his package and moved along the gallery towards the landing-place.

Rouletabille had instructed me to undo the curtain-cord when I saw anything. Was Rouletabille expecting this? It was not my business to question. All I had to do was obey instructions. I unfastened the window-cord; my heart beating the while as if it would burst. The man reached the landing-place, but, to my utter surprise—I had expected to see him continue to pass along the gallery—I saw him descend the stairs leading to the vestibule.

What was I to do? I looked stupidly at the heavy curtain which had shut the light from the window. The signal had been given, and I did not see Rouletabille appear at the corner of the off-turning gallery. Nobody appeared. I was exceedingly perplexed. Half an hour passed, an age to me. What was I to do now, even if I saw something? The signal once given I could not give it a second time. To venture into the gallery might upset all Rouletabille's plans. After all, I had nothing to reproach myself for, and if something had happened that my friend had not expected he could only blame himself. Unable to be of any further assistance to him by means of a signal, I left the dark closet and, still in my socks, made my way to the "off-turning" gallery.

There was no one there. I went to the door of Rouletabille's room and listened. I could hear nothing. I knocked gently. There was no answer. I turned the door-handle and the door opened. I entered. Rouletabille lay extended at full length on the floor.

# XXII

## The Incredible Body

I bent in great anxiety over the body of the reporter and had the joy to find that he was deeply sleeping, the same unhealthy sleep that I had seen fall upon Frederic Larsan. He had succumbed to the influence of the same drug that had been mixed with our food. How was it then, that I, also, had not been overcome by it? I reflected that the drug must have been put into our wine; because that would explain my condition. I never drink when eating. Naturally inclined to obesity, I am restricted to a dry diet. I shook Rouletabille, but could not succeed in waking him. This, no doubt, was the work of Mademoiselle Stangerson.

She had certainly thought it necessary to guard herself against this young man as well as her father. I recalled that the steward, in serving us, had recommended an excellent Chablis which, no doubt, had come from the professor's table.

More than a quarter of an hour passed. I resolved, under the pressing circumstances, to resort to extreme measures. I threw a pitcher of cold water over Rouletabille's head. He opened his eyes. I beat his face, and raised him up. I felt him stiffen in my arms and heard him murmur: "Go on, go on; but don't make any noise." I pinched him and shook him until he was able to stand up. We were saved!

"They sent me to sleep," he said. "Ah! I passed an awful quarter of an hour before giving way. But it is over now. Don't leave me."

He had no sooner uttered those words than we were thrilled by a frightful cry that rang through the chateau,—a veritable death cry.

"Malheur!" roared Rouletabille; "we shall be too late!"

He tried to rush to the door, but he was too dazed, and fell against the wall. I was already in the gallery, revolver in hand, rushing like a madman towards Mademoiselle Stangerson's room. The moment I arrived at the intersection of the "off-turning" gallery and the "right" gallery, I saw a figure leaving her apartment, which, in a few strides had reached the landing-place.

I was not master of myself. I fired. The report from the revolver made a deafening noise; but the man continued his flight down the stairs. I ran behind him, shouting: "Stop!—stop! or I will kill you!" As I rushed after him down the stairs, I came face to face with Arthur Rance coming from the left wing of the chateau, yelling: "What is it? What is it?" We arrived almost at the same time at the foot of the staircase. The window of the vestibule was open. We distinctly saw the form of a man running away. Instinctively we fired our revolvers in his direction. He was not more than ten paces in front of us; he staggered and we thought he was going to fall. We had sprung out of the window, but the man dashed off with renewed vigour. I was in my socks, and the American was barefooted. There being no hope of overtaking him, we fired our last cartridges at him. But he still kept on running, going along the right side of the court towards the end of the right wing of the chateau, which had no other outlet than the door of the little chamber occupied by the forest-keeper. The man, though he was evidently wounded by our bullets, was now twenty yards ahead of us. Suddenly, behind us, and above our heads, a window in the gallery opened and we heard the voice of Rouletabille crying out desperately:

"Fire, Bernier!—Fire!"

At that moment the clear moonlight night was further lit by a broad flash. By its light we saw Daddy Bernier with his gun on the threshold of the donjon door.

He had taken good aim. The shadow fell. But as it had reached the end of the right wing of the chateau, it fell on the other side of the angle of the building; that is to say, we saw it about to fall, but not the actual sinking to the ground. Bernier, Arthur Rance and myself reached the other side twenty seconds later. The shadow was lying dead at our feet.

Aroused from his lethargy by the cries and reports, Larsan opened the window of his chamber and called out to us. Rouletabille, quite awake now, joined us at the same moment, and I cried out to him:

"He is dead!—is dead!"

"So much the better," he said. "Take him into the vestibule of the chateau." Then as if on second thought, he said: "No!—no! Let us put him in his own room."

Rouletabille knocked at the door. Nobody answered. Naturally, this did not surprise me.

"He is evidently not there, otherwise he would have come out," said the reporter. "Let us carry him to the vestibule then."

Since reaching the dead shadow, a thick cloud had covered the moon and darkened the night, so that we were unable to make out the features. Daddy Jacques, who had now joined us, helped us to carry the body into the vestibule, where we laid it down on the lower step of the stairs. On the way, I had felt my hands wet from the warm blood flowing from the wounds.

Daddy Jacques flew to the kitchen and returned with a lantern. He held it close to the face of the dead shadow, and we recognised the keeper, the man called by the landlord of the Donjon Inn the Green Man, whom, an hour earlier, I had seen come out of Arthur Rance's chamber carrying a parcel. But what I had seen I could only tell Rouletabille later, when we were alone.

Rouletabille and Frederic Larsan experienced a cruel disappointment at the result of the night's adventure. They could only look in consternation and stupefaction at the body of the Green Man.

Daddy Jacques showed a stupidly sorrowful face and with silly lamentations kept repeating that we were mistaken—the keeper could not be the assailant. We were obliged to compel him to be quiet. He could not have shown greater grief had the body been that of his own son. I noticed, while all the rest of us were more or less undressed and barefooted, that he was fully clothed.

Rouletabille had not left the body. Kneeling on the flagstones by the light of Daddy Jacques's lantern he removed the clothes from the body and laid bare its breast. Then snatching the lantern from Daddy Jacques, he held it over the corpse and saw a gaping wound. Rising suddenly he exclaimed in a voice filled with savage irony:

"The man you believe to have been shot was killed by the stab of a knife in his heart!"

I thought Rouletabille had gone mad; but, bending over the body, I quickly satisfied myself that Rouletabille was right. Not a sign of a bullet anywhere—the wound, evidently made by a sharp blade, had penetrated the heart.

# XXIII

## THE DOUBLE SCENT

I had hardly recovered from the surprise into which this new discovery had plunged me, when Rouletabille touched me on the shoulder and asked me to follow him into his room.

"What are we going to do there?"

"To think the matter over."

I confess I was in no condition for doing much thinking, nor could I understand how Rouletabille could so control himself as to be able calmly to sit down for reflection when he must have known that Mademoiselle Stangerson was at that moment almost on the point of death. But his self-control was more than I could explain. Closing the door of his room, he motioned me to a chair and, seating himself before me, took out his pipe. We sat there for some time in silence and then I fell asleep.

When I awoke it was daylight. It was eight o'clock by my watch. Rouletabille was no longer in the room. I rose to go out when the door opened and my friend re-entered. He had evidently lost no time.

"How about Mademoiselle Stangerson?" I asked him.

"Her condition, though very alarming, is not desperate."

"When did you leave this room?"

"Towards dawn."

"I guess you have been hard at work?"

"Rather!"

"Have you found out anything?"

"Two sets of footprints!"

"Do they explain anything?"

"Yes."

"Have they anything to do with the mystery of the keeper's body?"

"Yes; the mystery is no longer a mystery. This morning, walking round the chateau, I found two distinct sets of footprints, made at the same time, last night. They were made by two persons walking side by side. I followed them from the court towards the oak grove. Larsan joined me. They were the same kind of footprints as were made at the time of the assault in the 'Yellow Room'—one set was from clumsy boots and the other was made by neat ones, except that the big toe of one of the sets was of a different size from the one measured in the 'Yellow Room' incident. I compared the marks with the paper patterns I had previously made.

"Still following the tracks of the prints, Larsan and I passed out of the oak grove and reached the border of the lake. There they turned off to a little path leading to the high road to Epinay where we lost the traces in the newly macadamised highway.

"We went back to the chateau and parted at the courtyard. We met again, however, in Daddy Jacques's room to which our separate trains of thinking had led us both. We found the old servant in bed. His clothes on the chair were wet through and his boots very muddy. He certainly did not get into that state in helping us to carry the body of the keeper. It was not raining then. Then his face showed extreme fatigue and he looked at us out of terror-stricken eyes.

"On our first questioning him he told us that he had gone to bed immediately after the doctor had arrived. On pressing him, however, for it was evident to us he was not speaking the truth, he confessed that he had been away from the chateau. He explained his absence by saying that he had a headache and went out into the fresh air, but had gone no further than the oak grove. When we then described to him the whole route he had followed, he sat up in bed trembling.

"'And you were not alone!' cried Larsan.

"'Did you see it then?' gasped Daddy Jacques.

"'What?' I asked.

"'The phantom—the black phantom!'

"Then he told us that for several nights he had seen what he kept calling the black phantom. It came into the park at the stroke of midnight and glided stealthily through the trees; it appeared to him to pass through the trunks of the trees. Twice he had seen it from his window, by the light of the moon and had risen and followed the strange apparition. The night before last he had almost overtaken it; but it had vanished at the corner of the donjon. Last night, however, he had not left the chateau, his mind being disturbed by a presentiment that some new crime would be attempted. Suddenly he saw the black phantom rush out from somewhere in the middle of the court. He followed it to the lake and to the high road to Epinay, where the phantom suddenly disappeared.

"'Did you see his face?' demanded Larsan.

"'No!—I saw nothing but black veils.'

"'Did you go out after what passed on the gallery?'

"'I could not!—I was terrified.'

"'Daddy Jacques,' I said, in a threatening voice, 'you did not follow it; you and the phantom walked to Epinay together—arm in arm!'

"'No!' he cried, turning his eyes away, 'I did not. It came on to pour, and—I turned back. I don't know what became of the black phantom.'"

"We left him, and when we were outside I turned to Larsan, looking him full in the face, and put my question suddenly to take him off his guard:

"'An accomplice?'

"'How can I tell?' he replied, shrugging his shoulders. 'You can't be sure of anything in a case like this. Twenty-four hours ago I would have sworn that there was no accomplice!' He left me saying he was off to Epinay."

"Well, what do you make of it?" I asked Rouletabille, after he had ended his recital. "Personally I am utterly in the dark. I can't make anything out of it. What do you gather?"

"Everything! Everything!" he exclaimed. "But," he said abruptly, "let's find out more about Mademoiselle Stangerson."

# XXIV

## ROULETABILLE KNOWS THE TWO HALVES OF THE MURDERER

Mademoiselle Stangerson had been almost murdered for the second time. Unfortunately, she was in too weak a state to bear the severer injuries of this second attack as well as she had those of the first. She had received three wounds in the breast from the murderer's knife, and she lay long between life and death. Her strong physique, however, saved her; but though she recovered physically it was found that her mind had been affected. The slightest allusion to the terrible incident sent her into delirium, and the arrest of Robert Darzac which followed on the day following the tragic death of the keeper seemed to sink her fine intelligence into complete melancholia.

Robert Darzac arrived at the chateau towards half-past nine. I saw him hurrying through the park, his hair and clothes in disorder and his face a deadly white. Rouletabille and I were looking out of a window in the gallery. He saw us, and gave a despairing cry: "I'm too late!"

Rouletabille answered: "She lives!"

A minute later Darzac had gone into Mademoiselle Stangerson's room and, through the door, we could hear his heart-rending sobs.

"There's a fate about this place!" groaned Rouletabille. "Some infernal gods must be watching over the misfortunes of this family!— If I had not been drugged, I should have saved Mademoiselle Stangerson. I should have silenced him forever. And the keeper would not have been killed!"

Monsieur Darzac came in to speak with us. His distress was terrible. Rouletabille told him everything: his preparations for Mademoiselle Stangerson's safety; his plans for either capturing or for disposing of the assailant for ever; and how he would have succeeded had it not been for the drugging.

"If only you had trusted me!" said the young man, in a low tone. "If you had but begged Mademoiselle Stangerson to confide in me!—But, then, everybody here distrusts everybody else, the daughter distrusts her father, and even her lover. While you ask me to protect her she is doing all she can to frustrate me. That was why I came on the scene too late!"

At Monsieur Robert Darzac's request Rouletabille described the whole scene. Leaning on the wall, to prevent himself from falling, he had made his way to Mademoiselle Stangerson's room, while we were running after the supposed murderer. The ante-room door was open and when he entered he found Mademoiselle Stangerson lying partly thrown over the desk. Her dressing-gown was dyed with the blood flowing from her bosom. Still under the influence of the drug, he felt he was walking in a horrible nightmare.

He went back to the gallery automatically, opened a window, shouted his order to fire, and then returned to the room. He crossed the deserted boudoir, entered the drawing-room, and tried to rouse Monsieur Stangerson who was lying on a sofa. Monsieur Stangerson rose stupidly and let himself be drawn by Rouletabille into the room where, on seeing his daughter's body, he uttered a heart-rending cry. Both united their feeble strength and carried her to her bed.

On his way to join us Rouletabille passed by the desk. On the floor, near it, he saw a large packet. He knelt down and, finding the wrapper loose, he examined it, and made out an enormous quantity of papers and photographs. On one of the papers he read: "New differential electroscopic condenser. Fundamental properties of substance intermediary between ponderable matter and imponderable ether." Strange irony of fate that the professor's precious papers should be restored to him at the very time when an attempt was being made to deprive him of his daughter's life! What are papers worth to him now?

The morning following that awful night saw Monsieur de Marquet once more at the chateau, with his Registrar and gendarmes. Of course we were all questioned. Rouletabille and I had already agreed on what to say. I kept back any information as to my being in the dark closet and said nothing about the drugging. We did not wish to suggest in any way that Mademoiselle Stangerson had been expecting her nocturnal visitor. The poor woman might, perhaps, never recover, and it was none of our business to lift the veil of a secret the preservation of which she had paid for so dearly.

Arthur Rance told everybody, in a manner so natural that it astonished me, that he had last seen the keeper towards eleven o'clock of that fatal night. He had come for his valise, he said, which he was to take for him early next morning to the Saint-Michel station, and had been kept out late running after poachers. Arthur Rance had, indeed, intended to leave the chateau and, according to his habit, to walk to the station.

Monsieur Stangerson confirmed what Rance had said, adding that he had not asked Rance to dine with him because his friend had taken his final leave of them both earlier in the evening. Monsieur Rance had had tea served him in his room, because he had complained of a slight indisposition.

Bernier testified, instructed by Rouletabille, that the keeper had ordered him to meet at a spot near the oak grove, for the purpose of looking out for poachers. Finding that the keeper did not keep his appointment, he, Bernier, had gone in search of him. He had almost arrived at the donjon, when he saw a figure running swiftly in a direction opposite to him, towards the right wing of the chateau. He heard revolver shots from behind the figure and saw Rouletabille at one of the gallery windows. He heard Rouletabille call out to him to fire, and he had fired. He believed he had killed the man until he learned, after Rouletabille had uncovered the body, that the man had died from a knife thrust. Who had given it he could not imagine. "Nobody could have been near the spot without my seeing him." When the examining magistrate reminded him that the spot where the body was found was very dark and that he himself had not been able to recognise the keeper before firing, Daddy Bernier replied that neither had they seen the other body; nor had they found it. In the narrow court where five people were standing it would have been strange if the other body, had it been there, could have escaped. The only door that opened into the court was that of the keeper's room, and that door was closed, and the key of it was found in the keeper's pocket.

However that might be, the examining magistrate did not pursue his inquiry further in this direction. He was evidently convinced that we had missed the man we were chasing and we had come upon the keeper's body in our chase. This matter of the keeper was another matter entirely. He wanted to satisfy himself about that without any further delay. Probably it fitted in with the conclusions he had already arrived at as to the keeper and his intrigues with the wife of Mathieu, the landlord of the Donjon Inn. This Mathieu, later in the afternoon, was arrested and taken to Corbeil in spite of his rheumatism. He had been heard to threaten the keeper, and though no evidence against him had been found at his inn, the evidence of carters who had heard the threats was enough to justify his retention.

The examination had proceeded thus far when, to our surprise, Frederic Larsan returned to the chateau. He was accompanied by one of the employeeees of the railway. At that moment Rance and I were in the vestibule discussing Mathieu's guilt or innocence, while Rouletabille stood apart buried, apparently, in thought. The examining magistrate and his Registrar were in the little green drawing-room, while Darzac was with the doctor and Stangerson in the lady's chamber. As Frederic Larsan entered the vestibule with the railway employeee, Rouletabille and I at once recognised him by the small blond beard. We exchanged meaningful glances. Larsan had himself announced to the examining magistrate by the gendarme and entered with the railway servant as Daddy Jacques came out. Some ten minutes went by during which Rouletabille appeared extremely impatient. The door of the drawing-room was then opened and we heard the magistrate calling to the gendarme who entered. Presently he came out, mounted the stairs and, coming back shortly, went in to the magistrate and said:

"Monsieur,—Monsieur Robert Darzac will not come!"

"What! Not come!" cried Monsieur de Marquet.

"He says he cannot leave Mademoiselle Stangerson in her present state."

"Very well," said Monsieur de Marquet; "then we'll go to him."

Monsieur de Marquet and the gendarme mounted the stairs. He made a sign to Larsan and the railroad employeee to follow. Rouletabille and I went along too.

On reaching the door of Mademoiselle Stangerson's chamber, Monsieur de Marquet knocked. A chambermaid appeared. It was Sylvia, with her hair all in disorder and consternation showing on her face.

"Is Monsieur Stangerson within?" asked the magistrate.

"Yes, Monsieur."

"Tell him that I wish to speak with him."

Stangerson came out. His appearance was wretched in the extreme.

"What do you want?" he demanded of the magistrate. "May I not be left in peace, Monsieur?"

"Monsieur," said the magistrate, "it is absolutely necessary that I should see Monsieur Darzac at once. If you cannot induce him to come, I shall be compelled to use the help of the law."

The professor made no reply. He looked at us all like a man being led to execution, and then went back into the room.

Almost immediately after Monsieur Robert Darzac came out. He was very pale. He looked at us and, his eyes falling on the railway servant, his features stiffened and he could hardly repress a groan.

We were all much moved by the appearance of the man. We felt that what was about to happen would decide the fate of Monsieur Robert Darzac. Frederic Larsan's face alone was radiant, showing a joy as of a dog that had at last got its prey.

Pointing to the railway servant, Monsieur de Marquet said to Monsieur Darzac:

"Do you recognise this man, Monsieur?"

"I do," said Monsieur Darzac, in a tone which he vainly tried to make firm. "He is an employeee at the station at Epinay-sur-Orge."

"This young man," went on Monsieur de Marquet, "affirms that he saw you get off the train at Epinay-sur-Orge—"

"That night," said Monsieur Darzac, interrupting, "at half-past ten—it is quite true."

An interval of silence followed.

"Monsieur Darzac," the magistrate went on in a tone of deep emotion, "Monsieur Darzac, what were you doing that night, at Epinay-sur-Orge—at that time?"

Monsieur Darzac remained silent, simply closing his eyes.

"Monsieur Darzac," insisted Monsieur de Marquet, "can you tell me how you employeeed your time, that night?"

Monsieur Darzac opened his eyes. He seemed to have recovered his self-control.

"No, Monsieur."

"Think, Monsieur! For, if you persist in your strange refusal, I shall be under the painful necessity of keeping you at my disposition."

"I refuse."

"Monsieur Darzac!—in the name of the law, I arrest you!"

The magistrate had no sooner pronounced the words than I saw Rouletabille move quickly towards Monsieur Darzac. He would certainly have spoken to him, but Darzac, by a gesture, held him off. As the gendarme approached his prisoner, a despairing cry rang through the room:

"Robert!—Robert!"

We recognised the voice of Mademoiselle Stangerson. We all shuddered. Larsan himself turned pale. Monsieur Darzac, in response to the cry, had flown back into the room.

The magistrate, the gendarme, and Larsan followed closely after. Rouletabille and I remained on the threshold. It was a heart-breaking sight that met our eyes. Mademoiselle Stangerson, with a face of deathly pallor, had risen on her bed, in spite of the restraining efforts of two doctors and her father. She was holding out her trembling arms towards Robert Darzac, on whom Larsan and the gendarme had laid hands. Her distended eyes saw—she understood—her lips seemed to form a word, but nobody made it out; and she fell back insensible.

Monsieur Darzac was hurried out of the room and placed in the vestibule to wait for the vehicle Larsan had gone to fetch. We were all overcome by emotion and even Monsieur de Marquet had tears in his eyes. Rouletabille took advantage of the opportunity to say to Monsieur Darzac:

"Are you going to put in any defense?"

"No!" replied the prisoner.

"Very well, then I will, Monsieur."

"You cannot do it," said the unhappy man with a faint smile.

"I can—and I will."

Rouletabille's voice had in it a strange strength and confidence.

"I can do it, Monsieur Robert Darzac, because I know more than you do!"

"Come! Come!" murmured Darzac, almost angrily.

"Have no fear! I shall know only what will benefit you."

"You must know nothing, young man, if you want me to be grateful."

Rouletabille shook his head, going close up to Darzac.

"Listen to what I am about to say," he said in a low tone, "and let it give you confidence. You do not know the name of the murderer. Mademoiselle Stangerson knows it; but only half of it; but I know his two halves; I know the whole man!"

Robert Darzac opened his eyes, with a look that showed he had not understood a word of what Rouletabille had said to him. At that moment the conveyance arrived, driven by Frederic Larsan. Darzac and the gendarme entered it, Larsan remaining on the driver's seat. The prisoner was taken to Corbeil.

# XXV

## Rouletabille Goes on a Journey

That same evening Rouletabille and I left the Glandier. We were very glad to get away and there was nothing more to keep us there. I declared my intention to give up the whole matter. It had been too much for me. Rouletabille, with a friendly tap on my shoulder, confessed that he had nothing more to learn at the Glandier; he had learned there all it had to tell him. We reached Paris about eight o'clock, dined, and then, tired out, we separated, agreeing to meet the next morning at my rooms.

Rouletabille arrived next day at the hour agreed on. He was dressed in a suit of English tweed, with an ulster on his arm, and a valise in his hand. Evidently he had prepared himself for a journey.

"How long shall you be away?" I asked.

"A month or two," he said. "It all depends."

I asked him no more questions.

"Do you know," he asked, "what the word was that Mademoiselle Stangerson tried to say before she fainted?"

"No—nobody heard it."

"I heard it!" replied Rouletabille. "She said 'Speak!'"

"Do you think Darzac will speak?"

"Never."

I was about to make some further observations, but he wrung my hand warmly and wished me good-bye. I had only time to ask him one question before he left.

"Are you not afraid that other attempts may be made while you're away?"

"No! Not now that Darzac is in prison," he answered.

With this strange remark he left. I was not to see him again until the day of Darzac's trial at the court when he appeared to explain the inexplicable.

# XXVI

## In Which Joseph Rouletabille Is
## Awaited with Impatience

On the 15th of January, that is to say, two months and a half after the tragic events I have narrated, the "Epoque" printed, as the first column of the front page, the following sensational article: "The Seine-et-Oise jury is summoned today to give its verdict on one of the most mysterious affairs in the annals of crime. There never has been a case with so many obscure, incomprehensible, and inexplicable points. And yet the prosecution has not hesitated to put into the prisoner's dock a man who is respected, esteemed, and loved by all who knew him—a young savant, the hope of French science, whose whole life has been devoted to knowledge and truth. When Paris heard of Monsieur Robert Darzac's arrest a unanimous cry of protest arose from all sides. The whole Sorbonne, disgraced by this act of the examining magistrate, asserted its belief in the innocence of Mademoiselle Stangerson's fiancé. Monsieur Stangerson was loud in his denunciation of this miscarriage of justice. There is no doubt in the mind of anybody that could the victim speak she would claim from the jurors of Seine-et-Oise the man she wishes to make her husband and whom the prosecution would send to the scaffold. It is to be hoped that Mademoiselle Stangerson will shortly recover her reason, which has been temporarily unhinged by the horrible mystery at the Glandier. The question before the jury is the one we propose to deal with this very day.

"We have decided not to permit twelve worthy men to commit a disgraceful miscarriage of justice. We confess that the remarkable coincidences, the many convicting evidences, and the inexplicable silence on the part of the accused, as well as a total absence of any evidence for an alibi, were enough to warrant the bench of judges in assuming that in this man alone was centered the truth of the affair. The evidences are, in appearance, so overwhelming against Monsieur Robert Darzac that a detective so well informed, so intelligent, and generally so successful, as Monsieur Frederic Larsan, may be excused for having been misled by them. Up to now everything has gone against Monsieur Robert Darzac in the magisterial inquiry. Today, however, we are going to defend him before the jury, and we are going to bring to the witness stand a light that will illumine the whole mystery of the Glandier. For we possess the truth.

"If we have not spoken sooner, it is because the interests of certain parties in the case demand that we should take that course. Our readers may remember the unsigned reports we published relating to the 'Left foot of the Rue Oberkampf,' at the time of the famous robbery of the Credit Universel, and the famous case of the 'Gold Ingots of the Mint.' In both those cases we were able to discover the truth long before even the excellent ingenuity of Frederic Larsan had been able to unravel it. These reports were written by our youngest reporter, Joseph Rouletabille, a youth of eighteen, whose fame tomorrow will be world-wide. When attention was first drawn to the Glandier case, our youthful reporter was on the spot and installed in the chateau, when every other representative of the press had been denied admission. He worked side by side with Frederic Larsan. He was amazed and terrified at the grave mistake the celebrated detective was about to make, and tried to divert him from the false scent he was following; but the great Fred refused to receive instructions from this young journalist. We know now where it brought Monsieur Robert Darzac.

"But now, France must know—the whole world must know, that, on the very evening on which Monsieur Darzac was arrested, young Rouletabille entered our editorial office and informed us that he was about to go away on a journey. 'How long I shall be away,' he said, 'I cannot say; perhaps a month—perhaps two--perhaps three—perhaps I may never return. Here is a letter. If I am not back on the day on which Monsieur Darzac is to appear before the Assize Court, have this letter opened and read to the court, after all the witnesses have been heard. Arrange it with Monsieur Darzac's counsel. Monsieur Darzac is innocent. In this letter is written the name of the murderer; and—that is all I have to say. I am leaving to get my proofs—for the irrefutable evidence of the murderer's guilt.' Our reporter departed. For a long time we were without news from him; but, a week ago, a stranger called upon our manager and said: 'Act in accordance with the instructions of Joseph Rouletabille, if it becomes necessary to do so. The letter left by him holds the truth.' The gentleman who brought us this message would not give us his name.

"Today, the 15th of January, is the day of the trial. Joseph Rouletabille has not returned. It may be we shall never see him again. The press also counts its heroes, its martyrs to duty. It may be he is no longer living. We shall know how to avenge him. Our manager will, this afternoon, be at the Court of Assize at Versailles, with the letter—the letter containing the name of the murderer!"

Those Parisians who flocked to the Assize Court at Versailles, to be present at the trial of what was known as the "Mystery of 'The Yellow Room,' will certainly remember the terrible crush at the Saint-Lazare station. The ordinary trains were so full that special trains had to be made up. The article in the 'Epoque' had so excited the populace that discussion was rife everywhere even to the verge of blows. Partisans of Rouletabille fought with the supporters of Frederic Larsan. Curiously enough the excitement was due less to the fact that an innocent man was in danger of a wrongful conviction than to the interest taken in their own ideas as to the Mystery of the 'Yellow Room'. Each had his explanation to which each held fast. Those who explained the crime on Frederic Larsan's theory would not admit that there could be any doubt as to the perspicacity of the popular detective. Others who had arrived at a different solution, naturally insisted that this was Rouletabille's explanation, though they did not as yet know what that was.

With the day's "Epoque" in their hands, the "Larsans" and the "Rouletabilles" fought and shoved each other on the steps of the Palais de Justice, right into the court itself. Those who could not get in remained in the neighbourhood until evening and were, with great difficulty, kept back by the soldiery and the police. They became hungry for news, welcoming the most absurd rumours. At one time the rumour spread that Monsieur Stangerson himself had been arrested in the court and had confessed to being the murderer. This goes to show to what a pitch of madness nervous excitement may carry people. Rouletabille was still expected. Some pretended to know him; and when a young man with a "pass" crossed the open space which separated the crowd from the Court House, a scuffle took place. Cries were raised of "Rouletabille!—there's Rouletabille!" The arrival of the manager of the paper was the signal for a great demonstration. Some applauded, others hissed.

The trial itself was presided over by Monsieur de Rocouz, a judge filled with the prejudice of his class, but a man honest at heart. The witnesses had been called. I was there, of course, as were all who had, in any way, been in touch with the mysteries of the Glandier. Monsieur Stangerson—looking many years older and almost unrecognisable—Larsan, Arthur Rance, with his face ruddy as ever, Daddy Jacques,

Daddy Mathieu, who was brought into court handcuffed between two gendarmes, Madame Mathieu, in tears, the two Berniers, the two nurses, the steward, all the domestics of the chateau, the employeee of the Paris Post Office, the railway employeee from Epinay, some friends of Monsieur and Mademoiselle Stangerson, and all Monsieur Darzac's witnesses. I was lucky enough to be called early in the trial, so that I was then able to watch and be present at almost the whole of the proceedings.

The court was so crowded that many lawyers were compelled to find seats on the steps. Behind the bench of justices were representatives from other benches. Monsieur Robert Darzac stood in the prisoner's dock between policemen, tall, handsome, and calm. A murmur of admiration rather than of compassion greeted his appearance. He leaned forward towards his counsel, Maitre Henri Robert, who, assisted by his chief secretary, Maitre Andre Hesse, was busily turning over the folios of his brief.

Many expected that Monsieur Stangerson, after giving his evidence, would have gone over to the prisoner and shaken hands with him; but he left the court without another word. It was remarked that the jurors appeared to be deeply interested in a rapid conversation which the manager of the "Epoque" was having with Maitre Henri Robert. The manager, later, sat down in the front row of the public seats. Some were surprised that he was not asked to remain with the other witnesses in the room reserved for them.

The reading of the indictment was got through, as it always is, without any incident. I shall not here report the long examination to which Monsieur Darzac was subjected. He answered all the questions quickly and easily. His silence as to the important matters of which we know was dead against him. It would seem as if this reticence would be fatal for him. He resented the President's reprimands. He was told that his silence might mean death.

"Very well," he said; "I will submit to it; but I am innocent."

With that splendid ability which has made his fame, Maitre Robert took advantage of the incident, and tried to show that it brought out in noble relief his client's character; for only heroic natures could remain silent for moral reasons in face of such a danger. The eminent advocate however, only succeeded in assuring those who were already assured of Darzac's innocence. At the adjournment Rouletabille had not yet arrived. Every time a door opened, all eyes there turned towards it and back to the manager of the "Epoque," who sat impassive in his place. When he once was feeling in his pocket a loud murmur of expectation followed. The letter!

It is not, however, my intention to report in detail the course of the trial. My readers are sufficiently acquainted with the mysteries surrounding the Glandier case to enable me to go on to the really dramatic denouement of this ever-memorable day.

When the trial was resumed, Maitre Henri Robert questioned Daddy Mathieu as to his complicity in the death of the keeper. His wife was also brought in and was confronted by her husband. She burst into tears and confessed that she had been the keeper's mistress, and that her husband had suspected it. She again, however, affirmed that he had had nothing to do with the murder of her lover. Maitre Henri Robert thereupon asked the court to hear Frederic Larsan on this point.

"In a short conversation which I have had with Frederic Larsan, during the adjournment," declared the advocate, "he has made me understand that the death of the keeper may have been brought about otherwise than by the hand of Mathieu. It will be interesting to hear Frederic Larsan's theory."

Frederic Larsan was brought in. His explanation was quite clear.

"I see no necessity," he said, "for bringing Mathieu in this. I have told Monsieur de Marquet that the man's threats had biassed the examining magistrate against him. To me the attempt to murder Mademoiselle and the death of the keeper are the work of one and the same person. Mademoiselle Stangerson's murderer, flying through the court, was fired on; it was thought he was struck, perhaps killed. As a matter of fact, he only stumbled at the moment of his disappearance behind the corner of the right wing of the chateau. There he encountered the keeper who, no doubt, tried to seize him. The murderer had in his hand the knife with which he had stabbed Mademoiselle Stangerson and with this he killed the keeper."

This very simple explanation appeared at once plausible and satisfying. A murmur of approbation was heard.

"And the murderer? What became of him?" asked the President.

"He was evidently hidden in an obscure corner at the end of the court. After the people had left the court carrying with them the body of the keeper, the murderer quietly made his escape."

The words had scarcely left Larsan's mouth when from the back of the court came a youthful voice:

"I agree with Frederic Larsan as to the death of the keeper; but I do not agree with him as to the way the murderer escaped!"

Everybody turned round, astonished. The clerks of the court sprang towards the speaker, calling out silence, and the President angrily ordered the intruder to be immediately expelled. The same clear voice, however, was again heard:

"It is I, Monsieur President—Joseph Rouletabille!"

# XXVII

## In Which Joseph Rouletabille
## Appears in All His Glory

The excitement was extreme. Cries from fainting women were to be heard amid the extraordinary bustle and stir. The "majesty of the law" was utterly forgotten. The President tried in vain to make himself heard. Rouletabille made his way forward with difficulty, but by dint of much elbowing reached his manager and greeted him cordially. The letter was passed to him and pocketing it he turned to the witness-box. He was dressed exactly as on the day he left me even to the ulster over his arm. Turning to the President, he said:

"I beg your pardon, Monsieur President, but I have only just arrived from America. The steamer was late. My name is Joseph Rouletabille!"

The silence which followed his stepping into the witness-box was broken by laughter when his words were heard. Everybody seemed relieved and glad to find him there, as if in the expectation of hearing the truth at last.

But the President was extremely incensed:

"So, you are Joseph Rouletabille," he replied; "well, young man, I'll teach you what comes of making a farce of justice. By virtue of my discretionary power, I hold you at the court's disposition."

"I ask nothing better, Monsieur President. I have come here for that purpose. I humbly beg the court's pardon for the disturbance of which I have been the innocent cause. I beg you to believe that nobody has a greater respect for the court than I have. I came in as I could." He smiled.

"Take him away!" ordered the President.

Maitre Henri Robert intervened. He began by apologising for the young man, who, he said, was moved only by the best intentions. He made the President understand that the evidence of a witness who had slept at the Glandier during the whole of that eventful week could not be omitted, and the present witness, moreover, had come to name the real murderer.

"Are you going to tell us who the murderer was?" asked the President, somewhat convinced though still sceptical.

"I have come for that purpose, Monsieur President!" replied Rouletabille.

An attempt at applause was silenced by the usher.

"Joseph Rouletabille," said Maitre Henri Robert, "has not been regularly subpoenaed as a witness, but I hope, Monsieur President, you will examine him in virtue of your discretionary powers."

"Very well!" said the President, "we will question him. But we must proceed in order."

The Advocate-General rose:

"It would, perhaps, be better," he said, "if the young man were to tell us now whom he suspects."

The President nodded ironically:

"If the Advocate-General attaches importance to the deposition of Monsieur Joseph Rouletabille, I see no reason why this witness should not give us the name of the murderer."

A pin drop could have been heard. Rouletabille stood silent looking sympathetically at Darzac, who, for the first time since the opening of the trial, showed himself agitated.

"Well," cried the President, "we wait for the name of the murderer." Rouletabille, feeling in his waistcoat pocket, drew his watch and, looking at it, said:

"Monsieur President, I cannot name the murderer before half-past six o'clock!"

Loud murmurs of disappointment filled the room. Some of the lawyers were heard to say: "He's making fun of us!"

The President in a stern voice, said:

"This joke has gone far enough. You may retire, Monsieur, into the witnesses' room. I hold you at our disposition."

Rouletabille protested.

"I assure you, Monsieur President," he cried in his sharp, clear voice, "that when I do name the murderer you will understand why I could not speak before half-past six. I assert this on my honour. I can, however, give you now some explanation of the murder of the keeper. Monsieur Frederic Larsan, who has seen me at work at the Glandier, can tell you with what care I studied this case. I found myself compelled to differ with him in arresting Monsieur Robert Darzac, who is innocent. Monsieur Larsan knows of my good faith and knows that some importance may be attached to my discoveries, which have often corroborated his own."

Frederic Larsan said:

"Monsieur President, it will be interesting to hear Monsieur Joseph Rouletabille, especially as he differs from me."

A murmur of approbation greeted the detective's speech. He was a good sportsman and accepted the challenge. The struggle between the two promised to be exciting.

As the President remained silent, Frederic Larsan continued:

"We agree that the murderer of the keeper was the assailant of Mademoiselle Stangerson; but as we are not agreed as to how the murderer escaped, I am curious to hear Monsieur Rouletabille's explanation."

"I have no doubt you are," said my friend.

General laughter followed this remark. The President angrily declared that if it was repeated, he would have the court cleared.

"Now, young man," said the President, "you have heard Monsieur Frederic Larsan; how did the murderer get away from the court?"

Rouletabille looked at Madame Mathieu, who smiled back at him sadly.

"Since Madame Mathieu," he said, "has freely admitted her intimacy with the keeper—"

"Why, it's the boy!" exclaimed Daddy Mathieu.

"Remove that man!" ordered the President.

Mathieu was removed from the court. Rouletabille went on:

"Since she has made this confession, I am free to tell you that she often met the keeper at night on the first floor of the donjon, in the room which was once an oratory. These meetings became more frequent when her husband was laid up by his rheumatism. She gave him morphine to ease his pain and to give herself more time for the meetings. Madame Mathieu came to the chateau that night, enveloped in a large black shawl which served also as a disguise. This was the phantom that disturbed Daddy Jacques. She knew how to imitate the mewing of Mother Angenoux' cat and she would make the cries to advise the keeper of her presence. The recent repairs of the donjon did not interfere with their meetings in the keeper's old room, in the donjon, since the new room assigned to him at the end of the right wing was separated from the steward's room by a partition only.

"Previous to the tragedy in the courtyard Madame Mathieu and the keeper left the donjon together. I learnt these facts from my examination of the footmarks in the court the next morning. Bernier, the concierge, whom I had stationed behind the donjon—as he will explain himself—

could not see what passed in the court. He did not reach the court until he heard the revolver shots, and then he fired. When the woman parted from the man she went towards the open gate of the court, while he returned to his room.

"He had almost reached the door when the revolvers rang out. He had just reached the corner when a shadow bounded by. Meanwhile, Madame Mathieu, surprised by the revolver shots and by the entrance of people into the court, crouched in the darkness. The court is a large one and, being near the gate, she might easily have passed out unseen. But she remained and saw the body being carried away. In great agony of mind she neared the vestibule and saw the dead body of her lover on the stairs lit up by Daddy Jacques' lantern. She then fled; and Daddy Jacques joined her.

"That same night, before the murder, Daddy Jacques had been awakened by the cat's cry, and, looking through his window, had seen the black phantom. Hastily dressing himself he went out and recognised her. He is an old friend of Madame Mathieu, and when she saw him she had to tell him of her relations with the keeper and begged his assistance. Daddy Jacques took pity on her and accompanied her through the oak grove out of the park, past the border of the lake to the road to Épinay. From there it was but a very short distance to her home.

"Daddy Jacques returned to the chateau, and, seeing how important it was for Madame Mathieu's presence at the chateau to remain unknown, he did all he could to hide it. I appeal to Monsieur Larsan, who saw me, next morning, examine the two sets of footprints."

Here Rouletabille turning towards Madame Mathieu, with a bow, said:

"The footprints of Madame bear a strange resemblance to the neat footprints of the murderer."

Madame Mathieu trembled and looked at him with wide eyes as if in wonder at what he would say next.

"Madame has a shapely foot, long and rather large for a woman. The imprint, with its pointed toe, is very like that of the murderer's."

A movement in the court was repressed by Rouletabille. He held their attention at once.

"I hasten to add," he went on, "that I attach no importance to this. Outward signs like these are often liable to lead us into error, if we do not reason rightly. Monsieur Robert Darzac's footprints are also like the murderer's, and yet he is not the murderer!"

The President turning to Madame Mathieu asked:

"Is that in accordance with what you know occurred?"

"Yes, Monsieur President," she replied, "it is as if Monsieur Rouletabille had been behind us."

"Did you see the murderer running towards the end of the right wing?"

"Yes, as clearly as I saw them afterwards carrying the keeper's body."

"What became of the murderer?—You were in the courtyard and could easily have seen.

"I saw nothing of him, Monsieur President. It became quite dark just then."

"Then Monsieur Rouletabille," said the President, "must explain how the murderer made his escape."

Rouletabille continued:

"It was impossible for the murderer to escape by the way he had entered the court without our seeing him; or if we couldn't see him we must certainly have felt him, since the court is a very narrow one enclosed in high iron railings."

"Then if the man was hemmed in that narrow square, how is it you did not find him?—I have been asking you that for the last half hour."

"Monsieur President," replied Rouletabille, "I cannot answer that question before half-past six!"

By this time the people in the court-room were beginning to believe in this new witness. They were amused by his melodramatic action in thus fixing the hour; but they seemed to have confidence in the outcome. As for the President, it looked as if he also had made up his mind to take the young man in the same way. He had certainly been impressed by Rouletabille's explanation of Madame Mathieu's part.

"Well, Monsieur Rouletabille," he said, "as you say; but don't let us see any more of you before half-past six."

Rouletabille bowed to the President, and made his way to the door of the witnesses' room.

I quietly made my way through the crowd and left the court almost at the same time as Rouletabille. He greeted me heartily, and looked happy.

"I'll not ask you, my dear fellow," I said, smiling, "what you've been doing in America; because I've no doubt you'll say you can't tell me until after half-past six."

"No, my dear Sainclair, I'll tell you right now why I went to America. I went in search of the name of the other half of the murderer!"

"The name of the other half?"

"Exactly. When we last left the Glandier I knew there were two halves to the murderer and the name of only one of them. I went to America for the name of the other half."

I was too puzzled to answer. Just then we entered the witnesses' room, and Rouletabille was immediately surrounded. He showed himself very friendly to all except Arthur Rance to whom he exhibited a marked coldness of manner. Frederic Larsan came in also. Rouletabille went up and shook him heartily by the hand. His manner toward the detective showed that he had got the better of the policeman. Larsan smiled and asked him what he had been doing in America, Rouletabille began by telling him some anecdotes of his voyage. They then turned aside together apparently with the object of speaking confidentially. I, therefore, discreetly left them and, being curious to hear the evidence, returned to my seat in the court-room where the public plainly showed its lack of interest in what was going on in their impatience for Rouletabille's return at the appointed time.

On the stroke of half-past six Joseph Rouletabille was again brought in. It is impossible for me to picture the tense excitement which appeared on every face, as he made his way to the bar. Darzac rose to his feet, frightfully pale.

The President, addressing Rouletabille, said gravely:

"I will not ask you to take the oath, because you have not been regularly summoned; but I trust there is no need to urge upon you the gravity of the statement you are about to make."

Rouletabille looked the President quite calmly and steadily in the face, and replied:

"Yes, Monsieur."

"At your last appearance here," said the President, "we had arrived at the point where you were to tell us how the murderer escaped, and also his name. Now, Monsieur Rouletabille, we await your explanation."

"Very well, Monsieur," began my friend amidst a profound silence. "I had explained how it was impossible for the murderer to get away without being seen. And yet he was there with us in the courtyard."

"And you did not see him? At least that is what the prosecution declares."

"No! We all of us saw him, Monsieur le President!" cried Rouletabille.

"Then why was he not arrested?"

"Because no one, besides myself, knew that he was the murderer. It would have spoiled my plans to have had him arrested, and I had then no proof other than my own reasoning. I was convinced we had the murderer before us and that we were actually looking at him. I have now brought what I consider the indisputable proof."

"Speak out, Monsieur! Tell us the murderer's name."

"You will find it on the list of names present in the court on the night of the tragedy," replied Rouletabille.

The people present in the court-room began showing impatience. Some of them even called for the name, and were silenced by the usher.

"The list includes Daddy Jacques, Bernier the concierge, and Mr. Arthur Rance," said the President. "Do you accuse any of these?"

"No, Monsieur!"

"Then I do not understand what you are driving at. There was no other person at the end of the court."

"Yes, Monsieur, there was, not at the end, but above the court, who was leaning out of the window."

"Do you mean Frederic Larsan!" exclaimed the President.

"Yes! Frederic Larsan!" replied Rouletabille in a ringing tone. "Frederic Larsan is the murderer!"

The court-room became immediately filled with loud and indignant protests. So astonished was he that the President did not attempt to quiet it. The quick silence which followed was broken by the distinctly whispered words from the lips of Robert Darzac:

"It's impossible! He's mad!"

"You dare to accuse Frederic Larsan, Monsieur?" asked the President. "If you are not mad, what are your proofs?"

"Proofs, Monsieur?—Do you want proofs? Well, here is one," cried Rouletabille shrilly. "Let Frederic Larsan be called!"

"Usher, call Frederic Larsan."

The usher hurried to the side door, opened it, and disappeared. The door remained open, while all eyes turned expectantly towards it. The clerk re-appeared and, stepping forward, said:

"Monsieur President, Frederic Larsan is not here. He left at about four o'clock and has not been seen since."

"That is my proof!" cried Rouletabille, triumphantly.

"Explain yourself?" demanded the President.

"My proof is Larsan's flight," said the young reporter. "He will not come back. You will see no more of Frederic Larsan."

"Unless you are playing with the court, Monsieur, why did you not accuse him when he was present? He would then have answered you."

"He could give no other answer than the one he has now given by his flight."

"We cannot believe that Larsan has fled. There was no reason for his doing so. Did he know you'd make this charge?"

"He did. I told him I would."

"Do you mean to say that knowing Larsan was the murderer you gave him the opportunity to escape?"

"Yes, Monsieur President, I did," replied Rouletabille, proudly. "I am not a policeman, I am a journalist; and my business is not to arrest people. My business is in the service of truth, and is not that of an executioner. If you are just, Monsieur, you will see that I am right. You can now understand why I refrained until this hour to divulge the name. I gave Larsan time to catch the 4:17 train for Paris, where he would know where to hide himself, and leave no traces. You will not find Frederic Larsan," declared Rouletabille, fixing his eyes on Monsieur Robert Darzac. "He is too cunning. He is a man who has always escaped you and whom you have long searched for in vain. If he did not succeed in outwitting me, he can yet easily outwit any police. This man who, four years ago, introduced himself to the Surete, and became celebrated as Frederic Larsan, is notorious under another name—a name well known to crime. Frederic Larsan, Monsieur President, is Ballmeyer!"

"Ballmeyer!" cried the President.

"Ballmeyer!" exclaimed Robert Darzac, springing to his feet. "Ballmeyer!—It was true, then!"

"Ah! Monsieur Darzac; you don't think I am mad, now!" cried Rouletabille.

Ballmeyer! Ballmeyer! No other word could be heard in the courtroom. The President adjourned the hearing.

Those of my readers who may not have heard of Ballmeyer will wonder at the excitement the name caused. And yet the doings of this remarkable criminal form the subject-matter of the most dramatic narratives of the newspapers and criminal records of the past twenty years. It had been reported that he was dead, and thus had eluded the police as he had eluded them throughout the whole of his career.

Ballmeyer was the best specimen of the high-class "gentleman swindler." He was adept at sleight of hand tricks, and no bolder or more ruthless crook ever lived. He was received in the best society, and was a member of some of the most exclusive clubs. On many of his depredatory expeditions he had not hesitated to use the knife and the mutton-bone. No difficulty stopped him and no "operation" was too dangerous. He had been caught, but escaped on the very morning of his trial, by throwing pepper into the eyes of the guards who were conducting him to Court. It was known later that, in spite of the keen hunt after him by the most expert of detectives, he had sat that same evening at a first performance in the Theatre Francais, without the slightest disguise.

He left France, later, to "work" America. The police there succeeded in capturing him once, but the extraordinary man escaped the next day. It would need a volume to recount the adventures of this master-criminal. And yet this was the man Rouletabille had allowed to get away! Knowing all about him and who he was, he afforded the criminal an opportunity for another laugh at the society he had defied! I could not help admiring the bold stroke of the young journalist, because I felt certain his motive had been to protect both Mademoiselle Stangerson and rid Darzac of an enemy at the same time.

The crowd had barely recovered from the effect of the astonishing revelation when the hearing was resumed. The question in everybody's mind was: Admitting that Larsan was the murderer, how did he get out of the "Yellow Room"?

Rouletabille was immediately called to the bar and his examination continued.

"You have told us," said the President, "that it was impossible to escape from the end of the court. Since Larsan was leaning out of his window, he had left the court. How did he do that?"

"He escaped by a most unusual way. He climbed the wall, sprang onto the terrace, and, while we were engaged with the keeper's body, reached the gallery by the window. He then had little else to do than to open the window, get in and call out to us, as if he had just come from his own room. To a man of Ballmeyer's strength all that was mere child's play. And here, Monsieur, is the proof of what I say."

Rouletabille drew from his pocket a small packet, from which he produced a strong iron peg.

"This, Monsieur," he said, "is a spike which perfectly fits a hole still to be seen in the cornice supporting the terrace. Larsan, who thought and prepared for everything in case of any emergency, had fixed this spike into the cornice. All he had to do to make his escape good was to plant one foot on a stone which is placed at the corner of the chateau, another on this support, one hand on the cornice of the keeper's door and the other on the terrace, and Larsan was clear of the ground. The rest was easy. His acting after dinner as if he had been drugged was make believe. He was not drugged; but he did drug me. Of course he had to make it appear as if he also had been drugged so that no suspicion should fall on him for my condition. Had I not been thus overpowered, Larsan would never have entered Mademoiselle Stangerson's chamber that night, and the attack on her would not have taken place."

A groan came from Darzac, who appeared to be unable to control his suffering.

"You can understand," added Rouletabille, "that Larsan would feel himself hampered from the fact that my room was so close to his, and from a suspicion that I would be on the watch that night. Naturally, he could not for a moment believe that I suspected him! But I might see him leaving his room when he was about to go to Mademoiselle Stangerson. He waited till I was asleep, and my friend Sainclair was busy trying to rouse me. Ten minutes after that Mademoiselle was calling out, 'Murder!'"

"How did you come to suspect Larsan?" asked the President.

"My pure reason pointed to him. That was why I watched him. But I did not foresee the drugging. He is very cunning. Yes, my pure reason pointed to him; but I required tangible proof so that my eyes could see him as my pure reason saw him."

"What do you mean by your pure reason?"

"That power of one's mind which admits of no disturbing elements to a conclusion. The day following the incident of 'the inexplicable gallery,' I felt myself losing control of it. I had allowed myself to be diverted by fallacious evidence; but I recovered and again took hold of the right end. I satisfied myself that the murderer could not have left the gallery, either naturally or supernaturally. I narrowed the field of consideration to that small circle, so to speak. The murderer could not be outside that circle. Now who was in it? There was, first, the murderer. Then there were Daddy Jacques, Monsieur Stangerson, Frederic Larsan, and myself. Five persons in all, counting in the murderer. And yet, in the gallery, there were but four. Now since it had been demonstrated to me that the fifth could not have escaped, it was evident that one of the four present in the gallery must be a double—he must be himself and the murderer also. Why had I not seen this before? Simply because the phenomenon of the double personality had not occurred before in this inquiry.

"Now who of the four persons in the gallery was both that person and the assassin? I went over in my mind what I had seen. I had seen at one and the same time, Monsieur Stangerson and the murderer, Daddy Jacques and the murderer, myself and the murderer; so that the murderer, then, could not be either Monsieur Stangerson, Daddy Jacques, or myself. Had I seen Frederic Larsan and the murderer at the same time?—No!—Two seconds had passed, during which I lost sight of the murderer; for, as I have noted in my papers, he arrived two seconds before Monsieur Stangerson, Daddy Jacques, and myself at the meeting-point of the two galleries. That would have given Larsan time to go through the 'off-turning' gallery, snatch off his false beard, return, and hurry with us as if, like us, in pursuit of the murderer. I was sure now I had got hold of the right end in my reasoning. With Frederic Larsan was now always associated, in my mind, the personality of the unknown of whom I was in pursuit—the murderer, in other words.

"That revelation staggered me. I tried to regain my balance by going over the evidences previously traced, but which had diverted my mind and led me away from Frederic Larsan. What were these evidences?

"1st. I had seen the unknown in Mademoiselle Stangerson's chamber. On going to Frederic Larsan's room, I had found Larsan sound asleep.

"2nd. The ladder.

"3rd. I had placed Frederic Larsan at the end of the 'off-turning' gallery and had told him that I would rush into Mademoiselle Stangerson's room to try to capture the murderer. Then I returned to Mademoiselle Stangerson's chamber where I had seen the unknown.

"The first evidence did not disturb me much. It is likely that, when I descended from my ladder, after having seen the unknown in Mademoiselle Stangerson's chamber, Larsan had already finished what he was doing there. Then, while I was re-entering the chateau, Larsan went back to his own room and, undressing himself, went to sleep.

"Nor did the second evidence trouble me. If Larsan were the murderer, he could have no use for a ladder; but the ladder might have been placed there to give an appearance to the murderer's entrance from without the chateau; especially as Larsan had accused Darzac and Darzac was not in the chateau that night. Further, the ladder might have been placed there to facilitate Larsan's flight in case of absolute necessity.

"But the third evidence puzzled me altogether. Having placed Larsan at the end of the 'off-turning gallery,' I could not explain how he had taken advantage of the moment when I had gone to the left wing of the chateau to find Monsieur Stangerson and Daddy Jacques, to return to Mademoiselle Stangerson's room. It was a very dangerous thing to do. He risked being captured,—and he knew it. And he was very nearly captured. He had not had time to regain his post, as he had certainly hoped to do. He had then a very strong reason for returning to his room. As for myself, when I sent Daddy Jacques to the end of the 'right gallery,' I naturally thought that Larsan was still at his post. Daddy Jacques, in going to his post, had not looked, when he passed, to see whether Larsan was at his post or not.

"What, then, was the urgent reason which had compelled Larsan to go to the room a second time? I guessed it to be some evidence of his presence there. He had left something very important in that room. What was it? And had he recovered it? I begged Madame Bernier who was accustomed to clean the room to look, and she found a pair of eye-glasses—this pair, Monsieur President!"

And Rouletabille drew the eye-glasses, of which we know, from his pocket.

"When I saw these eye-glasses," he continued, "I was utterly nonplussed. I had never seen Larsan wear eye-glasses. What did they mean? Suddenly I exclaimed to myself: 'I wonder if he is long-sighted?' I had never seen Larsan write. He might, then, be long-sighted. They would certainly know at the Surete, and also know if the glasses were his. Such evidence would be damning. That explained Larsan's return. I know now that Larsan, or Ballmeyer, is long-sighted and that these glasses belonged to him.

"I now made one mistake. I was not satisfied with the evidence I had obtained. I wished to see the man's face. Had I refrained from this, the second terrible attack would not have occurred."

"But," asked the President, "why should Larsan go to Mademoiselle Stangerson's room, at all? Why should he twice attempt to murder her?"

"Because he loves her, Monsieur President."

"That is certainly a reason, but—"

"It is the only reason. He was madly in love, and because of that, and—other things, he was capable of committing any crime."

"Did Mademoiselle Stangerson know this?"

"Yes, Monsieur; but she was ignorant of the fact that the man who was pursuing her was Frederic Larsan, otherwise, of course, he would not have been allowed to be at the chateau. I noticed, when he was in her room after the incident in the gallery, that he kept himself in the shadow, and that he kept his head bent down. He was looking for the lost eye-glasses. Mademoiselle Stangerson knew Larsan under another name."

"Monsieur Darzac," asked the President, "did Mademoiselle Stangerson in any way confide in you on this matter? How is it that she has never spoken about it to anyone? If you are innocent, she would have wished to spare you the pain of being accused."

"Mademoiselle Stangerson told me nothing," replied Monsieur Darzac.

"Does what this young man says appear probable to you?" the President asked.

"Mademoiselle Stangerson has told me nothing," he replied stolidly.

"How do you explain that, on the night of the murder of the keeper," the President asked, turning to Rouletabille, "the murderer brought back the papers stolen from Monsieur Stangerson?—How do you explain how the murderer gained entrance into Mademoiselle Stangerson's locked room?"

"The last question is easily answered. A man like Larsan, or Ballmeyer, could have had made duplicate keys. As to the documents, I think Larsan had not intended to steal them, at first. Closely watching Mademoiselle with the purpose of preventing her marriage with Monsieur Robert Darzac, he one day followed her and Monsieur into the Grands Magasins de la Louvre. There he got possession of the reticule which she lost, or left behind. In that reticule was a key with a brass head. He did not know there was any value attached to the key till the advertisement in the newspapers revealed it. He then wrote to Mademoiselle, as the advertisement requested. No doubt he asked for a meeting, making known to her that he was also the person who had for some time pursued her with his love. He received no answer. He went to the Post Office and ascertained that his letter was no longer there. He had already taken complete stock of Monsieur Darzac, and, having decided to go to any lengths to gain Mademoiselle Stangerson, he had planned that, whatever might happen, Monsieur Darzac, his hated rival, should be the man to be suspected.

"I do not think that Larsan had as yet thought of murdering Mademoiselle Stangerson; but whatever he might do, he made sure that Monsieur Darzac should suffer for it. He was very nearly of the same height as Monsieur Darzac and had almost the same sized feet. It would not be difficult, to take an impression of Monsieur Darzac's footprints, and have similar boots made for himself. Such tricks were mere child's play for Larsan, or Ballmeyer.

"Receiving no reply to his letter, he determined, since Mademoiselle Stangerson would not come to him, that he would go to her. His plan had long been formed. He had made himself master of the plans of the chateau and the pavilion. So that, one afternoon, while Monsieur and Mademoiselle Stangerson were out for a walk, and while Daddy Jacques was away, he entered the latter by the vestibule window. He was alone, and, being in no hurry, he began examining the furniture. One of the pieces, resembling a safe, had a very small keyhole. That interested him! He had with him the little key with the brass head, and, associating one with the other, he tried the key in the lock. The door opened. He saw nothing but papers. They must be very valuable to have been put away in a safe, and the key to which to be of so much importance. Perhaps a thought of blackmail occurred to him as a useful possibility in helping him in his designs on Mademoiselle Stangerson. He quickly made a parcel of the papers and took it to the lavatory in the vestibule. Between the time of his first examination of the pavilion and the night of the murder of the keeper, Larsan had had time to find out what those papers contained. He could do nothing with them, and they were rather compromising. That night he took them back to the chateau. Perhaps he hoped that, by returning the papers he might obtain some gratitude from Mademoiselle Stangerson. But whatever may have been his reasons, he took the papers back and so rid himself of an encumbrance."

Rouletabille coughed. It was evident to me that he was embarrassed. He had arrived at a point where he had to keep back his knowledge of Larsan's true motive. The explanation he had given had evidently been unsatisfactory. Rouletabille was quick enough to note the bad impression he had made, for, turning to the President, he said: "And now we come to the explanation of the Mystery of the 'Yellow Room'!"

A movement of chairs in the court with a rustling of dresses and an energetic whispering of "Hush!" showed the curiosity that had been aroused.

"It seems to me," said the President, "that the Mystery of the 'Yellow Room', Monsieur Rouletabille, is wholly explained by your hypothesis.

Frederic Larsan is the explanation. We have merely to substitute him for Monsieur Robert Darzac. Evidently the door of the 'Yellow Room' was open at the time Monsieur Stangerson was alone, and that he allowed the man who was coming out of his daughter's chamber to pass without arresting him—perhaps at her entreaty to avoid all scandal."

"No, Monsieur President," protested the young man. "You forget that, stunned by the attack made on her, Mademoiselle Stangerson was not in a condition to have made such an appeal. Nor could she have locked and bolted herself in her room. You must also remember that Monsieur Stangerson has sworn that the door was not open."

"That, however, is the only way in which it can be explained. The 'Yellow Room' was as closely shut as an iron safe. To use your own expression, it was impossible for the murderer to make his escape either naturally or supernaturally. When the room was broken into he was not there! He must, therefore, have escaped."

"That does not follow."

"What do you mean?"

"There was no need for him to escape—if he was not there!"

"Not there!"

"Evidently, not. He could not have been there, if he were not found there."

"But, what about the evidences of his presence?" asked the President.

"That, Monsieur President, is where we have taken hold of the wrong end. From the time Mademoiselle Stangerson shut herself in the room to the time her door was burst open, it was impossible for the murderer to escape. He was not found because he was not there during that time."

"But the evidences?"

"They have led us astray. In reasoning on this mystery we must not take them to mean what they apparently mean. Why do we conclude the murderer was there?—Because he left his tracks in the room? Good! But may he not have been there before the room was locked. Nay, he must have been there before! Let us look into the matter of these traces and see if they do not point to my conclusion.

"After the publication of the article in the 'Matin' and my conversation with the examining magistrate on the journey from Paris to Epinaysur-Orge, I was certain that the 'Yellow Room' had been hermetically sealed, so to speak, and that consequently the murderer had escaped before Mademoiselle Stangerson had gone into her chamber at midnight.

"At the time I was much puzzled. Mademoiselle Stangerson could not have been her own murderer, since the evidences pointed to some other person. The assassin, then, had come before. If that were so, how was it that Mademoiselle had been attacked after? or rather, that she appeared to have been attacked after? It was necessary for me to reconstruct the occurrence and make of it two phases—each separated from the other, in time, by the space of several hours. One phase in which Mademoiselle Stangerson had really been attacked—the other phase in which those who heard her cries thought she was being attacked. I had not then examined the 'Yellow Room'. What were the marks on Mademoiselle Stangerson? There were marks of strangulation and the wound from a hard blow on the temple. The marks of strangulation did not interest me much; they might have been made before, and Mademoiselle Stangerson could have concealed them by a collarette, or any similar article of apparel. I had to suppose this the moment I was compelled to reconstruct the occurrence by two phases. Mademoiselle Stangerson had, no doubt, her own reasons for so doing, since she had told her father nothing of it, and had made it understood to the examining magistrate that the attack had taken place in the night, during the second phase. She was forced to say that, otherwise her father would have questioned her as to her reason for having said nothing about it.

"But I could not explain the blow on the temple. I understood it even less when I learned that the mutton-bone had been found in her room. She could not hide the fact that she had been struck on the head, and yet that wound appeared evidently to have been inflicted during the first phase, since it required the presence of the murderer! I thought Mademoiselle Stangerson had hidden the wound by arranging her hair in bands on her forehead.

"As to the mark of the hand on the wall, that had evidently been made during the first phase—when the murderer was really there. All the traces of his presence had naturally been left during the first phase; the mutton-bone, the black footprints, the Basque cap, the handkerchief, the blood on the wall, on the door, and on the floor. If those traces were still all there, they showed that Mademoiselle Stangerson—who desired that nothing should be known—had not yet had time to clear them away. This led me to the conclusion that the two phases had taken place one shortly after the other. She had not had the opportunity, after leaving her room and going back to the laboratory to her father, to get back again to her room and put it in order. Her father was all the time with her, working. So that after the first phase she did not re-enter her chamber till midnight. Daddy Jacques was there at ten o'clock, as he was every night; but he went in merely to close the blinds and light the night-light. Owing to her disturbed state of mind she had forgotten that Daddy Jacques would go into her room and had begged him not to trouble himself. All this was set forth in the article in the 'Matin.' Daddy Jacques did go, however, and, in the dim light of the room, saw nothing.

"Mademoiselle Stangerson must have lived some anxious moments while Daddy Jacques was absent; but I think she was not aware that so many evidences had been left. After she had been attacked she had only time to hide the traces of the man's fingers on her neck and to hurry to the laboratory. Had she known of the bone, the cap, and the handkerchief, she would have made away with them after she had gone back to her chamber at midnight. She did not see them, and undressed by the uncertain glimmer of the night light. She went to bed, worn-out by anxiety and fear—a fear that had made her remain in the laboratory as late as possible.

"My reasoning had thus brought me to the second phase of the tragedy, when Mademoiselle Stangerson was alone in the room. I had now to explain the revolver shots fired during the second phase. Cries of 'Help!—Murder!' had been heard. How to explain these? As to the cries, I was in no difficulty; since she was alone in her room these could result from nightmare only. My explanation of the struggle and noise that were heard is simply that in her nightmare she was haunted by the terrible experience she had passed through in the afternoon. In her dream she sees the murderer about to spring upon her and she cries, 'Help! Murder!' Her hand wildly seeks the revolver she had placed within her reach on the night-table by the side of her bed, but her hand, striking the table, overturns it, and the revolver, falling to the floor, discharges itself, the bullet lodging in the ceiling. I knew from the first that the bullet in the ceiling must have resulted from an accident. Its very position suggested an accident to my mind, and so fell in with my theory of a nightmare. I no longer doubted that the attack had taken place before Mademoiselle had retired for the night. After wakening from her frightful dream and crying aloud for help, she had fainted.

"My theory, based on the evidence of the shots that were heard at midnight, demanded two shots—one which wounded the murderer at the time of his attack, and one fired at the time of the nightmare. The evidence given by the Berniers before the examining magistrate was to the effect that only one shot had been heard. Monsieur Stangerson testified to hearing a dull sound first followed by a sharp ringing sound. The dull sound I explained by the falling of the marble-topped table; the ringing sound was the shot from the revolver. I was now convinced I was right. The shot that had wounded the hand of the murderer and had caused it to bleed so that he left the bloody imprint on the wall was fired by Mademoiselle in self-defence, before the second phase, when she had been really attacked. The shot in the ceiling which the Berniers heard was the accidental shot during the nightmare.

"I had now to explain the wound on the temple. It was not severe enough to have been made by means of the mutton-bone, and Mademoiselle had not attempted to hide it. It must have been made during the second phase. It was to find this out that I went to the 'Yellow Room', and I obtained my answer there."

Rouletabille drew a piece of white folded paper from his pocket, and drew out of it an almost invisible object which he held between his thumb and forefinger.

"This, Monsieur President," he said, "is a hair—a blond hair stained with blood;—it is a hair from the head of Mademoiselle Stangerson. I found it sticking to one of the corners of the overturned table. The corner of the table was itself stained with blood—a tiny stain—hardly visible; but it told me that, on rising from her bed, Mademoiselle Stangerson had fallen heavily and had struck her head on the corner of its marble top.

"I still had to learn, in addition to the name of the assassin, which I did later, the time of the original attack. I learned this from the examination of Mademoiselle Stangerson and her father, though the answers given by the former were well calculated to deceive the examining magistrate—Mademoiselle Stangerson had stated very minutely how she had spent the whole of her time that day. We established the fact that the murderer had introduced himself into the pavilion between five and six o'clock. At a quarter past six the professor and his daughter had resumed their work. At five the professor had been with his daughter, and since the attack took place in the professor's absence from his daughter, I had to find out just when he left her. The professor had stated that at the time when he and his daughter were about to re-enter the laboratory he was met by the keeper and held in conversation about the cutting of some wood and the poachers. Mademoiselle Stangerson was not with him then since the professor said: 'I left the keeper and rejoined my daughter who was at work in the laboratory.'

"It was during that short interval of time that the tragedy took place. That is certain. In my mind's eye I saw Mademoiselle Stangerson re-enter the pavilion, go to her room to take off her hat, and find herself faced by the murderer. He had been in the pavilion for some time waiting for her. He had arranged to pass the whole night there. He had taken off Daddy Jacques's boots; he had removed the papers from the cabinet; and had then slipped under the bed. Finding the time long, he had risen, gone again into the laboratory, then into the vestibule, looked into the garden, and had seen, coming towards the pavilion, Mademoiselle Stangerson—alone. He would never have dared to attack her at that hour, if he had not found her alone. His mind was made up. He would be more at ease alone with Mademoiselle Stangerson in the pavilion, than he would have been in the middle of the night, with Daddy Jacques sleeping in the attic. So he shut the vestibule window. That explains why neither Monsieur Stangerson, nor the keeper, who were at some distance from the pavilion, had heard the revolver shot.

"Then he went back to the 'Yellow Room'. Mademoiselle Stangerson came in. What passed must have taken place very quickly. Mademoiselle tried to call for help; but the man had seized her by the throat. Her hand had sought and grasped the revolver which she had been keeping in the drawer of her night-table, since she had come to fear the threats of her pursuer. The murderer was about to strike her on the head with the mutton-bone—a terrible weapon in the hands of a Larsan or Ballmeyer; but she fired in time, and the shot wounded the hand that held the weapon. The bone fell to the floor covered with the blood of the murderer, who staggered, clutched at the wall for support—imprinting on it the red marks—and, fearing another bullet, fled.

"She saw him pass through the laboratory, and listened. He was long at the window. At length he jumped from it. She flew to it and shut it. The danger past, all her thoughts were of her father. Had he either seen or heard? At any cost to herself she must keep this from him. Thus when Monsieur Stangerson returned, he found the door of the 'Yellow Room' closed, and his daughter in the laboratory, bending over her desk, at work!"

Turning towards Monsieur Darzac, Rouletabille cried: "You know the truth! Tell us, then, if that is not how things happened."

"I don't know anything about it," replied Monsieur Darzac.

"I admire you for your silence," said Rouletabille, "but if Mademoiselle Stangerson knew of your danger, she would release you from your oath. She would beg of you to tell all she has confided to you. She would be here to defend you!"

Monsieur Darzac made no movement, nor uttered a word. He looked at Rouletabille sadly.

"However," said the young reporter, "since Mademoiselle is not here, I must do it myself. But, believe me, Monsieur Darzac, the only means to save Mademoiselle Stangerson and restore her to her reason, is to secure your acquittal."

"What is this secret motive that compels Mademoiselle Stangerson to hide her knowledge from her father?" asked the President.

"That, Monsieur, I do not know," said Rouletabille. "It is no business of mine."

The President, turning to Monsieur Darzac, endeavoured to induce him to tell what he knew.

"Do you still refuse, Monsieur, to tell us how you employeeed your time during the attempts on the life of Mademoiselle Stangerson?"

"I cannot tell you anything, Monsieur."

The President turned to Rouletabille as if appealing for an explanation.

"We must assume, Monsieur President, that Monsieur Robert Darzac's absences are closely connected with Mademoiselle Stangerson's secret, and that Monsieur Darzac feels himself in honour bound to remain silent. It may be that Larsan, who, since his three attempts, has had everything in training to cast suspicion on Monsieur Darzac, had fixed on just those occasions for a meeting with Monsieur Darzac at a spot most compromising. Larsan is cunning enough to have done that."

The President seemed partly convinced, but still curious, he asked:

"But what is this secret of Mademoiselle Stangerson?"

"That I cannot tell you," said Rouletabille. "I think, however, you know enough now to acquit Monsieur Robert Darzac! Unless Larsan should return, and I don't think he will," he added, with a laugh.

"One question more," said the President. "Admitting your explanation, we know that Larsan wished to turn suspicion on Monsieur Robert Darzac, but why should he throw suspicion on Daddy Jacques also?"

"There came in the professional detective, Monsieur, who proves himself an unraveller of mysteries, by annihilating the very proofs he had accumulated. He's a very cunning man, and a similar trick had often enabled him to turn suspicion from himself. He proved the innocence of one before accusing the other. You can easily believe, Monsieur, that so complicated a scheme as this must have been long and carefully thought out in advance by Larsan. I can tell you that he had long been engaged on its elaboration. If you care to learn how he had gathered information, you will find that he had, on one occasion, disguised himself as the commissionaire between the 'Laboratory of the Surete' and Monsieur Stangerson, of whom 'experiments' were demanded. In this way he had been able before the crime, on two occasions to take stock of the pavilion. He had 'made up' so that Daddy Jacques had not recognised him. And yet Larsan had found the opportunity to rob the old man of a pair of old boots and a cast-off Basque cap, which the servant had tied up in a handkerchief, with the intention of carrying them to a friend, a charcoal-burner on the road to Epinay. When the crime was discovered, Daddy Jacques had immediately recognised these objects as his. They were extremely compromising, which explains his distress at the time when we spoke to him about them. Larsan confessed it all to me. He is an artist at the game. He did a similar thing in the affair of the 'Credit Universel,' and in that of the 'Gold Ingots of the Mint.' Both these cases should be revised. Since Ballmeyer or Larsan has been in the Surete a number of innocent persons have been sent to prison."

# XXVIII

## In Which It Is Proved That One Does Not Always Think of Everything

Great excitement prevailed when Rouletabille had finished. The court-room became agitated with the murmurings of suppressed applause. Maitre Henri Robert called for an adjournment of the trial and was supported in his motion by the public prosecutor himself. The case was adjourned. The next day Monsieur Robert Darzac was released on bail, while Daddy Jacques received the immediate benefit of a "no cause for action." Search was everywhere made for Frederic Larsan, but in vain. Monsieur Darzac finally escaped the awful calamity which, at one time, had threatened him. After a visit to Mademoiselle Stangerson, he was led to hope that she might, by careful nursing, one day recover her reason.

Rouletabille, naturally, became the "man of the hour." On leaving the Palais de Justice, the crowd bore him aloft in triumph. The press of the whole world published his exploits and his photograph. He, who had interviewed so many illustrious personages, had himself become illustrious and was interviewed in his turn. I am glad to say that the enormous success in no way turned his head.

We left Versailles together, after having dined at "The Dog That Smokes." In the train I put a number of questions to him which, during our meal, had been on the tip of my tongue, but which I had refrained from uttering, knowing he did not like to talk "shop" while eating.

"My friend," I said, "that Larsan case is wonderful. It is worthy of you."

He begged me to say no more, and humorously pretended an anxiety for me should I give way to silly praise of him because of a personal admiration for his ability.

"I'll come to the point, then," I said, not a little nettled. "I am still in the dark as to your reason for going to America. When you left the Glandier you had found out, if I rightly understand, all about Frederic Larsan; you had discovered the exact way he had attempted the murder?"

"Quite so. And you," he said, turning the conversation, "did you suspect nothing?"

"Nothing!"

"It's incredible!"

"I don't see how I could have suspected anything. You took great pains to conceal your thoughts from me. Had you already suspected Larsan when you sent for me to bring the revolvers?"

"Yes! I had come to that conclusion through the incident of the 'inexplicable gallery.' Larsan's return to Mademoiselle Stangerson's room, however, had not then been cleared up by the eye-glasses. My suspicions were the outcome of my reasoning only; and the idea of Larsan being the murderer seemed so extraordinary that I resolved to wait for actual evidence before venturing to act. Nevertheless, the suspicion worried me, and I sometimes spoke to the detective in a way that ought to have opened your eyes. I spoke disparagingly of his methods. But until I found the eye-glasses I could but look upon my suspicion of him in the light of an absurd hypothesis only. You can imagine my elation after I had explained Larsan's movements. I remember well rushing into my room like a mad-man and crying to you: 'I'll get the better of the great Fred. I'll get the better of him in a way that will make a sensation!'

"I was then thinking of Larsan, the murderer. It was that same evening that Darzac begged me to watch over Mademoiselle Stangerson. I made no efforts until after we had dined with Larsan, until ten o'clock. He was right there before me, and I could afford to wait. You ought to have suspected, because when we were talking of the murderer's arrival, I said to you: 'I am quite sure Larsan will be here tonight.'

"But one important point escaped us both. It was one which ought to have opened our eyes to Larsan. Do you remember the bamboo cane? I was surprised to find Larsan had made no use of that evidence against Robert Darzac. Had it not been purchased by a man whose description tallied exactly with that of Darzac? Well, just before I saw him off at the train, after the recess during the trial, I asked him why he hadn't used the cane evidence. He told me he had never had any intention of doing so; that our discovery of it in the little inn at Epinay had much embarrassed him. If you will remember, he told us then that the cane had been given him in London. Why did we not immediately say to ourselves: 'Fred is lying. He could not have had this cane in London. He was not in London. He bought it in Paris'? Then you found out, on inquiry at Cassette's, that the cane had been bought by a person dressed very like Robert Darzac, though, as we learned later, from Darzac himself, it was not he who had made the purchase. Couple this with the fact we already knew, from the letter at the poste restante, that there was actually a man in Paris who was passing as Robert Darzac, why did we not immediately fix on Fred himself?

"Of course, his position at the Surete was against us; but when we saw the evident eagerness on his part to find convicting evidence against Darzac, nay, even the passion he displayed in his pursuit of the man, the lie about the cane should have had a new meaning for us. If you ask why Larsan bought the cane, if he had no intention of manufacturing evidence against Darzac by means of it, the answer is quite simple. He had been wounded in the hand by Mademoiselle Stangerson, so that the cane was useful to enable him to close his hand in carrying it. You remember I noticed that he always carried it?

"All these details came back to my mind when I had once fixed on Larsan as the criminal. But they were too late then to be of any use to me. On the evening when he pretended to be drugged I looked at his hand and saw a thin silk bandage covering the signs of a slight healing wound. Had we taken a quicker initiative at the time Larsan told us that lie about the cane, I am certain he would have gone off, to avoid suspicion. All the same, we worried Larsan or Ballmeyer without our knowing it."

"But," I interrupted, "if Larsan had no intention of using the cane as evidence against Darzac, why had he made himself up to look like the man when he went in to buy it?"

"He had not specially 'made up' as Darzac to buy the cane; he had come straight to Cassette's immediately after he had attacked Mademoiselle Stangerson. His wound was troubling him and, as he was passing along the Avenue de l'Opera, the idea of the cane came to his mind and he acted on it. It was then eight o'clock. And I, who had hit upon the very hour of the occurrence of the tragedy, almost convinced that Darzac was not the criminal, and knowing of the cane, I still never suspected Larsan. There are times. . ."

"There are times," I said, "when the greatest intellects— . . ." Rouletabille shut my mouth. I still continued to chide him, but, finding he did not reply, I saw he was no longer paying any attention to what I was saying. I found he was fast asleep.

## XXIX

## The Mystery of Mademoiselle Stangerson

During the days that followed I had several opportunities to question him as to his reason for his voyage to America, but I obtained no more precise answers than he had given me on the evening of the adjournment of the trial, when we were on the train for Paris. One day, however, on my still pressing him, he said:

"Can't you understand that I had to know Larsan's true personality?"

"No doubt," I said, "but why did you go to America to find that out?"

He sat smoking his pipe, and made no further reply. I began to see that I was touching on the secret that concerned Mademoiselle Stangerson. Rouletabille evidently had found it necessary to go to America to find out what the mysterious tie was that bound her to Larsan by so strange and terrible a bond. In America he had learned who Larsan was and had obtained information which closed his mouth. He had been to Philadelphia.

And now, what was this mystery which held Mademoiselle Stangerson and Monsieur Robert Darzac in so inexplicable a silence? After so many years and the publicity given the case by a curious and shameless press; now that Monsieur Stangerson knows all and has forgiven all, all may be told. In every phase of this remarkable story Mademoiselle Stangerson had always been the sufferer.

The beginning dates from the time when, as a young girl, she was living with her father in Philadelphia. A visitor at the house, a Frenchman, had succeeded by his wit, grace and persistent attention, in gaining her affections. He was said to be rich and had asked her of her father. Monsieur Stangerson, on making inquiries as to Monsieur Jean Roussel, found that the man was a swindler and an adventurer. Jean Roussel was but another of the many names under which the notorious Ballmeyer, a fugitive from France, tried to hide himself. Monsieur Stangerson did not know of his identity with Ballmeyer; he learned that the man was simply undesirable for his daughter. He not only refused to give his consent to the marriage but denied him admission into the house. Mathilde Stangerson, however, had fallen in love. To her Jean Roussel was everything that her love painted him. She was indignant at her father's attitude, and did not conceal her feelings. Her father sent her to stay with an aunt in Cincinnati. There she was joined by Jean Roussel and, in spite of the reverence she felt for her father, ran away with him to get married.

They went to Louisville and lived there for some time. One morning, however, a knock came at the door of the house in which they were and the police entered to arrest Jean Roussel. It was then that Mathilde Stangerson, or Roussel, learned that her husband was no other than the notorious Ballmeyer!

The young woman in her despair tried to commit suicide. She failed in this, and was forced to rejoin her aunt in Cincinnati, The old lady was overjoyed to see her again. She had been anxiously searching for her and had not dared to tell Monsieur Stangerson of her disappearance. Mathilde swore her to secrecy, so that her father should not know she had been away. A month later, Mademoiselle Stangerson returned to her father, repentant, her heart dead within her, hoping only one thing: that she would never again see her husband, the horrible Ballmeyer. A report was spread, a few weeks later, that he was dead, and she now determined to atone for her disobedience by a life of labour and devotion for her father. And she kept her word.

All this she had confessed to Robert Darzac, and, believing Ballmeyer dead, had given herself to the joy of a union with him. But fate had resuscitated Jean Roussel—the Ballmeyer of her youth. He had taken steps to let her know that he would never allow her to marry Darzac—that he still loved her.

Mademoiselle Stangerson never for one moment hesitated to confide in Monsieur Darzac. She showed him the letter in which Jean Roussel asked her to recall the first hours of their union in their beautiful and charming Louisville home. "The presbytery has lost nothing of its charm, nor the garden its brightness," he had written. The scoundrel pretended to be rich and claimed the right of taking her back to Louisville. She had told Darzac that if her father should know of her dishonour, she would kill herself. Monsieur Darzac had sworn to silence her persecutor, even if he had to kill him. He was outwitted and would have succumbed had it not been for the genius of Rouletabille.

Mademoiselle Stangerson was herself helpless in the hands of such a villain. She had tried to kill him when he had first threatened and then attacked her in the "Yellow Room". She had, unfortunately, failed, and felt herself condemned to be for ever at the mercy of this unscrupulous wretch who was continually demanding her presence at clandestine interviews. When he sent her the letter through the Post Office, asking her to meet him, she had refused. The result of her refusal was the tragedy of the "Yellow Room". The second time he wrote asking for a meeting, the letter reaching her in her sick chamber, she had avoided him by sleeping with her servants. In that letter the scoundrel had warned her that, since she was too ill to come to him, he would come to her, and that he would be in her chamber at a particular hour on a particular night. Knowing that she had everything to fear from Ballmeyer, she had left her chamber on that night. It was then that the incident of the "inexplicable gallery" occurred.

The third time she had determined to keep the appointment. He asked for it in the letter he had written in her own room, on the night of the incident in the gallery, which he left on her desk. In that letter he threatened to burn her father's papers if she did not meet him. It was to rescue these papers that she made up her mind to see him. She did not for one moment doubt that the wretch would carry out his threat if she persisted in avoiding him, and in that case the labours of her father's lifetime would be for ever lost. Since the meeting was thus inevitable, she resolved to see her husband and appeal to his better nature. It was for this interview that she had prepared herself on the night the keeper was killed. They did meet, and what passed between them may be imagined. He insisted that she renounce Darzac. She, on her part, affirmed her love for him. He stabbed her in his anger, determined to convict Darzac of the crime. As Larsan he could do it, and had so managed things that Darzac could never explain how he had employeeed the time of his absence from the chateau. Ballmeyer's precautions were most cunningly taken.

Larsan had threatened Darzac as he had threatened Mathilde—with the same weapon, and the same threats. He wrote Darzac urgent letters, declaring himself ready to deliver up the letters that had passed between him and his wife, and to leave them for ever, if he would pay him his price. He asked Darzac to meet him for the purpose of arranging the matter, appointing the time when Larsan would be with Mademoiselle Stangerson. When Darzac went to Epinay, expecting to find Ballmeyer or Larsan there, he was met by an accomplice of Larsan's, and kept waiting until such time as the "coincidence" could be established.

It was all done with Machiavellian cunning; but Ballmeyer had reckoned without Joseph Rouletabille.

Now that the Mystery of the "Yellow Room" has been cleared up, this is not the time to tell of Rouletabille's adventures in America. Knowing the young reporter as we do, we can understand with what acumen he had traced, step by step, the story of Mathilde Stangerson and Jean Roussel. At Philadelphia he had quickly informed himself as to Arthur William Rance. There he learned of Rance's act of devotion and the reward he thought himself entitled to for it. A rumour of his marriage with Mademoiselle Stangerson had once found its way into the drawing-rooms of Philadelphia. He also learned of Rance's continued attentions to her and his importunities for her hand. He had taken to drink, he had said, to drown his grief at his unrequited love. It can now be understood why Rouletabille had shown so marked a coolness of demeanour towards Rance when they met in the witnesses' room, on the day of the trial.

The strange Roussel-Stangerson mystery had now been laid bare. Who was this Jean Roussel? Rouletabille had traced him from Philadelphia to Cincinnati. In Cincinnati he became acquainted with the old aunt, and had found means to open her mouth. The story of Ballmeyer's arrest threw the right light on the whole story. He visited the "presbytery"—a small and pretty dwelling in the old colonial style—which had, indeed, "lost nothing of its charm." Then, abandoning his pursuit of traces of Mademoiselle Stangerson, he took up those of Ballmeyer. He followed them from prison to prison, from crime to crime. Finally, as he was about leaving for Europe, he learned in New York that Ballmeyer had, five years before, embarked for France with some valuable papers belonging to a merchant of New Orleans whom he had murdered.

And yet the whole of this mystery has not been revealed. Mademoiselle Stangerson had a child, by her husband,—a son. The infant was born in the old aunt's house. No one knew of it, so well had the aunt managed to conceal the event.

What became of that son?—That is another story which, so far, I am not permitted to relate.

About two months after these events, I came upon Rouletabille sitting on a bench in the Palais de Justice, looking very depressed.

"What's the matter, old man?" I asked. "You are looking very downcast. How are your friends getting on?"

"Apart from you," he said, "I have no friends."

"I hope that Monsieur Darzac—"

"No doubt."

"And Mademoiselle Stangerson—How is she?"

"Better—much better."

"Then you ought not to be sad."

"I am sad," he said, "because I am thinking of the perfume of the lady in black—"

"The perfume of the lady in black!—I have heard you often refer to it. Tell me why it troubles you."

"Perhaps—some day; some day," said Rouletabille.

And he heaved a profound sigh.

# A Note About the Author

Gaston Leroux (1868–1927) was a French journalist and writer of detective fiction. Born in Paris, Leroux attended school in Normandy before returning to his home city to complete a degree in law. After squandering his inheritance, he began working as a court reporter and theater critic to avoid bankruptcy. As a journalist, Leroux earned a reputation as a leading international correspondent, particularly for his reporting on the 1905 Russian Revolution. In 1907, Leroux switched careers in order to become a professional fiction writer, focusing predominately on novels that could be turned into film scripts. With such novels as *The Mystery of "The Yellow Room"* (1908), Leroux established himself as a leading figure in detective fiction, eventually earning himself the title of Chevalier in the Legion of Honor, France's highest award for merit. *The Phantom of the Opera* (1910), his most famous work, has been adapted countless times for theater, television, and film, most notably by Andrew Lloyd Webber in his 1986 musical of the same name.

# A Note from the Publisher

Spanning many genres, from non-fiction essays to literature classics to children's books and lyric poetry, Mint Edition books showcase the master works of our time in a modern new package. The text is freshly typeset, is clean and easy to read, and features a new note about the author in each volume. Many books also include exclusive new introductory material. Every book boasts a striking new cover, which makes it as appropriate for collecting as it is for gift giving. Mint Edition books are only printed when a reader orders them, so natural resources are not wasted. We're proud that our books are never manufactured in excess and exist only in the exact quantity they need to be read and enjoyed.

# bookfinity™

## Discover more of your favorite classics with Bookfinity™.

- Track your reading with custom book lists.
- Get great book recommendations for your personalized Reader Type.
- Add reviews for your favorite books
- AND MUCH MORE!

Visit **bookfinity.com** and take the fun Reader Type quiz to get started.

Enjoy our classic and modern companion pairings!

Classic & Modern

9 781513 282930